AQUARIUS

THE OLDEST SOUL BOOK THREE

TIFFANY FITZHENRY

Printed in the United States of America

First printing, 2017

All rights reserved. Published by Hierarchy Publishing, LLC

ISBN 978-1-944216-16-0 (Paperback)
ISBN 978-1-944216-17-7 (Hardcover)
ISBN 978-1-944216-20-7 (Kindle)
ISBN 978-1-944216-14-6 (Epub)

Hierarchy Publishing, LLC
1029 Peachtree Parkway, #346
Peachtree City, GA 30269
www.hierarchypublishing.com

Cover image copyright © Aleksandar Mijatovic/Shutterstock.com
Cover Design by Vanessa Mendozzi
Formatting by Polgarus Studio
The Oldest Soul original artwork, symbols, and interior illustrations copyright

For Mary

I am not afraid ... I was born to do this.

— Joan of Arc

PREFACE

Speeding towards Antiquus in the dead of the night, Phoenix at the wheel, we careened sharply up winding mountain roads. According to Ansel, a man I'd known all my life but had never meet in person, Cian was weak. He was so unwell that even though humanity had descended into chaos and was in the midst of violent collapse, Phoenix, Roman, and I were racing halfway across the country to get to him.

With what remained of America burning to the ground before my eyes, it hit me that Cian's death was imminent. Losing Cian was my worst fear.

I had dreaded the day he'd leave me for as long as I could remember. The prospect of having to deal with Shamus all on my own was a nightmare so terrifying I couldn't even dream it. The mere thought always left me reeling and pale.

This was the one thing that scared me most—

And as I sat alone in the back seat of my jeep on that dark, cold night, fire on the horizon, wind swirling my hair around wildly, I wondered how, for so long, I hadn't seen it. And I finally understood that this destiny, my worst fear, what I was racing towards at that very moment, I had been racing towards my whole life. And that there never was any way out of it—even if it killed me.

Destiny is death, I thought. It was something Cian had said so many times I often heard the words in my sleep.

"You are meant to die at the hand of the very thing that enslaves you. That's all your destiny is, Eve. It is you choosing your death, the one death that can give you life, your *real life*," he tried to explain again and again. I never understood it. Not until that fateful night when I finally realized *this* is the march of death, and there is only forward.

The once terrifying thought caused a strange settling inside me instead. It felt as though I was finally coming into myself, the deepest part of who I was. What I found, echoing within the hollows of this depth, was a knowing. Resisting my destiny was futile, and I should be eager to get on with it.

A funny thing happened after that: I could see very clearly. More clearly than I ever could before. I saw that Cian had been racing towards it too, towards leaving me and Shamus behind to work out our long-held differences on our own, once and for all.

Cian had been aging over the years leading up to that night, more and more rapidly with each passing day. Now, I could see it all so perfectly, that he'd been doing it on purpose. He was aging *by will*.

I'd almost suspected as much just after I turned twelve, when he seemed to go from forty to seventy in the span of a single year. By the night of my thirteenth birthday I was all but certain, if only in the back of my mind, that he was heading out, that he had already made his exit plans.

By the time I was thirteen years old Cian was already set to leave me because he knew that I was ready—because I *am* ready, I realized.

I AM, a loud voice thundered inside me.

"Whomever can wake the dead will win the war," I proclaimed abruptly to Phoenix and Roman from the back seat. Words that sounded just how they felt. As if they were bursting forth from another universe, emerging from the shadows of other realms where they'd been stashed, lying dormant, in centuries of primordial sleep.

PART ONE

FIRE & BLOOD

EVE

ONE

— ❋ —

I warned Roman that there would be suffering. Well, I tried to, anyway.

It was a ridiculous thing to do, of course, trying to caution him when he would still have to walk every step of the journey, regardless. Giving him an ominous, blanket warning like that for the unavoidable, no less. There's really no act more futile and nothing quite so useless to anyone. And yet, to the man I loved, to my soul's eternal mate, *this* was the last thing I said as he watched me pixilate into nothing. Fade away. Dissolve like some dream—or horrible nightmare.

"Roman," I pleaded, begging him to focus. But he just stood there, lost in shock, helpless. I knew he was terrified about what was happening to me. I saw it. How the whites of his brilliant jade eyes burned red with fear. But, in that moment, I also saw something else; I saw what was coming … *after* the ascent. The hardest human existence has ever been, the hardest it will ever be. *The last epoch.*

"There will be suffering," I sputtered out, my ridiculous, wasted warning. I knew my words would be lost, but I couldn't help myself. Not once I knew that Roman was staying behind.

Now, he leaves the small desert hut he calls home, sword at his side, sealing the wooden door tight behind him. After securing his goggles over his eyes, he turns to face another day in the place where life is as unrelenting and cruel as the merciless landscape. Primitus, the desolate desert dwelling of New Souls. One of only two states in which humans now live under one government, Aurora.

He wraps a long scarf around his head and neck, expertly twisting the gauzy, tan fabric in circles until he's completely covered, careful not to leave any exposed skin. Then he tucks the ends into the front and back of his shirt, a solid tan, button-down, military-style fatigue.

He gives another tap on the handle of his sword, checking it one last time. Among all of Roman's many deadly tasks, trips to the ration tent rank near the top. He's preparing the same way he always does for the unpredictable trek ahead, methodically. And, as usual, I watch him. I'm standing less than a foot away, my back pressed against the mud brick wall beside the door. Close enough to touch or even kiss him, but he doesn't see me, he never does, because he can't—*not yet.* Though he's getting closer, he's not ready. So, I remain out of sight for now.

As he walks by me, I smell the familiar honeyed scent of him, his salty, sun-browned skin and warm, velvety sweet breath—the smell of home to my soul—I close my eyes and breathe it in, drowning myself in him. And for a moment, I dissolve into the universe, losing my place. It's like looking up from a page in a book. Instead of the usual world, psychedelic colors explode into shapes that bloom in my mind, and all around me, growing geometric patterns that begin as prisms and pyramids and folding out to become lilies and Christmas roses. Flowers that link him to me, their fragrances etched into my soul alongside the smell of him.

I watch as he looks side to side before stepping off into the sand. Soon he's trekking against the fierce wind, head down, making his way through the King sector, a never-ending grid of identical huts. His body, which is both leaner and stronger now, is pressed forward sharply into the ceaseless squall. The sand, blowing in sheets, pelts him without mercy. Like a mindless robot, he steps right over the spheres of burning brush, which he comes upon every few feet or so, white smoke parting around him. He studies his own boots as they plod along, how they disappear into the fine powdery sand. He watches the round, black, steel toe get swallowed away with each step, again and again.

This is Earth. What's left of it anyway, nearly one year after the ascent, though the hundreds of millions of souls still here know nothing of that. They know nothing of history or truth—this world's or their own. And nearly everything that would inform them is gone, torn down, burned and cast away to places no one dares go. Even what was in their minds has been altered or rearranged.

It is a stunning achievement, to be totally fair. Creating an entire world where not a single soul has the faintest idea who they truly are or where they come from or why they're here. Not the *real story* anyway. A world where the truth has been flung so far out of reach.

Is it any wonder then, that just as heavy and burdened as Roman's trudging steps are the thoughts that so often rule his mind? Like images of the mangled bodies he walked passed the day before, which are bathing his brain at the moment. Men butchered and left to rot. King souls, all of them, just like him. Warrior souls die too in these bloody battles over the most basic necessities of life, and on rare occasions, a Guardian or Gypsy Soul who finds the courage or will to try. But all of those bodies are quickly removed, dropped back in their own sectors in tall, heaping piles, from what Roman has heard, piles that regularly creep into his imagination. The slain King Souls are left out, lying where they died, decomposing for weeks sometimes in the scorching sun, their putrid rotting flesh melting from their bones.

"Stop it," he mumbles under his breath, "don't think of that," he tells himself, shaking his head a bit.

I watch the grisly thought implode. It dissolves from his mind, but its dull energy still lingers around him, a circle of low frequency waves emitting out several feet in all directions from the color light that surrounds him—his aura. Lately, his aura has been somewhere between green and blue during the waking hours and nearly purple when he sleeps. Right now, it's the bright yellowish-orange of anxiety and fear, like a flashing neon sign. It's nothing he can see. Not with having only third dimensional sight.

It's only natural for Roman to be thinking these thoughts, and to be afraid. King Souls lose their lives every day for a few cups of grain, an ounce of oil, a log of wood, or the rare barrel of water, which always seems to come just in time. Just as the spinning head and heavy limbs of severe dehydration start taking hold of him, the dreaded painful symptoms he began feeling yesterday.

More often than not, there's nothing at all in the ration

tent. He never knows if his long, tiresome trek across the sprawling King sector will be for naught. An utter waste of precious time and energy. But he does it anyway. Always precisely at his designated time. If he doesn't, it's hard to say which threat would be the first to do him in, the merciless sun, the blistering heat, the ever-worsening famine, or the strict religious and state laws under which he lives.

Roman's walking turns to more of a staggering as he becomes gripped by exhaustion. Looking up slowly, he glances ahead and finally sees the giant pristine structure looming in the distance. He also sees the faint outline of what look like other King Souls walking a hundred yards away, water barrels atop their shoulders. A mirage, the same one he always sees when he's this thirsty. He can't allow himself to believe there might really be water. The disappointment will be too crushing.

He reaches the largest of all the government tents and the only one with a somewhat regular supply of actual rations in it. The imposing beast is constructed of solid steel rods and crossbeams, and draped with heavy, gleaming white canvas. The fabric so dense it barely billows in the whipping desert winds. Some days, Roman notices how odd and out of place the whole thing looks against the backdrop of barrenness and ruin. Other days, like today, when his needs are particularly acute, he doesn't notice that at all.

The tents in the Warrior, Guardian, and Gypsy sectors are lesser in every respect. Small, poorly built, and almost never resupplied. Guardian Souls generally do not riot or protest, when there is never enough. In the Warrior and Gypsy sectors, however, the tents function mostly as gathering places for revolt and anarchy.

"They'd riot here too, the lower-souls, if they could. If not for the heavy presence of guards and drones protecting us," were words said often by the president of Primitus, Shamus, the man I once believed was my brother, who is a King Soul. A man with whom, like Roman, my soul is eternally entwined. It's one of the few things he says that's actually true. They would riot here, if not for the tight security and if souls from one sector were lawfully permitted to step foot in another.

The towering behemoth casts a long shadow on the sand, a rare swath of shade that's like a welcome mat when Roman finally reaches it, his body drenched in sweat, pants and shirt soaked through. He walks past several exiting King souls, water barrels atop their shoulders, as he makes it to the back of the short line in front of the entrance. The more acute the thirst, the more persistent the mirage. He's even imagined himself carrying water before, only to realize it's not really there. He knows all too well the devastating feeling of an imagined barrel of water turning out to be a fire log. He knows he can't believe what his eyes are telling him, so he pays them no mind as he nears the front.

Each side of the entrance is stamped with a golden emblem, the state seal of Primitus—a tribal sun encircled and flanked with muscled guards in titanium body armor, their faces masked.

"IN," the guard demands, a stiff arm extended out, a cautioning hand mashed into Roman's chest.

Roman pushes the sleeve of his shirt up, revealing his Incarnation Number. From the crook of his elbow to his wrist, over scarred skin, CCXCIX is written in blazing red ink. The Roman numeral 299, the result of his Animus test. The number of times his soul has incarnated, according to his DNA.

The emotionless brute eyes the scar beneath Roman's IN tattoo, then looks at him, moving a hand to rest on his weapon, a large automatic assault rifle.

"It's a burn," Roman explains, as he always must. But the guard doesn't move, except to tighten his finger on the trigger.

Eyeing one another carefully, Roman moves slowly. He raises both hands up in front of his chest, then moves to lift his other sleeve, keeping a close eye on the guard's movements. Roman reveals a large, blood-red, King Soul symbol branded deep into his left forearm. After examining the symbol, two lines and an arrow in the shape of a shield, then looking again at Roman's right arm, the guard removes his hand from his weapon and steps aside, permitting Roman to enter.

A few moments later Roman exits with a heavy wooden barrel atop his broad shoulders. *Water*. Real water. His heart is pounding out of his chest as he glances side to side, takes a deep breath, steps off, and begins wading through the sand. He's rejuvenated by what are now obsessive thoughts of water. But his senses are also on high alert, as the most coveted rations are also the most dangerous to possess—and nothing is more coveted than water.

There are a hundred yards of open space in all directions surrounding the tent. Roman, escorted by an overhead police drone, walks it undisturbed. But once he reenters the dizzying grid of huts, he's on his own. And it doesn't take long for him to hear the kicking sand of someone fast approaching behind him.

In one smooth, swift motion, he swings the barrel to the ground, and grabs the sword from his side. A split second later he's face to face with a hollow-cheeked man in tattered black combat clothes, a Warrior Soul, who has been lying in wait behind a hut. Their swords clash overhead between them. Roman notes two more Warriors dashing out from behind other nearby huts, racing towards him.

Three, he thinks to himself as they fast approach. He doesn't see any others. *Three I can handle. Three's not so bad.*

He often fends off more, though they're always Warrior Souls. It's his water they've come for, of course, and to express their disdain for his privileged existence. Which they do with every swing and jab of their weapons—steel swords, government issued, just like Roman's.

Water barrel at his feet, they surround him, jeering, spitting, jabbing their swords, and tightening their circle. A primordial, animal-like war dance. They're closing in fast, trapping him, or so they think.

Roman turns, suddenly, lunging at one of them. The one he's determined, *correctly*, to be the least brave. The scrawny man goes stumbling back, losing his footing and falling to the ground. Roman turns swiftly, bringing his blade down onto the skull of another, the one he's assessed as the most skilled. The one who was about to sink his sword into Roman's back. As the skilled fighter crumples to the ground like a deflated balloon, Roman half spins back, arcing his sword upward, and catches the last man in the center of the chin, the overconfident one. He slices skyward, removing half the man's head from his body, causing him to fall straight back into the sand like a board.

Roman trains his sights on the first man, the one on the ground, who's now back-peddling through the sand away from him. Breath heavy, eyes clear, Roman stares him down. Then, after a long beat, he waves him off with his sword. The man scrambles to his feet and runs in the other direction, tripping as he goes. Roman sheaths his sword back at his side, hoists the barrel up onto his shoulders, and moves on.

He eventually makes it back home, but only after three similar ambushes are thwarted, both him and the precious barrel of water safely in one piece.

As he reaches for the door, he has the overwhelming eerie feeling he's not alone when he's more than certain that he is, and it stops him dead in his tracks. He slowly lowers the barrel to the ground next to him and removes his goggles. He turns wearily, unwrapping his head cloth.

He scans every inch he can see of the desert before him, eyes squinting, brow furrowed, seeing no explanation for the strange sense of another presence, though it's so strong it can't be ignored. More and more frequently this feeling has been rushing through his body, these strange senses he doesn't have names for, bombarding him with information he can't interpret.

He was alarmed when it first began happening, then, gradually, he became more curious. Now, with it happening at least once every day without fail, he's determined to figure it out.

He takes a slow step in my direction, and his gaze starts to narrow. Another step closer. His eyes zero in on where I stand, less than three feet from him. He searches and scans, but he sees nothing, only unending desert in front of him. Unlike the mirages he so often sees, where his eyes show him things that aren't there, this time he knows something is there, but his eyes refuse to confirm it.

He rubs his sore neck and shoulders with one hand. I stare up at him as he looks right through me. Then I reach out, my fingers gently touching his chest, and run my hand down the front of him, my flat palm coming to rest on his stomach.

His face begins to change. His jaw releases, lips part, and eyes soften. He stops trying to figure out what's going on around him and starts simply feeling it. The rhythmic beating of his pulse beneath my hand makes my heart surge with love, my body with desire for his—a powerful wave of energy, a life force, stored deep inside us both like a coiled serpent. A rush of chills covers his skin, and all the hair on his body stands on end as he starts to feel it. Then I watch as it passes through him, like the silent detonation of an invisible atomic bomb.

He inhales sharply.

ROMAN

TWO

— ✵ —

I don't mind the world so much when everyone else is asleep; the quiet stillness all around me—only the hum inside my own chest—when all my thoughts melt away. There's something about being awake when no one else is, a feeling that's strangely familiar.

One might call this time early morning, but I don't. I have no proof of that. Because the sun never sets in the desert. Not anymore. Nor does it rise for that matter— here, or anywhere else. So, I secretly call it what it really is: the time when we're told to sleep.

The sun used to rise and set, *apparently*. Long ago, *allegedly*.

No one alive now remembers it. Even if they could, no one alive now would remotely care about such a thing. Because it is a useless thing to care about.

Concern with useless things will only make our problems worse, our demise swifter and more punishing; what is useless is dangerous.

I try telling myself this all the time, but it never sticks.

The truth, which I'll deny if anyone asks, is that I don't just *care* that the sun once circled us, I am captivated by the idea. I find it almost too strange to even imagine, and yet impossible to stop thinking about.

They say it would just come rising into sight, as if out of nowhere. That it would move slowly overhead from east to west. Then it would lower towards the ground and finally disappear altogether. Just vanish, gone. The most fascinating thing of all about this odd cycle is that during certain times, the colors of the world would actually change. Intriguing shades of violet and warm soothing ambers would be cast out in a shimmering blanket across the lands. The sun would become drenched in gold, its rich rays turning first to copper then burnt sapphire.

Imagine that.

Whenever I think of how breathtaking it must have been, *which is all the time,* the same thing happens. A sinkhole opens inside my chest. An unexplainable cavernous abyss, a bottomless pit of aching, of wanting for something. Something I can't seem to name. A thing, a feeling, a time, or maybe a person, unknown and out of reach, and I just can't grab onto it.

The same dreaded void I feel now as I look out at the staggering expanse of Primitus from my doorstep. My eyes go dizzy at the sight of hundreds of thousands of huts just like ours. All of them are the same, crammed together like bugs in a nest, and spanning miles into the flat sunbaked distance. The sweltering air and glaring sun blur them into a wavy black mesh, where one person's life is indistinguishable from the next.

Primitus. Where everything blisters endlessly. Primitus, always the same hot, hazy, sand-colored, static wasteland with the same nose-hair-singeing stink in the air—a hopeless, acrid stench that sticks to my lungs and leaches into my brain. It starts in the underbrush. The only thing that somehow still manages to grow in abundance. Bone-dry desert scrub which dots, and in some places lines, Primitus, and seems to serve no purpose at all, other than being the sun's kindling. It's forever scorched and always burning wild. Sizzling and snapping all over the sand-covered terrain, it smells like charred dirt and barrenness. We step over these stinking white-smoke fireballs everywhere we walk. While from overhead and in the distance, the smell of petrochemicals invades the air, noxious clay mixed with ammonia, dirt, and rock dust. A heady nauseating stench. It wafts down correlating to the bombings and raids, blanketing us in currents and waves.

But it's the metallic, iron-rich, salty smell of blood-sweat from the sector battles and endless tribal infighting that really rounds out the terrorizing aroma, makes it all feel so immediate and impending—the smell of not just death and aggression, chemicals and warfare, heat and fire, but of total human desperation. It's the exact smell of *suffering*, I've come to believe. The smell of the world burning down. Of humankind ending itself.

I find it impossible not to yearn for the way things were. For how the world used to be ... how I imagine it was before so much was lost.

They say even the sky used to be different. That it was blue. They say it looked like infinite azure glass. Like crystal indigo water running from one end of the world to the other. It wasn't always a stark white sheet of nothing, so they say.

And no matter how hard I try, I can't seem to stop myself from fixating on it, on all of these useless, trivial things—like the sun and the sky, *along with a few other unexplained things*. My nagging wonder persists, despite the risks. So much in fact, that when the world is asleep, when the sand and dust have settled down, I head outside against all good judgment to clear my mind and to study the sun and the sky.

I pull the door shut behind me as quietly as I can, then lay a small pelt of coyote skin on the front step. The step is coated with a thick layer of sand and dust, of course, but that's not the reason for the pelt. The mud-brick stone, which I slowly lower myself towards, is hot enough to fry a lizard egg—like everything else around here—if one were lucky enough to find a lizard egg, that is. And without the barrier of the pelt, it would singe my skin through my clothing in seconds.

The roof of our tiny hut is dome-shaped. It provides no shade at all. Shielding my eyes with my forearm, I look up and begin to examine the ever-present, ever-burning, fire-yellow orb.

The sun is always in the same spot in the sky. But at this precise time, I've discovered that it's just a little farther away, in what I secretly call its 'distant position.' It looks a pinch smaller. And the sky, usually a bone-white flatness overhead, appears to dim ever so slightly. As I watch, the blinding alabaster begins to soften just a touch, turning opaque. Then, I squint—I've learned this is the best way to see it—and a moment or so later *it* happens. The sky turns blue. Well, sort of.

I'm not entirely sure if I'm seeing it with my eyes or only my mind, but I soak it in anyway, the mesmerizing hint of whitewashed pale blue that stretches overhead in all directions and slips behind the distant mountains.

The sky's still blue, I tell myself, just barely louder than a thought. And then, all at once, as quickly as it starts, it ends. And the paper-white atmosphere returns, seeming even starker than before.

According to The Word, there used to be darkness for hours at a time. Instead of bright stone white like it is now when we sleep, the sky was black as soot and there were tiny dotted lights, like little pins of diamond fire, splayed out across the blackness—*stars.* They went as far as the eye could see in all directions. They were arranged in secret shapes, patterns, and pictures, which revealed things about the world. The stars told stories across generations, like lifelines from one ancient ancestor to another.

What I wouldn't give to have stars. I can almost imagine them … sometimes. If I really try. Though picturing something I've never seen before takes time, and there's no time for things like that, especially on a day like today. Plus, there's a Witness in the distance. It's a couple hundred yards out. With the glare of the sun its dull silver body looks almost black. It's zipping through the air towards me like a flying Fennec fox, past thousands of huts like ours. This aerial recorder is one of a seemingly unlimited fleet that constantly patrols each sector of Primitus: Gypsy, Warrior, Guardian, and King.

Drones to keep us safe. Witnesses to keep us honest. We could never be safe or honest without them, *apparently*.

This one appears to be minding its grid. Flying in its robotic, repeating, sleep-mode pattern. I don't think it sees me; not yet, anyway.

I stand up slow to avoid detection then head inside where even more oppressive heat awaits. It hardly seems possible that a more stifling, more bone-drying air could even exist. At times, I think the thick walls of sun-dried mud brick seem almost designed for the specific purpose of trapping it in.

When I duck through the doorway, I'm surprised to see her already standing in the kitchen, waiting for me. I am not surprised, however, to see her anxiously biting at her bottom lip or scratching at her freshly tattooed forearm. Though she decided to receive her sacred symbol months ago, it took until yesterday for it to finally be her turn to have it done. I wondered whether the government just moves that slowly, or if it's done on purpose to build anticipation.

Her other forearm was inked with her Incarnation Number when she came to me. The same number as mine, CCXCIX, 299. That's how King souls are paired, according to our soul age.

"Why didn't you leave the bandage on?" I ask her, but I already know why: the eagerness and the pride. The *excitement*. I shake my head.

She doesn't answer, just keeps clawing at her arm, biting at her lip and bouncing slightly. Filled with nerves and anticipation, eager for what lies ahead today—her pilgrimage. I lose myself watching her for a moment. The pain she's willing to endure, the constant threat of the unknown, putting her fate so willingly in the hands of others, no reason at all to trust that they know the truth any more than we do. Accepting their answers, all just to belong. I marvel at what it proves. How much we love to be claimed by groups, defined as something, anything. The lengths we'll go to for someone to tell us who we are and the strange comfort it brings. We're so easily convinced that all of it is real: Animus, Incarnation Numbers, who it says we are, and what that's supposed to mean about us. Staring at her bloody arm, the shredded painful flesh, my eyes lose focus, blurring everything together... *who says any of this is real?*

Then, shaking my head of the thought and telling myself, yet again, *concern with useless things will only make our problems worse, our demise swifter and more punishing; what is useless is dangerous.*

I turn my shoulder into the door and push hard to seal

it shut behind me. The wind is just beginning to pick up. Soon it could be blowing in sheets. Trying to slow the accumulation of sand and scorpions inside our hut is a constant losing battle. During the waking hours, the relentless on-and-off sandstorms are mostly *on*.

I turn back and look at her. She still hasn't given her arm a rest. Attacking it with her chewed, dirt-caked nails, as if just one more scratch will finally solve the nagging itch, despite that relief never comes.

"Stop. Scratching. It," I tell her, my words plain, simple, and rightfully annoyed. She looks up at me.

"It's infected," I inform her in a slow grave voice. Both her arms finally fall to her sides.

Her eyes widen with fear, and we exchange a perilous look. She swallows hard as the thought of what she's done finally registers.

I take in a deep breath and let it out.

"Does it hurt?" I ask, feeling sorry for her, assuring her we're still on the same team. *Of course,* we are on the same team, *always*, no matter what. She's my girl, after all. And I know it hurts a lot, that's clear when she nods 'yes' without hesitation.

Because of what I already knew today would bring, more *education*, I woke up with a deep feeling of dread, like a rotting block of spoiled meat liquefying in the bottom of my stomach. Now, with *this* on top of it, my dread turns darker and upgrades, officially, into fear.

"This is going to be a long day," I remark, because it's true, but only somewhat under my breath, letting her hear me. My own small way of resisting—all I've got at the moment.

I'd normally be heading into our room to wake her. She's never woken up this early. Ever. I can always steal a little time to shake the thoughts of gold-drenched suns glistening in violet skies out of my brain before being confronted with reality. Then again, this is the most anticipated day of her life, her pilgrimage day. The day she will swear her allegiance and her life and her blood and her womb, of course … all to The Cause. I knew today was going to be difficult … *for me*. I knew it would be overwhelming. I just didn't know it would start off with an instant sock in the gut.

"We'll, ah … we'll put some balm on it now, and again when you get home … later," I suggest, thinking what she'll have seen. How she may be changed.

She gives a trusting little nod.

"Sit down. Let's have a look," I instruct.

She immediately obliges, taking a seat on the one stool in front of the tiny counter next to the stove, her naïve innocent eyes devastating me suddenly, so deeply I abruptly look away. Crossing the small hut in a step or two, I draw a long matchstick out of the ceramic cylinder where we keep them and set about lighting the stove, which I always try to avoid. It makes the hut feel like an oven in which we are the slow-roasted main course for some otherworldly giant. But I don't have a choice. I need fire if I'm going to extract the oil from the stems, leaves, and flowers of the wild licorice to make the balm and stem the infection.

Reaching under the small ironstone washbasin to the open shelf below, I grab a round terra-cotta jar, the smallest one, which I know contains a few sprigs of the wild flowering plant. But when I lift the lid, it's empty.

"No, this can't be. Not today," I tell myself as I stare down into the empty jar, my back to her.

She's silent. *Remarkably so.*

"Either I used the last of it, and I forgot…" I start, which we both know is not true, "or *you* took it, for what I cannot possibly imagine, and you neglected to tell me."

Her silence continues, deafening silence. Predictable silence. Though I hardly expect her to own up, it still grinds my gears anyway. I take a deep breath and let it out, digesting our situation, which just went from pretty bad to lethal in a single instant.

Too angry to turn and look at her, "I am beginning to believe you'd rather be bitten by a Gila monster than to admit you made a mistake. Especially one this … *careless*," I say, when what we both know what I mean is *deadly*.

I wait, giving her a few more moments to confess. It soon becomes clear she doesn't plan to.

"You know, your silence doesn't actually surprise me," I scold, allowing her to hear the level of my frustration and anger in my voice. Something I rarely do. "It doesn't help me either. And I know you know that," I impress upon her. How is it possible to feel this alone while with another person? I look down again into the empty jar as if, by magic, the licorice root we need might have somehow appeared.

If I knew she were stewing in her silence, feeling remorse, I'd at least have the solace of her guilt. But I know her silence is not about stewing, it's about keeping a secret.

My head feels suddenly heavy, and there's a high-pitched ringing in my ears that grows more intrusive by the second.

The heat from the stove must be getting to me. I rest both my hands on the counter in front of me. Like everything else, the sandy stone surface is hot, only just possible to still touch without recoiling. I lean what feels like all my weight into it.

"We are supposed to be a team you and me. Remember?" I ask her, my eyes shut tight, trying to stop the room from spinning.

Our unconventional arrangement—another secret I keep hidden—is that of a partnership, like teammates.

"I need to hunt today," I remind her. "Now I can't," I add.

Wild licorice is one of the hardest and most time-consuming things to forage. The maddening task is a notorious one. Locating the illusive herb can often take weeks. Which is why the law requires that it be kept on hand at all times. Law requires *me* to have it on hand at all times—the male Keeper. Though it also requires I do not take more than my share. So now, I must find some for her arm immediately. I'll have to go into the western Black Rock Mountains where it grows. But, after her breakfast, we will also be entirely out of meat, and what few rabbits and coyotes can be found are not in the western range anymore, where the wild licorice is. They're only ever found along the eastern ridges now. But I've been hunting the barren eastern ridges for weeks, knowing our stores were dwindling. And every day I've come up empty.

So, she'll either starve to death or die of infection. Either way, in a few days' time she could easily be gone, her blood on my hands. I shake my head, trying not to think such a horrifying thought. Or about what goes on in Confinement for the men who end up there.

When the ringing in my ears finally stops, I bend down

and grab a handful of sand from the floor and toss it over the burning logs. The small fire is extinguished almost immediately. Returning the empty jar to its spot, I take a deep breath. Though I know it's likely impossible, I decide to try and restart our morning.

"So, remind me again why this is the most important day of your life…" I quip, realizing the second the words leave my lips that that was the wrong thing to say to try and lighten the mood.

"*Roman,*" she gasps.

I don't even have to see her face to be certain that her mouth is gaping wide open—the tone of her voice is always so telling. I also know, all too well, what's coming next, and how it will end—badly.

Still, out of respect for her, I half-turn my shoulders to show I'm listening but place my hands square on my hips to at least brace myself.

"Yes, Iris?" I indulge as politely as I can manage at this point, to which she begins slowly shaking her head at me, mouth gaping, eyes squinting, just glaring at me a few moments in disbelief.

"So much has been lost," she whispers finally, a sharp reprimand. The familiar refrain is one I don't deny.

"I know, Iris," I tell her. "Suffering is everywhere."

This is an objective matter—that there is suffering

literally everywhere. Anyone with eyes can see it. Anyone unlucky enough to be experiencing this world knows. But no one ever acknowledges it—that all of us are suffering—especially not directly.

So, she looks at me a bit cross. Then, she starts over again.

"So much has been lost," she repeats. "And it's all *Eve's* fault," she lectures, even more pious than normal.

EVE

THREE

I sit on the ground inside the hut, watching a young scorpion. He's somehow aware that *he* can see me and that Roman and Iris cannot.

"Aren't you clever," I remark, studying his odd behavior.

He keeps staring at me, more than a few seconds too long for an insect, then he scurries behind a little mound of sand. Eventually, he peeks out to see if I'm still here. When, invariably, he sees that I am, he runs straight over to Roman. Who keeps kicking him away, unknowingly, back towards me.

"Go on!" Roman shouts at him, growing aggravated, shooing him off with his foot and an avalanche of sand.

"That *was* the third time," I say, as he slides across the floor towards me. "You poor thing," I laugh. "Don't worry, you're not losing your little scorpion mind," I tell him, his black exoskeleton coated white with the fine dusty sand. "You're right, I am here, and they can't see me. But you can see me. And they can see *you*. I know, it's weird," I commiserate with him. He comes closer, listening.

"We're interdimensional," I tell him, then point to myself, "ascended human," and to him, "egoless being." Then, I point to Iris and Roman, "They aren't. Well, they are, technically, they just don't know it. Not yet," I tell him. "They may never," I worry aloud looking over at Roman, thinking of all we've still got to do. None of which can start until he knows I'm here. "Thanks for the help. I know you're trying to tell him, aren't you?" I say, wiping the sand off the little scorpion's head and back. "Join the club, buddy."

As I dust him off I notice how tiny, how young he really is. And seeing no mama scorpion around, I get up and go over to where Roman has placed the water barrel, on a table a few steps outside the kitchen. My new little best friend, Buddy, trailing behind me like a puppy.

Twisting the metal tap on the front of the barrel, ever so slightly, a drop of water drips to the ground. Then another. Buddy rushes under the barrel, drinking up the drops off the grains of sand.

From across the room Roman cocks his head, noticing the drip. He walks over, tightens the valve and goes back to where he was. Where he so often is. Standing behind the counter, listening to Iris. She's become increasingly intense, almost manic, about the state of the world and about everything she's learning in school.

Right now, she's deep into her usual diatribe about the current state of humanity, its incredible challenges, and how all of it is *my* fault. According to The Word it is, and The Word is all she knows.

"*The Events* are why we have no food. Why we starve, why nothing will grow, and why you haven't bagged a single animal in over a month," she proclaims.

Roman rubs the back of his neck and looks towards the ground. It's what he always does when he's uncomfortable, when he feels inadequate. When he doesn't know what else to do. He doesn't respond either, because he knows she's not finished. Not even close.

"*The Unthinkable* is why there are no births, and why we have to…" she stops. She can't finish that part of it, not while she's looking at Roman, anyway. She skips over it, moving on, "All of the destruction she caused to this planet, Roman … burning out the sky with her unholy water, murdering the innocent with her evil, wicked, blood moons," she recounts for him, yet again. Some of the highlights of what's known as The Destruction Story.

"If it wasn't for Animus," she starts, as she often does, but can't fill in a scenario as usual. There is no world without Animus in their minds, at least there's not supposed to be— one of the many things wiped from their consciousnesses. Frustrated, she reverts back to what she knows.

"One girl caused the complete destruction of an entire civilization, Roman, *just one girl!*" she shouts, her cheeks flushing white.

He looks at her blankly, careful to hide the sadness inside him, which he's always holding at bay. A mighty ocean of unspoken sympathy roils behind an old rickety dam that's failing. And every time he sees her like this, her own mind so clearly not hers, another crack is added.

"And why? Why did she do all of this?" she asks petulantly.

He looks at her, at a loss, shaking his head, "I don't know, Iris, to make the world fear girls?" he lets fly out. Then, off her stoic silence, "Because she was trying to prove she was a god..." Roman attempts to appease her, Iris picking up the heavy skepticism in his voice.

Looking about to blow her stack, "More specifically," she lectures, "that she *was* God," correcting him, then pauses dramatically.

He starts working on her breakfast.

She goes on, "You know, I really shudder to think how much more damage she'd have done if Animus hadn't revealed who she really was: the she-devil, the night owl, the *Lilit*," she proclaims, her voice rising with drama. When she's feeling overanxious, Iris treats Roman like she's treated at school. Like he's a student, and not a bright one at that, lecturing him endlessly, mostly with direct quotes she pirates from her teacher, Ms. Medea.

Roman, being Roman, knows that, and that he's a safe place in an unsafe world, so it's a battle he doesn't pick. And he'd probably never lose sight of it or lose his patience if their life wasn't so stressful.

"Eve actually believed she *was* God," Iris repeats, "that's unholy. That's why her IN was 6666, the mark of the beast, so we know she is the she-devil."

"Right," Roman drones, acting as if he's engaged in their conversation.

Though he's faking it somewhat well, nodding his head every now and again, a few seconds ago he began staring off, arms crossed, eyes fixed on the exact spot where I sit.

"And that's why we pray to Saint Jakob," Iris pontificates, growing even more agitated.

"Right, Saint Jakob," he murmurs back absently.

"Who is Saint Jakob?" she quizzes him.

Roman stares, unblinking, in my direction, "Ah, he's the guy... the one who, you know..." he struggles.

"Roman! *Saint Jakob*, the martyr! Who long ago gave his own life exiling her back into the underworld where she came from ... for us! Even though he found himself helplessly in love with her because of her magic. Of course, *her* soul was beyond saving."

Roman snaps his gaze back towards Iris.

"Wait, what did you say?" he asks. "How he was in love with her, how ... *Jakob*, was in love with ... *Eve*," he struggles, as if these words, ones he hears all the time, have suddenly sparked something inside him.

Lately, he's been awakening more and more, questioning things, not believing what he's told, but I've never seen him react like this before.

That's right Roman. You were there. You know the truth. It lives inside you, I stand up and start walking towards him. *That's not what happened. That's not who I am.*

Just as I get close, there's a sudden change in the air—a disturbance, far off, but unmistakable—alarming, even. And it's rapidly heading this way.

My little scorpion friend dashes over, huddling next to my foot.

"It's ok, Buddy," I tell him, not entirely sure that it is.

Then a spray of ultrasonic waves travels through the mud-brick walls, which aren't really there, of course. A semi-circular band of vibrations waft through the hut. As each wave band reaches me, it bounces off my energetic field, and then travels back out through the wall in the direction it came from.

"Echolocation … but you knew that before I did," I say, looking down at Buddy through my legs. Echolocation means bats, and bats eat scorpions. He runs to a find a new hiding place as I follow the waves through the wall.

Standing outside, seconds later, a canary-yellow bat goes streaking by. Then it tears back across the sky and circles high above me four times, slowly. Finally, it dives straight down, comes to a sudden stop, and hovers a foot from my face.

His amber yellow eyes are locked on mine.

There's something you need to see, his spirit tells mine.

Then he flies around me, hiding behind my back just as a small sliver of darkness appears directly in front of me, right where he was hovering. It begins to grow into a long vertical black line as the air slices apart revealing a portal— a rip in the curtain of this dimension, surrounded by the barren desert and blinding white sky of Primitus.

Around the edges of the long, black rift, a humming starts, as if it's suddenly become electrified. Staying safely behind me, the bat flies up a bit, looking over my shoulder. And we both watch as the portal continues to morph, expanding, rotating, and changing shape until it's a six-foot-tall, oblong, black disk. Then a glimmer of light appears in the middle. A dazzling, diamond-white speck, which expands into a swirling egg-shaped center. A brilliant yellow starry nebula. Brighter than a solar flare.

Soon, the whole thing starts to pulse and vibrate, looking more and more volatile, as if it's about to burst at the seams with the vastness of the cosmos, because it is. It begins to quake, violently, nearing collapse. I look over my shoulder at my new little friend, *time to enter*, I tell him, and he takes off in the other direction. Portals being a vacuum, I hover just one foot near it and am sucked in, instantly slipping through just as it slams shut behind me. I'm swallowed into a cocoon of dark matter and soundless space—the Noosphere. Where the soothing, airless silence is like going under water. All I hear is the sound of my consciousness, my own inward vibration. The constant high humming noise of soul in body. The ambient background of the womb, the most comforting noise there is. It reverberates in my ears, head, and chest.

Then suddenly tiny, brilliant, white star lights begin to become visible all around me, and the blackness gives way to the deepest, most majestic shade of midnight blue, each splendid twinkling pin light begins to stretch into a white beam as I travel beyond the speed of light. Though it feels as if I'm standing still, I warp past these growing stars, traveling faster and faster, extending the streaking white lines longer through the deep navy space that fades to a royal blue and starts to bend around me like the curve of a bell.

The Hall of Collective Records, the etheric warehouse of the Akashic, begins to materialize before me. It's a colossal white sanctuary of unending columns and peaks, a celestial Roman-style castle more solid and real than anything on Earth. Stronger than marble and mortar and the hillsides of earth, it is constructed out of billions of years of pure consciousness and built into the very fabric of the universe.

I float through the mammoth entrance, a space that's more expansive from side to side and higher from floor to ceiling than all of Earth's great mountains combined. Once I'm inside, stretched out before me are unending columned corridors. Each corridor leads to an incalculable stack of squares, like blocks that fit inside one another, and each block contains an infinite number of doors. Glancing down each corridor is like looking into a mirror of a mirror. Only this is no optical illusion. The blocks and doors, the columns and corridors don't just *appear* to go on and on without end, they actually do. All that is, all that ever was, and all that ever will be. And all of it is connected. Everything in the universe inseparably correlated with everything else in the universe, all events, people, conversations, thoughts, dreams, hopes, wars, tangled together on a quantum level, and all of it stored right here.

I don't know whether I'm standing still and the building

is moving or the other way around, but millions of corridors fly past me at warp speed, like shuffling through cards in a deck. One is pulsing, brilliant white, like a beacon in the distance.

The Hall of Collective Records is like a living library of sorts. The library itself helps you locate what you're looking for, even if you don't know. Sometimes I come in search of something specific. Other times, such as this one, I'm led and shown.

When I reach the corridor, or it reaches me, everything stops—like the sudden halt of a bullet train, minus the g-forces. I look to my right. The gleaming white door beside me is lit with a blinding glow, as if directly on the other side sits the sun.

As I reach for the handle, a shining golden doorknob, millions of dazzling, tiny, blue star lights illuminate all around the door. The instant I touch it, I'm beyond the door.

The first thing I notice is short, stubby grass and jagged pebble fragments beneath my feet. I look up to find myself lingering on the fringe of a circle of stone ruins a hundred feet in diameter. I'm in a place I know very well: an ancient monolithic structure called Adam's Calendar, which is a strange grouping of enormous hand-carved craggy stones and boulders that sit on a plateau atop a mountain in South Africa.

But Adam's Calendar is much more than meets the eye. I learned that when Cian brought Shamus and I to this mysterious ancient site in 2009. On September 9, to be specific. He hadn't told us much about the spot we were visiting. Only that it was a very important place.

On that evening, the wind howled, whistling as it whipped by us as we walked up the pass. Bustling air, invigorating and cool, seemed to be hurrying us along, directing us, pushing us towards whatever was at the top. The way the sky was lit with purple fire from the setting sun was a sight I will never forget. From end-to-end, the horizon was painted the most majestic violet, a stark, in your face, electric blaze so rare and so intense, it felt like the sun itself was trying to tell us something.

"September 9, 2009 ... nine, nine, nine," Cian pointed out about the date of that day as we traversed the long rocky path upward. "Nine is an important number. It represents completion, the end of a cycle. Nine being 3×3 or the Triple Triad, is all-powerful. Completion, fulfillment, attainment, the beginning and the end, the whole number, a celestial number—the Earthly Paradise."

"And I'm nine ... nine years old. That's a strange coincidence," I commented.

Cian turned and smiled at me.

"There are no coincidences. Come on, you know that,

Eve," he remarked with a wink, further sparking my curiosity about the number nine and its connection to me and to this now even more intriguing place we were heading to.

Here's what rapidly went through my head next:

September 9, 2009

9 9 9

$9 \times 3 = 27$

$2 + 7 = \underline{9}$

$9 \times 9 \times 9 = 729$

$7 + 2 + 9 = 18$

$1 + 8 = \underline{9}$

What if I use 2009 for the year, instead of just nine?

$9 \times 9 \times 9 \times 2 \times (0 + 0 + 9) = 13, 122$

$1 + 3 + 1 + 2 + 2 = \underline{9}$

$9 + 9 + 9 + 2 + 0 + 0 + 9 = 38$

$3 + 8 = \underline{11}$

$1 + 1 = \underline{2}$

"Two," I said.

"Two, two what? What are you blabbering about now, Eve?" Shamus taunted, trying to provoke me.

"Two," Cian looked back at me and confirmed, sounding amazed.

"Two *and nine*," I elaborated, my finger in the air like I'd just discovered a new continent.

"Two *and nine*," Shamus mocked, perfectly mimicking me.

"Yes, Eve. Exactly." Cian's voice lifted, energized, "Two and nine." The particular sound of his words when he was inspired by something I'd figured out was stronger than a drug. It was the song of my heart, and I yearned to hear it constantly.

"What does that even mean, two and nine … two and nine what?" Shamus quipped from behind me as we crested the hill. "See, this is why you don't have any friends," he snarled as Adam's Calendar came into view. But I'd already learned to ignore his insults. I barely heard them. All I was thinking of was the number two and the number nine as Cian began to tell us more about the odd sight before us.

"The peculiar circular arrangement of these oversized, hand-carved stones aligns with mathematical precision to the cardinal directions, north, south, east and west, *and* with the solstices and equinoxes, as well as the constellation Orion in the night sky. And when studied from above, the shapes, lines and patterns they create explode with sacred geometry and distances that measure the golden ratio, Phi. The divine proportion, found throughout the human face and body and all through nature," he said as he walked us directly through the center of the site heading to the southwestern side of the main circle towards a staggering cliff with a sheer drop, several thousand feet straight down a wall of jagged rock.

We stood motionless as we stared out beyond the cliff, where a sprawling, lush, green valley stretched on almost forever and finally gave way to another rugged mountain range like a mirror of the one we stood upon, far in the distance.

After a moment, Cian went on, "The center point," he said as he turned about face, directing our sight to the middle of the circle, "is at precisely thirty-one degrees."

"The same longitudinal line the Great Pyramids of Giza are built along," I added, waiting for Shamus's rude, ignorant remark. Cian even paused for it, but it never came. When I glanced over at him, Shamus looked focused, remarkably so. His eyes fixed laser-like on the center point of the circle, his head tilted to one side, brow furrowed. Any other time Shamus would have mocked me. He always mocked me for the odd things I knew, always. This was the one time he didn't.

After another beat of Shamus's silence, "Yes, Eve, that's right," Cian said. "Thirty-one degrees."

Thirty-one, I thought, three plus one equals *four*. I looked down at the ground and also filed away the number *four* with this spot in the back of my mind. For some reason, I filed this number away secretly.

As if he was giving me a moment to do so, Cian waited until I was done covertly storing away the number *four*, then, he went on.

"It's a straight shot along this line, at thirty-one degrees from the very tip of the highest pyramid in Giza, located at the north end of the African continent, to right here," he said, amazement in his voice as he pointed to the ground beneath our feet.

"Adam's Calendar," Shamus said with eerie thoughtfulness.

"Adam's Calendar," Cian echoed. "And like the pyramids, this spot is a part of something very important: a grid of lines that cover the earth."

Cian had talked about ley lines many times before, only now, Shamus was actually listening, so, he went over it again.

"This grid is ancient. It is a matrix of lines demarcating energy, subtle forces that form a pattern around the globe. Advanced ancient civilizations built megalithic stone structures at specific points along these grid lines, like Stonehenge, Easter island, Machu Picchu, to name just a few. Most people don't know they exist, and perhaps a handful know that they all connect. Even fewer people are aware that they are set 6666 kilometers apart along this grid, and they intersect with nodal points like this one," he said of Adam's Calendar. "Almost no one knows that there is a divine code embedded in our number system, vortex-based mathematics, the thumbprint of God. And I am one of only two people who know the true significance of this place, the oldest man-made structure on the planet ... this *creation,*" he said, emphasizing the word, "a staggering sixteen times older than the pyramids of Giza, where the single most important event in human history occurred," he impressed upon us. "And yet, it's not taught, not talked about, barely acknowledged. In many cases, its very existence is even denied..." he said, prompting me to ponder why. He paused, reflecting deeply on the last thing he said, the denial, as we both watched him. I wondered why it was veiled in so much secrecy. Then he looked at us both with the most serious expression I'd ever seen on his face.

"It is the birthplace of the sun," he revealed finally, his voice reverent. Then, he went completely quiet, seeming to slip into a kind of silent meditation for the remainder of the time we were there.

Now, I've been brought back to Adam's Calendar once again. This time within The Hall of Collective Records. For what purpose, I've yet to determine.

Two, I think to myself, as I take in the familiar place, the balmy night air, pondering the deeper meaning of the connection between Adam's Calendar and the numbers two and nine. Then, I see them, the *two* of them, Ansel North, member of the Aion Dorea's darker faction, and Cian, both around twenty years younger, standing side by side at the very center point of the circle.

Thirty-one degrees, I remember.

They're facing southwest, towards the outer cropping of stones that mimic the stars of Orion. As I stand watching, half-hidden behind a boulder twenty yards away, a warm gentle wind blows in, bringing with it the smell of earth and fresh rain. Like the smell of creation itself.

Ansel, head downcast, shifts back and forth uncomfortably, hands on his hips. Cian stares, unblinking, at a fallen monolith on the outer circle, hands resting in a peaceful clasp behind his back. Cian's gaze rests on a stone in front of them, one he mentioned specifically in 2009. The one he told us marks the vernal, or spring, equinox sunrise and is carved to resemble the Horus hawk head from Egypt.

"Thank you for meeting me, old friend," Ansel starts off abruptly.

"Nonsense, old friend. It was on my way," Cian replies, a little smile spreading across his face. The remote Adam's Calendar is not on the way to anywhere, clearly.

Ansel eyes Cian, who continues staring at the Horus stone.

"I'm here, as you've no doubt guessed, to talk you out of this whole thing," Ansel tells him, wiping away the nervous sweat from his brow with the back of his hand.

"Ah, so you drew the short straw," Cian jokes, his eyes staying fixed on the same stone. "That one right there, that's Horus," Cian informs him, but Ansel doesn't look at it. Instead, he carefully studies Cian's profile for a moment.

"There is no talking you out of it, is there?" Ansel surmises.

"That's not how these things work. You *know* that, old friend," Cian casually reports, his gaze unchanged.

"And *you know* that *this* is different. Very different," Ansel warns, a new sharpness in his tone, frustration and anger.

But Cian stays quiet, as if there's nothing more to say.

"I don't like it, Cian," Ansel confesses, "and I'm not the only one," he blurts out finally. "Rasuil and Sourial, they are highly against it. You raising this ... *girl*," he says, and suddenly I realize ... they're talking about me.

"And Druscilla, and Bael, too, right?" Cian ventures. "Can't imagine they like it much either." His voice is remarkably playful given Ansel's strained and dire tone.

"Of course, they don't!" Ansel blows up, finally losing it.

Again, and much to Ansel's dismay, Cian has no reply.

"You know, I cannot understand for the life of me why you are being so casual about this. We are all deeply troubled by the whole thing. By the whole idea of *her* coming back," he spits out. "*Now*, of all times, the winter solstice, the end of the millennium!"

"Relax," Cian interjects, "she isn't even born yet," he reminds him.

"Born?" Ansel questions.

"Here," Cian clarifies. "She isn't even *here* yet."

"But she is coming? You're certain?" Ansel demands.

"She is," Cian confirms, then he checks the watch on his wrist. "Speaking of which…"

"This is madness, Cian! *Madness*! How will you continue with your work? Tell me that. If you miss just one—*just one*," Ansel threatens.

"I'll manage. I always have," Cian assures him. He pauses, taking in the bundle of nerves that is Ansel. "But, you're not being honest with me, my old friend … *my dear brother*. It's not my ability to do my job that has you so … worried, is it?" Cian gathers as he looks him over in a familiar way. A way that makes me wonder about what Cian just said, if he and Ansel are actually brothers.

This time, it's Ansel who has no reply.

Cian goes on. "It's what she's coming to accomplish … that's what's got you feeling so … *alarmed*," Cian assesses.

Ansel fidgets under Cian's gaze.

Cian finally looks away, setting his sights on Orion, the real one, out in the night sky.

"You are alarmed, are you not?" Cian asks.

Ansel's voice trembling and low, "What does she *want*? That's the question," he finally admits.

Cian, checking his watch again. "Come on old friend, you know that. It is the very same thing she has always wanted since the beginning," he drones as if the answer is rudimentary, basic knowledge, but Ansel seems lost. Finally, "Truth," Cian clarifies, looking surprised that he needed to.

Ansel squares his body to Cian defensively.

"Truth," Cian repeats, "she wants the truth..." he shakes his head, looking Ansel over curiously. "It's not something we can stop, Ansel, not permanently, nor should we try to. Or *want* to ... not forever," Cian asserts, turning his whole body to face Ansel. "You know there's no stopping it, right? That nothing anyone does will stop the truth. One way or another, the truth always gets told eventually."

They stare at each other in tense silence, until finally, Ansel turns away. Now *he* stares off at Orion glimmering in the night sky, the same way Cian was doing before. Knowing Cian's gaze is still trained on him after several moments of heaviness between them, Ansel inhales deeply, then lets it all out in a long audible sign.

"Walk with me, old friend," Ansel says, stepping in the direction of the ledge. "Dear *brother*," he says, thinking better of it. And Cian obliges, seemingly without worry, keeping at Ansel's side, even slightly in front of him, all the way to the very edge of the cliff.

"I suppose you're right," Ansel starts, standing behind Cian, a couple inches off his shoulder. "I suspected you would be, *of course*. But we had to voice our concerns, you understand."

"I do," Cian reassures him, his toes perched over what looks like the edge of the world, if not the universe.

Staring out into the vastness, wind whipping over them from the distant valley far below, blowing their clothes and hair wildly, they share a long silence.

"I just want you to be aware, things are changing, Ansel," Cian reveals. "Everything is starting to shift. Can you feel it?" he asks.

Ansel doesn't answer. After a long beat, Cian goes on.

"It's a bit hard to tell yet. It's only just begun. But if you start now, really paying attention ... you'll see it happening. Slow, at first, for a few more years. But when the quickening begins, everyone will be able to feel it. And then, well, after that, it won't be much longer until…"

"Until they all wake up." Ansel assumes, staring into the void, his voice monotone.

"Yes, one day. But it won't be because of her," Cian reveals.

"How do you know that?" Ansel questions him.

Cian studies Ansel. "I just know. I'm certain of it," he says.

Seeming both relieved and newly anxious, "Who then, who?" Ansel demands.

Cian studies him with disbelief.

"You *know* the answer to that, Ansel." He shakes his head in wonder. "Have you *really* forgotten?" he asks, almost to himself, then turns his gaze back out over the cliff. "No one is coming to save them," Cian says finally. "The answer to your question, to your frantic concern … is… no one," he clarifies.

"Well, explain to me then why you're—" Ansel starts in again, sounding frustrated and confused. But Cian just cuts him off.

"*Rest assured*," he snaps, then pauses, calming himself, "she won't save them," he repeats, again, trying at patience. Then, after a few moments of quiet, "You really can see it all from up here, can't you?

I watch Ansel ball his hands into secret fists of rage.

"Yes," he agrees with Cian.

"Like the whole entire world is laid out before us, right in front of this very spot—what a spectacular view it is," Cian remarks.

Ansel nods, jaw clenched, "Tell me, what will she be named?" he asks.

Cian looks right at him. "She already has a name," he asserts in a matter of fact way. His words, again, seem to threaten Ansel, a threat Cian appears committed to meeting head on. For a long moment, they just look at one another.

"Yes, that is true," Ansel concedes. "She does, but … well, what about … what about, say… *Eve?*" he says, sounding as if, by his suggestion, he's trying to make a threat of his own.

Cian thinks it over and slowly nods in agreement.

"All right," he says, finally.

"You'll name her Eve?" Ansel questions him, surprised that he would agree.

"Yes," Cian replies. "*Eve* … Yes, I think that's perfect," he assesses thoughtfully. Then he looks up. "Well, it appears it's time." He seems to gather this from the stars. Shifting his weight onto his heels as he gazes straight up and almost back at the vast bowl of stars over his head. "Oh yes, the time has come. I'd better be going."

Ansel shifts his weight ever so slightly onto his toes. Both his elbows cock back just a hair, like he's preparing to throw Cian off the cliff.

I reach down and pick up a tiny pebble next to my foot and hurl it at the stone closest to them. It makes a little *tick* noise as it hits, bouncing off, then ticks twice more as it skips across the ground.

They turn their heads in my direction. Ansel looks straight past me as I peek between the two huge stones I hide behind. Cian gazes right into my eyes. Then, he smiles and nods as if wanting me to be sure. He can see me, and Ansel can't.

"Eve it is," Cian says, his gaze still locked on mine. Then he looks again at his watch, and without another word, he turns and walks off towards the trail that leads down the mountain.

Ansel grimaces as he watches Cian go, tightens his balled-up fists in rage, then flies through the air towards Cian's back.

Right in the center of the circle, Cian whips around and leaps skyward just in time, colliding with Ansel in mid-air, their feet at least six feet from the earth. Twisting and turning in a wrestling embrace, they rise even higher before they come slamming back down with the force of an earthquake. Both men land like crushing boulders, their bodies squared, feet light, hands raised, prepared to fight.

Still as statues, neither of them makes even the slightest move. Suddenly Cian knocks Ansel off his feet, diving into his torso, having flown towards him faster than I could see. They slide along the ground, Ansel on his back, Cian on top of him, his fists gripping Ansel's shirt, racing towards the cliff. When Ansel's neck reaches the edge, his head hanging over, Cian stops them, somehow, on a dime.

Ansel's arms are stretched out by his sides grabbing what earth he can claw along the ledge. Cian's back blocking most my view, I walk out from behind the boulder to get a closer look. I need to see it all, every part of their exchange, to fully understand why I'm here.

Cian has Ansel pinned on his back at the edge of the cliff. Looming over him, it's as if he's grown along with his intensity. Cian appears noticeably larger, much stronger, and much more powerful than Ansel.

"All of this is going to end," he booms, his voice like a mighty cannon, his words a warning shot across the bow. "The entire third dimension, it will end. It was never meant to last forever! It'll end just the way it began, and there is *nothing* you can do to stop it," Cian warns.

I keep moving closer and notice I'm not far from the center of the circle, when there's a great clap of thunder, like a bomb exploding overhead. Then a bolt of lightning out over the cliff streaks sideways across the night sky, as if slicing the heavens directly in half. Then, the landscape begins to change, slowly at first, and then more and more rapidly. Trees of all shapes and sizes, coming up and going down. The sky strobing between day and night, exploding with violent storms that dissipate as quickly as they form. Ice and snow covering the land and then melting away, as millennia elapse in reverse. Everything winding back to another time, another moment that took place at this very spot. I watch the world around me peel off what looks like a hundred thousand years, *or more.*

It begins slowing down as lush green grass grows up around me. When the grass is waist-high, everything stops, and I look around. The stones of Adam's Calendar are now gone, as are Ansel and Cian. Sounds of animals and birds fill the air, loud and exotic. Large leafy plants and towering trees, both in varieties that appear prehistoric, surround me.

The air feels different, empty and still, eerily so, like something is missing. Like there's nothing but plants and animals and the undisturbed vibration of the earth. What's missing is people, humans. They're not here yet. But, stranger still, is how familiar it all feels, hauntingly familiar. It's unmistakable, the feeling of home.

I wander over towards where the center of Adam's Calendar would be, and as I watch my own hand push back the tall thick grass, I know I've walked these steps before. Pushing back this very grass, living in this very place, at this very time—in my first life.

When I get to the middle, where I just watched Cian and Ansel's fight begin, all the grass has been pulled away, torn out or smashed down, as if another struggle just occurred here, a much older one, an ancient struggle. The open space is five or six feet around, where a large patch of bare, kicked-up earth is filled with rusty brown dirt pushed up in piles next to pools of thick red. A small hand-spear, a rudimentary weapon the size of a big rock, laying nearby. Everything is soaked red.

"Blood," I whisper to myself as I realize. It's splattered on the grass. It's all over the ground. It's everywhere, blood. And it hits me all at once—who Cian and Ansel are. Who they *were*. The *two* of them.

They *were brothers*. The first.

FOUR

With a renewed sense of urgency I return to the hut.

Hearing Roman's thoughts echoing off the walls, filling the tiny space as I enter, *Is there really no end to the number of times I'll have to hear it?* he wonders to himself, nearing his breaking point.

"*So* much has been lost, Roman, and *it is* all Eve's fault," she repeats, as if by some chance he didn't hear her the first ten times.

I stand next to him, wrapping my arm around his shoulders, closing my eyes.

I'm here with you, Roman. But I'm also everywhere. You're everywhere too, but you just don't know it. There are things we're doing, together, outside this realm, this boxed-in little dimension. These things we're doing are important, and only you and I can do them. But this you, trapped here, you're living a dream, a little sliver of existence. You call it life. Roman, it's not real, because it's not the whole thing you're seeing here—it's just a fraction. One tiny fractured possibility of the whole beautiful concept that is life. Real life, I whisper to him, feeling my soul growing impatient.

I know that Roman comes with me into Aquarius—the multidimensional plane where all ascended souls gather. I can see us there together. I know it happens. But, there are things I don't know, even as an ascended being. Things that are not up to me. Like when it will happen, and how. That's all up to Roman.

His soul feels impatient too, like mine, but it's not finished here, not yet. His mind is telling him the impatience he feels brewing inside himself is with Iris. He's still so dug in to this world and its illusions.

She's a child, I whisper, *and she's afraid, Roman. You understand that, and you know why. Your impatience isn't really because of Iris. It's all the parts of your soul that are already growing impatient with the few parts left that are not.*

He hears the things I tell him, just not with his ears. It's all stored in the recesses of his mind, in his unconscious. Then, when and if he has the same thought or idea on his own, when the idea becomes conscious, he'll recognize it like a long-lost friend. Like those things you just somehow know deep in your heart to be true. You don't really know why you know. You just do. Things you feel in your bones, that no one can convince you otherwise. Things known by the soul.

It's the world she's a product of ... that's causing her to be this way. You know that, I remind him as his frustration grows.

Iris's tiny arms are crossed tightly in front of her short, thin body, a deep wrinkle on her brow. The intensity of her stare rivals the unyielding scorch of the desert sun.

Lately, no matter where their conversation starts, this is where it ends—her staring up at him, liquid gray eyes like molten steel, scanning his face with alarm after firing off these same old words. Words she believes more than anything else. Then, she gawks at him in silence. After which there's more staring and more silence in what has become their daily ritual standoff.

In all fairness to Iris, she really isn't asking for much. All she wants is to hear him say something that, to her, couldn't be more ordinary. Words no one here thinks anything of at all, the very words on which their whole world is built. She's waiting for him to say the *second* part in particular. That it's all Eve's fault—*my fault*—the grueling and grim state of their lives, the reason so much has been lost.

All she wants is for him to agree and to proclaim it. And, why wouldn't she? This *is* what they're teaching the children after all. It's what every person in Primitus believes, and everyone else for that matter, across all of Aurora. He knows she is correct. Though lately, Roman has begun to understand that simply being *correct* within a society doesn't have a whole lot to do with whether something is actually *true*.

So, he doesn't say it, as usual. He just gives a small nod, a mild agreement, that much he can seem to manage. But, as usual, it doesn't work. Her eyes widen, and her mouth falls open.

"You're correct," he decides to throw in, which has about the same effect as a single drop of water would have on a raging fire.

The storm gathers first in her shoulders then spreads to her face, quickly consuming her molten granite eyes, "So much has been lost! And it's all Eve's fault!" she fires off, furious, narrowing her gaze and waiting in silence for him to affirm his beliefs by repeating the words.

But as much as he'd like to, for Iris's sake, *You just can't say it, can you?* I smile up at him.

"You never say it!" Iris finally explodes. Her voice louder than ever, louder than either of them is comfortable with.

"You're right," he replies after a few moments of heavy silence. "I never do say it," he admits to her surprise, to mine as well, and a bit to his own, apparently, his heart beating faster. "Not every word of it, anyway, and not loud and proud, how we're supposed to," he goes on, feeling the resentment he usually works harder to repress, for being told what to think and what to believe. "You see, typically, I'll mumble the first part, you know, under my breath, then just let my voice trail off completely. My silence is always drowned out by the enthusiasm of the others," he reveals to her, knowing instantly he's gone too far.

"What are you saying?" she grills him. "You're an unbeliever?" she accuses. It's what she worries about constantly, what she's suspected for as long as she can remember.

"I'm just saying it always … gives me pause," he tries, hoping to diffuse the situation.

"It gives you pause? The most important pillar of our beliefs?"

"Yes. It just, sort of, stops me dead in my tracks," he admits.

"I don't even know what to say to that," she tells him. "I don't know what that means, Roman."

She is at a complete loss with him, and he's at quite a loss with himself as well. Trying to explain things to her even he doesn't fully understand.

"Why are we always fighting, fighting about ideas, beliefs, and words?" he asks her with a sigh. "There are a lot of other things we have to be concerned about."

"Because it's what matters, more than anything else. We *have to* believe if we've even got a shot at surviving. Because so much has been lost. And because it is all Eve's fault," she implores him, desperate for him to believe. "Why do you have to be different? Why aren't you just like everyone else?" she asks. He hears the sadness hidden in her cutting words.

"I don't know," he honestly tells her.

"A perfect world, Roman, *a paradise*. What humans had! And all of it was destroyed! By this wicked, evil girl," she implores him. "And now I finally get to see it ... I finally get to see what she's done..." Iris shakes her head at him, her eyes welling, feeling betrayed. "Do you *really not* believe?" she whispers, equal parts inquiry and accusation with a hint of amazement, all drenched in fear.

Again, he stays quiet. He just can't bring himself to say it. And again, it makes her blood boil.

"Say it," she challenges. "Say it's all Eve's fault."

He knows he's not going to say it, that he just can't bring himself to. So, he turns around quickly and busies himself with her breakfast. Foraged wild bush berries and the last bit of coyote meat they've got. His thoughts go to hunting and gathering, to his responsibilities, to the wild licorice and wondering how in the world he's going to find some before her infection gets even worse.

"Roman…" she whispers, "How could you *not* believe?" the trembling in her voice calls him out of his own mind and back into reality.

"I just wish they didn't take you there, that's all," he admits, voice low, but feels bad the second he says it. She's been waiting for this, and at eleven, she's finally old enough.

"Why? Tell me that. Why not?" she demands.

He turns around and looks at her. Her thick, long mop of light brown hair pulled, as best she can manage, into a knot on top of her small, delicate head. Her tiny body is still that of a child. No more than eighty pounds. His heart aches at the sight of her. His mind goes numb and red at the thought of anyone ever hurting her and the primal knowledge of how easy it would be to do.

He swallows a sudden lump in his throat, his eyes welling.

"I wish they didn't take you there because I've been there. I've seen it. And it is a very hard thing to see," he warns, knowing it's likely lost on her. "I just want to protect you, Iris, from … *everything*… especially from all of that death…" he trails off, not wanting his words to pull his mind any closer. Not wanting to revisit the place where the human remains of the fallen civilization serve as a supposed reminder of the stakes of their existence—the survival of the human race—the sheer impossibility of accomplishing it, all that's against them, and the kind of fate that awaits them all if they don't.

"And *that* is exactly why it's so important, Roman," she says, right on cue. "If we don't see all the destruction and all the death with our own eyes, as awful as it is, we might forget what she's done. Or worse, we might even begin to question The Word."

He sets her breakfast on the stone counter in front of her, the metal plate making a clanking sound as he does. It's a meager meal. And he has nothing to give her for lunch. She looks up from the bare rations of scrappy sun-cured coyote meat and tiny shriveled bush berries.

"I'm sorry, Roman," she mumbles, to his surprise. Words he can't recall ever hearing from her before.

He turns to look at her. She begins to fidget, suddenly uncomfortable with the conversation she just started.

"Go on," he encourages, much like a father might. Iris takes a deep breath. She's worried about what she has to tell him, but knows she has no choice.

"About the wild licorice," she finally admits after a moment, "I—"

Then suddenly she stops. Her eyes widen and move one side to the other as she tries to decipher what she feels happening under her where she sits. Her heart quickens at the terrifying thought of what this warm wet feeling might be, this sudden gush she feels rush out of her. She jumps off her seat and darts for the back room.

Roman walks a few slow steps towards where she ran.

"Iris?" he calls to her, but she doesn't answer.

There's no door separating the bedroom from the rest of the hut. There's just a smooth mud-brick wall that divides the circular structure in two, a single archway in the middle of it.

He stands next to the arched opening with his back against the wall, listening. Worrying. *Knowing* ... in the pit of his stomach. Knowing exactly what this is. The one thing they've both been dreading. It's been happening to all the girls in her class lately, one right after the other.

"Iris..." he says again, even more gently. "What is it?" He whispers to her through the wall, hearing the faint sound of her sniffling. He takes a deep breath, trying to calm his frayed nerves, his churning sick stomach. He tries to imagine how she must be feeling and realizes he can't. "Talk to me," he says, his voice soft and comforting, like a cool inviting river.

She stays quiet, her lips pressed tight together. If she speaks, she'll burst out sobbing.

"Iris, talk to me. What happened?" he asks her again,

then rests his forehead on the wall in front of him.

"It's nothing," she blurts out finally, trying her best to sound casual, frustrated at the sound of her shaky, weak voice. How she knows it gives her away. Roman knows her every different pitch and tone, he knows this one is dire alarm, and he knows exactly what it's telling him.

He lifts his head off the wall, wondering to himself if this day that's hardly begun could honestly get any worse and fearing for where it may be heading. He hears her shuffling around, moving about their room. The sound of her drawer opening and closing. Then, another few moments pass, the hut smothered in anxious quiet.

Roman stands motionless outside the doorway, not wanting to intrude. To give her privacy. He's always tries to be so mindful of things like that, though it's often hard in the tiny living space they share. With him being a grown man and her a young girl.

Iris, for all her brash antagonizing, secretly knows how lucky she is, that out of all the King Soul men, her Keeper is Roman. Because he *is* different, he thinks differently, and so he sees her differently. Not how the world is telling him to see her—the sum of her female parts, a means to an end. He sees *her*, who she really is. A young girl who's not yet a woman in almost any sense of the word, and nowhere near it. He knows she's sharp and smart, but he also knows she talks so big because she feels rather small. That she's strong-willed and tough, but also anxious and fearful. He sees all of her, how fierce she is, but also how fragile. And Iris knows that makes her lucky.

He looks down at his side to see her standing in the middle of the doorway, right next to him. Her gray eyes glazed and icy, staring straight ahead. Her skin drained so white it reminds Roman of the alabaster sky he stared at so intently just a short time ago.

"Is it?" he starts, and she cuts him off with an obedient, affirming nod. Like a little soldier, he thinks, a heartbreaking thought.

By her shocked, sickened look, he knows she doesn't want him to say the word any more than he wants to say it himself. So, he doesn't say it. Instead, he watches her, trying to read her emotions. Trying to find the best way to reach her and to bring her back, feeling as if she's floated off the planet far away from him. She stares, stunned, out into the stale dry air ahead, unblinking. Her tiny chest rises and falls at what Roman perceives to be about twice its normal rate.

"Servus," she whispers, finally, her voice heavy with defeat and disbelief. But even her voice, which sounds gutted, doesn't reveal how hollowed-out she feels. But Roman doesn't need her words to understand. He already knows how she feels, or at least how she must. They both fall silent. Both stifled and crushed under the enormous weight of it—all that it means.

Iris will now be fully enlisted in The Cause. Although for both of them, it defies all natural feelings. From now on it will be Roman's job to try to impregnate her and her job to cooperate, to submit. As her Keeper, he's always been free to "do what he pleased with her." His only requirement is to keep her alive, fed, in "moderate health," and to be sure she attended to her education. But from now on, doing to her what he finds utterly incomprehensible, what sends a shiver down his spine and rage boiling through his veins, will be required of him by law. She'll be submitted to daily checks, and all of it will be monitored. He's been living in fear of this turn of events for as long as he can remember.

She imagined when this moment arrived that logic would save her. Logic and the education she's so enthusiastically embraced, but neither has come to rescue her. She feels abandoned by both, desperate and lost, set adrift in a hostile sea with nothing to cling to.

"The Cause is everything," she starts, voice trembling, words she recites regularly but falls silent, unable to make herself finish the rest of the verse. "Servus is a duty and an honor, the highest honor a woman can attain." Her mind is splintered, fractured in a way she's never imagined it could be. Her deeply engrained beliefs, snagged violently by her heart's protest of this reality.

This fabled day, when her status would be changed, lingered out before her in her mind, almost dream-like, with a kind of magical mystery. As if the whole thing were just imaginary. A fairy tale, a story you know so well it feels real but that you suspect deep down is not. But the lead brick sitting in the pit of her stomach tells her, this once-fabled idea, this imaginary thing, is terrifyingly real.

On top of her sadness, fear, and worry is the guilt.

"The fate of the world depends on it," she breathes out, telling herself she has no right to all the things she's feeling.

Her attempt to rally herself and those damn words nearly knock all the wind out of Roman's chest in a baffled sigh. The level to which her education has taught her to rewire her natural feelings never ceases to amaze him.

Iris has been taught that the regulated, state-controlled process is the only way to ensure that humanity will succeed in finally reproducing once more. That, and their blind belief.

Servus is what God has called them to do, to submit themselves and their bodies to the government of Primitus for monitoring, and to their Keeper, as soon as they become "useful" to The Cause. When she adds it all up, when she puts it on paper, when she's listening in class, it all makes sense. But now in this moment, nothing makes sense to her.

What she knows in her head is directly opposed to what she suddenly feels in every other fiber of her being.

She can't look at Roman. She can only stare ahead absently, her gaze glazed over, because that's what she's trying to feel. Nothing. Only, it's not working. *Really* not working.

Finally, she begins to break.

"This is supposed to be the best day of my life," she mumbles, eyes welling at once. "How could the worst thing in the world happen?" she whispers to him. Her secret forbidden feelings.

Roman's heart is broken, seeing her like this, trying her best to right herself with the impossible. Trying with everything she has to accept the utterly unacceptable and watching her continue to come up short, and perceiving how she's actually blaming herself.

He places one knee on the ground, squaring himself in front of her and takes both of her trembling hands in his. He gives them a warm comforting squeeze.

She looks down at her balled-up fists, rolls one of them over and opens it, revealing the missing sprig of wild licorice crumpled up in her tiny, sweaty palm.

"What in the world were you doing with this?" he whispers, shaking his head in wonder.

Finally, for the first time since she walked out of the

room, she looks at him in his eyes, sadness overwhelming them both.

"Eliza is a liar," she spits, voice trembling, tears falling down both cheeks. It's all she can manage before her anger starts to bubble into rage. She purses her lips tight together as if to seal in her torrent of emotions and offers him the flattened, dried-up herb.

"Eliza, a girl from your class," Roman assumes. Iris nods grudgingly, feeling suddenly motion sick, as if the whole hut is spinning in a slow wobbly circle.

He thinks of wiping away her tears, but he doesn't. He doesn't want to make her feel more vulnerable than she already does.

"She lives next door," she says, barely moving her little mouth, afraid if she lets her anger out there's no telling what other emotions will escape with it. Then she pulls one of her hands from his and wipes each side of her face with the back of it.

Roman, assuming that this girl must have told Iris some kind of wives' tale, presses her for more. He knows it's best to release at least some of her feelings, and he figures the anger at a schoolmate is a safe place to start.

"What did she lie about?" he asks.

But Iris doesn't want to tell him. She realizes, quite suddenly, the way children do, that it makes her seem as if she isn't fully behind The Cause. That she doesn't fully believe in all she's been taught. All she's been preaching to him.

"It's nothing," she says. "Forget it."

Roman studies her a moment.

"You're sure?" he offers, looking prepared to move on.

His eyes, soft and encouraging, remind her that if there's one person she can tell, it's him.

"She told me that if I hid wild licorice in the bed underneath where I slept, that ... that it wouldn't come. That *this* wouldn't happen," she blurts out, furious. Then she immediately shifts her eyes to his, trying to gauge his reaction.

He nods, slow and thoughtful.

"Well, I can certainly understand why you'd want to believe something like that," he says, Iris hanging on his every word feeling uneasy with what's suddenly in the air between them. How her act validates the doubts Roman clearly has about the way things are and what they are supposed to believe.

"I hate her," she seethes, trying to fling the focus onto someone other than herself, all the while worrying about what Roman might think this means. How it appears. Like she doesn't want to do her part. Like maybe she even questions The Word.

"I'm not an unbeliever," she spits out suddenly. "It's just a dumb little game. I knew it wouldn't work, obviously."

"Right," he gives her.

"And anyway, Eliza says the strangest, most bizarre, most stupid things," Iris vents as Roman takes the plant from her small hand. He wants to ask about the strange bizarre things Eliza says. But for Iris's sanity in this moment, he decides not to. It's best just to move on.

"I'll take care of your arm when you get home tonight," he tells her, holding up the plant and she nods. "After you've finally seen it, all the destruction, with your own eyes," he reminds her, watching as she works to realign herself to her deeply engrained beliefs from this brand-new vantage point.

"You need to register me," she tells him with a swallow, her voice dutiful and thin. By law, Roman must change her status to Servus today after assembly, changing her officially from a girl being educated to a woman in the eyes of the government, a woman doing her part for The Cause. If he fails to register her, he'll be thrown in Confinement, and Iris will be placed with another grown male King Soul.

Tears well fast and quickly spill over her dark black lashes.

"Sshhh, it's ok," he starts.

"How?" she demands. "How is this ok?" She stares off,

feeling lost again, in the terrifying space between what she knows and what she feels. She starts to cry openly now, unable to hold it back any longer. As he watches her small body convulse with anguish, his heart aches, feelings of anger burning in his chest.

"You're right, Iris, it's not. There's nothing ok about this," he agrees as he watches her crying and trembling. "It's wrong. It's all wrong," he asserts, feeling more definitive the more he watches her. And more defiant.

"I won't do it," he says, sounding as though it's already resolved in his mind.

Her swollen watery eyes flick up to meet his.

"We're not going to do it. I'm not going to register you," he tells her, his words hanging like a live grenade in the still air between them.

ROMAN

FIVE

———— ✠ ————

I know this girl as well as I know myself, and right now I can't predict which way she'll swing, towards duty or defiance.

With one of my knees on the ground we are eye level. Iris scans my face, her expression twists.

"We can't," she whispers, terror filling her teary eyes.

I stay quiet a moment, allowing her to think some more.

"Can we?" she asks, a question I'm amazed to hear from her. "But even if we can, should we? I mean, we *shouldn't*, right?" she starts to reason, looking torn apart by all she's been taught. "It's not the right thing to do."

"What is right? What does that even mean, Iris?" I ask her.

"What? You know the difference between right and wrong?" she tries to tell me.

"No actually, I don't think I do," I confide, taking her in—her innocence. "You see, what I think is wrong is called right, and what I feel in my heart is right, that's all wrong," I start, knowing that after this, there's no going back. "Let me tell you something, Iris. It is right to try and beat a system that's wrong," I say, watching her. "A bad system," I go on. "One that you … that you don't believe in," I tell her finally, for the first time. "You're right, Iris. You've had it right all along. I don't believe, not in The Word or The Cause or The Destruction Story. I used to, at some point. But not anymore."

Her mouth falls open. Her eyes scan the room.

"Don't say that, Roman," she whispers, begging me. "Please, take it back." She panics, her eyes well, and her mouth falling into a tearful pout. Her bottom lip quivers. Seeing her so panicked and sad at me admitting what I truly believe puts a lump in my throat. Despite it, I stay quiet, my steady gaze on her, unwavering.

"You want to be registered?" I ask. Her silence is her answer.

All the things we've argued about constantly sit squarely between us now, all of it laid bare. I knew eventually it might be, but this was always the one thing I was most unsure about. How she would react when the time came, when I would finally have to tell her that I didn't believe.

That I wasn't going to be able to do what was required of me. Any of it.

"Iris, what you're being taught … it's all … I think it's just some kind of made-up story," I say tenderly, feeling freer and more certain of it as the words leave my mouth for the first time.

"A made-up story? But Roman, there are no births, no pregnancies, there is no food, everything has been ruined. How can you say—"

"We're not being told the truth. I don't know how I know, but I do. The things that are expected of us, all of it just creates more suffering. It can't be the real answer to these problems. There is another answer. I know it's out there. And I feel like, somehow, I can find it," I venture.

She stands there quietly, weighing it all.

"You don't really want to be registered, do you?" I ask, "Monitored," I add, reminding her of what she already knows, all the things that begin the moment I change her status. The horrible things.

"No … I don't want to be registered," she admits stiffly. Terrified.

"Ok. Then we are not registering you. We tell no one," I say, warningly. "We have to be in this together, united. You know that, right?" I remind her, feeling suddenly weary. "We have to really be a team."

She nods in agreement. Then suddenly, out of nowhere, she throws her arms around me, burying her face in my shirt, crying onto my shoulder. I hold on to her tightly. I want her to feel safe, to feel secure. I want to give that to her, even if I know it's not real.

She lifts her head with the strangest look on her face. She places her small hand on the center of my chest.

I reach down the front of my shirt and pull up a key.

"Where did that come from?" she asks, sounding more open than she normally would about something she knows goes against policy. Private, personal effects must all be declared with the government, and since she's never seen this before, she knows it's undeclared.

"I don't know exactly where it came from," I struggle to tell her.

"How long have you had it?" she quizzes me, reaching out towards the key.

"For … as long as I can remember," I tell her. I place it in her hand, letting her look it over.

"Why do you wear it? What does it mean?"

"I'm not sure, actually."

"Well, what does it unlock?" she asks.

"I don't know, but I know it's something important," I say. "Very important."

"How? How do you know that?" she challenges, her

trademark intensity returning. Iris always wants answers. And like everyone, she wants something to believe in. So, I decide to tell her what I know. *Everything.*

"Well," I start, gingerly. "There's this girl. I dream about her when I sleep, a girl my own age. And I am almost certain that she gave it to me," I tell her.

"Another girl?" she asks, seeming almost wounded.

"Yes, a grown girl my own age," I say. She nods.

"When did she give it to you? Was it in a dream?" she asks, her eyes widening at the thought.

"No, in another life, I think, maybe."

"Another life?" she marvels, intrigued.

"Perhaps. Or in this lifetime, but in some other place, in a place other than this," I struggle to explain, as frustrated as I usually am when I try to understand the origin of the key.

"A place other than this?"

"Yes. Before Passus," I tell her. "The girl I talk with in my dreams, she explains to me that the world of Passus, the world where we now stand, is not all there ever was, or even … all that there is," I say, trying to read her reaction but finding little evidence of how she feels from her pensive look. Everything she's been taught sits directly opposed to what I'm telling her.

"Before Passus? Right here … but before?" There's sheer wonder in her voice.

"Another world existed, Iris, before what we know as Passus. I lived in it. You too. We all did," I explain. Her mouth drops open at the thought. "We had … other lives. They weren't perfect, but things weren't this bad. And Iris … I don't think it was that long ago," I divulge.

"What happened?" she asks.

"Something. I'm not sure what," I admit. "But it wasn't The Destruction, not as we know it, as it's told. It was different, something else entirely."

"How can you be so sure?" she asks.

"I'm sure. We're being lied to, Iris. And I won't stop until I find the truth," I declare out loud for the first time, this intense desire that's been growing inside me.

Iris goes silent. She stares at me, knowing that this changes everything. Then, she gazes at the ground a moment.

"Roman?" she asks, looking back up at me, her gray eyes softened and vulnerable. A way I've never seen them before.

"Yeah?"

"Her name," she requests, "the girl you dream about … the girl who is your own age who tells you all these things. The girl who gave you the key, what is her name?"

"Her name is Eve," I say, looking right into her eyes as they widen with terror.

Just then, there's a knock on the door. The last thing

I'm expecting. There's never once been a knock on the door of the hut Iris and I share. And so, the knock, that's truly more of an incessant pounding, jars us both beyond our own skin, throwing the already trying moment into a full-fledged crisis.

She quickly hands back the key. I replace it around my neck and hide it securely under my shirt.

"Roman," she whispers, her eyes begging me to somehow know who is behind the door and exactly what it is they want. Then something occurs to her and fear grips her small narrow face.

"What if they already know? What if they're coming for me—" she breaks off, terrified.

"Shhh, it's ok. It's ok. No one knows," I whisper gently to her. She's shaking. Her eyes are lost in terror. I hold her shoulders and look calmly into her face.

"Everything is going to be okay."

"How do you know that?" she shrills, too loudly. And we both look towards the door.

"Listen to me," I whisper. "Listen, I promise you. I am not going to let anything happen to you. You believe me, Iris, right?"

After studying me for a moment she nods her head.

"Go back," I whisper, motioning her towards the bedroom.

Though she's afraid to part with me, after a second she does as I tell her. I can almost hear her heart fluttering like a jackrabbit's against her chest as she backs into the rounded room, always keeping her eyes on me, her lifeline. There are no corners in which to hide, so Iris tucks herself close to the head of our bamboo and straw bed. Her back sealed tight against the mud-brick wall.

I grab my head cloth and wrap it around my head and neck securing it into the front of my shirt and into the back under my collar and I head for the door.

The second I lift the latch, the door flies open with a blast of wind, which then tears through the hut in a maddening swirl that upends our few belongings. It's all I can do just to hang on to the handle as the door slams against the wall into its full open position.

Before me stands the man from the neighboring hut directly to our right. Cicero. We've never spoken before. His girl, who I now know is Eliza, is the same age as Iris and in the same class at school. I know nothing else about him.

His lanky body is covered from head to toe in the same clothes as me, the same clothes that all King Soul men wear; a pair of thick cargo trousers, a long sleeve military-style shirt, red King Soul armband around his bicep, protective eyewear goggles, otherwise known as Oculum, and a head cloth that wraps around covering the neck, and head. Clothes designed to protect us from the whipping sand and the brutal sun. Clothes, that as King Souls, we are highly privileged to have.

After an awkward beat, Cicero leans in. He speaks quietly, his voice low but commanding, like the boom of a distant cannon.

"What they're saying..." he starts, then pauses. He begins shaking his head, "You ever get the feeling ... well," he parses out, seeming to struggle with what he wants to say. He shifts his weight from one foot to the other. Then finally, "You think maybe this is just ... to get us angry? To make things worse, always worse..." he trails off, lost in thought. "You ever feel like we're being lied to?" he asks finally.

"What are they saying?" I stammer out.

"Don't you know what's happened?" he asks, sounding surprised.

"No," I tell him, both of us knowing that I should. I should have had my Oculum on by now. We're expected to wear them at all times, even while we sleep.

He shifts his weight slightly to the right, looking past me to where my Oculum headset is lying dormant on the kitchen counter. Then he shifts his weight back and looks me square in the face.

"Busy killing scorpions," I lie, kicking one off my foot, not wanting to give away any clues about what I was busy with instead, with Iris.

"What happened?" I ask.

With his headset covering his eyes I can't read his expression. I'm lost as to what he's thinking or what he may be trying to tell me.

"The Aurora Treaty… it's not happening. Antiquus tore it up," he tells me, sounding glib. "I'm almost not surprised, given that that's about the worst thing that could possibly happen. All the fighting and bloodshed, the constant bombing, that's nothing. Think we were already at war?" he says, shaking his head, then gives a quick glance over his shoulder and behind him. He turns back and stares at me a moment longer. "That's nothing, compared to what's coming," he says. Then he pivots on his heels and is gone.

In his place, I spot a Witness barreling down the row, straight towards me. It's much closer to our hut than the one I saw this morning. This one is just a few rows away and closing in fast.

Always assume they're not after you. It's what I tell Iris constantly. *They're just collecting data, looking for threats. Primitus must be protected. That's their job. You're not doing anything wrong. You're not a threat.*

I grab the door and start pushing it shut against the brutal gusts, keeping an eye on the Witness's course. It continues approaching rapidly, like a predator—right towards me. With all my might and weight, I push on the door, and get it past the critical halfway point just as the Witness takes a sharp turn in the direction of Cicero's hut.

I finish the strenuous job of closing and sealing the door and turn around, breathing hard. Sweat is dripping from my brow. I can feel it soaking my head cloth.

"What is it?" Iris whispers from the archway, her voice trembling.

"We need to get going," I tell her.

"Is that Witness after him?" she speculates. "It looked like it was coming for him? Or for us!?" She panics.

"I don't think it's after us. But we need to get going," I say. "Now." I grab my hunting bag and crossbow.

"What did he say to you?"

Her question stops me. I look over at her.

"He said … he said he thought we were being lied to," I say, how his words perfectly echo the very ones I was saying to Iris seconds before sends a chill over my whole body.

All the color drains out of Iris's face.

"We need to go about our day as normally as possible, all right?" I say, as I help Iris with her head cloth. "And that means we cannot be late," I warn. We both rush to prepare to leave the hut.

"All right," she says, the voice of resolve through a look of terror.

"Don't worry about your arm," I tell her, "just do *not* touch it," I warn with a stern look. "We don't want it getting any worse. I'll fix it tonight, all right?"

"Okay," she agrees with a trusting nod.

"I am going to have something for us to eat," I pledge, leery of making such promises but feeling the need to give her something to look forward to knowing the day she's about to face.

"A rabbit?" she suggests hopefully, a twinkle in her eyes.

"Not sure I'm in a position to take requests," I joke, trying to remember the last time I laid eyes on a rabbit.

"I would *really* like some rabbit," she says.

"Me too," I admit. "I'll see what I can do." I smile. It feels good to know how much faith she has in me— misplaced as it may be.

"Ready?" I ask. We're both about to pull our goggles over our eyes.

"Roman?" she stops me.

"What is it?"

"I'm so glad you're my Keeper," she breaths out, her smoky gray eyes starting to well up once again.

"Me too, Iris," I tell her.

SIX

—— ❁ ——

Through the blinding wall of sand, dust, and silt blowing towards us at thirty miles per hour, it's impossible to navigate anywhere. But with a series of directional signals, arrows, and green and red lines, and by creating a virtual reality of images where huts, burning brush, and other objects exist, our goggles guide us through the King sector with perfect precision.

The day's news, updates, and threat level in a scrolling feed appear along the sides of our view. Fire, weather, and wind advisories chirp and chime on the left. The threat level today is a red ten, telling us to maintain the height of vigilance, that we are as unsafe as possible.

"It's always red ten," Iris whispers to me, and I nod. I'd noticed that long ago, but she never had. Not until today. The threat level is measured in yellow, orange, and red and numbers one through ten. But it's always red ten. Always.

The latest news and current events appear on the right side of our view, delivered every day by the same women in a white jacket with dark red hair and sage green eyes, named Sourial. I find her hauntingly familiar, as if I know her. Of course, I don't. Oculum is fully personalized, so she talks directly to me, which is the reason for this odd familiar feeling. Or so I tell myself.

Right now, she's warning me about foreign terrorists.

"Today's threat level is a red ten, Roman, the highest and most dangerous. An insurgency of Dragon Souls, in numbers unknown, are heading towards Primitus. An attack is imminent, and they could strike at any time. According to state intelligence, these foreign terrorists are believed to be targeting King Souls, and they are said to be heavily armed," she warns as Iris and I are approaching the center square, the enormous gathering place where I drop her off every day. The presence of guards is heavier than usual.

"In other state news," Sourial goes on, "a lawless gang of Warrior Souls launched yet another attack on the latest government supply trucks from Aurora, intercepting the rations and killing ten government agents and five state guards. Ration restrictions will begin tomorrow as a result of these attacks. Sectors effected will be King and Guardian.

The sheer number of Gypsy Souls place the heaviest strain on the already limited resources for all other Primitans."

I look down at Iris, knowing I have no more food at home, and no rations coming anytime soon, and my heart sinks. I have to catch something today. I have to catch her a rabbit.

"The violence and senseless killings continued around the clock throughout the Warrior sector, with over ninety percent of the stolen rations believed to have been destroyed by arson. Hundreds of Warrior Souls were killed in the anarchy," she concludes. The close-up shot never breaks from her face.

"Ever wonder why she just tells us the news but never shows us anything?" I whisper to Iris. And watch as her mouth drops open.

"There are cameras everywhere…" she realizes, shaking her head in wonder, and I watch another layer of blind acceptance peel away from her mind just as Primitus Castle comes into view. It rises high above everything else and sits a few hundred yards beyond the center square. Even through the sheets of sand it's easy to spot the enormous white structure looming ahead in the distance. The white flags that adorn the top of the imposing palace, like the sails of a mighty ship, thrash and snap violently in the wind.

Iris is lagging a bit today. I can tell she doesn't feel well.

"Keep close," I tell her, and she hustles up beside me as we begin to fold into the large wave of King Souls, millions of them, just like Iris and I, all heading to the same place.

The center square is the King Soul gathering place. It's a sprawling swathe of desert paved in brick, divided into ten cells and surrounded by large screens and high guard towers. The brick is always a welcome change once we reach it. Drudging our heavy boots through the sand never seems to get any easier. The center square is the closest anyone can get to Primitus Castle. As King Souls, we can actually see it with our own eyes, and the balcony where the leader of Primitus and his High Council are seated. Lower souls have never laid eyes on it. Their gathering places are miles from here.

We assemble according to our Incarnation Numbers, arranged in cells, one through ten. According to The Word, King Souls have lived between two hundred and two hundred ninety-nine lifetimes. Iris and I, with our INs of 299, are in cell ten. As are Cicero and Eliza. I catch a glimpse of them standing just ahead of us as The Aurora Creed begins, the words appearing in our viewfinders as well as all the gigantic screens surrounding us.

"Out of the ground she came," the millions of King Souls begin, speaking in unison, "seeking destruction, an evil unto the world, the oldest evil, a demon, the she-devil."

I always watch Iris during The Creed—how she proclaims so proudly each and every word. This time though, she looks up at me, her mouth not moving at all. Neither is mine. We lock eyes, bonded by our silence, vowing to be united in our dissent, whatever it may bring upon us. Everyone else goes on.

"From Eve came forth the great flood, the sky burned white by the wall of her unholy water. *So much has been lost, and it's all Eve's fault.* Our fate she sealed in red when the moon she turned to blood. The innocent perished, the land and souls grew barren. *So much has been lost, and it's all Eve's fault.* She brought the wind upon us. She is the bearer of disease, illness, and death, destroyer of paradise. *So much has been lost, and it's all Eve's fault.*," the colossal crowd of millions proclaims, then falls silent.

In unison, they all bow their heads, looking towards the ground. After several seconds and all together, they look back up and continue.

"Souls will be saved from imminent extinction," they assert, their voices rising. "We believe in The Word and in The Cause. We believe God bestowed Animus upon the world for the separation of souls, Old from New, to end unordered soul assimilation, to purify and order us by our blood. We believe our Incarnation Numbers are the truth of who we are. We believe in one world, *Passus*, in one government, *Aurora*, and in two states of souls, *Old* and *New*." their voices building to a roar. "One world, one government, one truth!"

After the creed, each cell is called one by one. The process is orderly and precise, the overhead drones see to that.

When the number ten appears in our viewfinders, Iris glances up quickly then walks off with all the other girls around us. They are herded towards the front where they'll be handed off to Ms. Medea and taken away for their lesson. The female King Souls who are already in Servus to The Cause are led under guard to lab tents for daily testing and monitoring.

Iris will be loaded onto a cargo plane with all the other girls in her class and flown over the ruins. My stomach drops at the thought of it, at what she'll see, and how fearful it will make her. I keep my eyes on her for as long as I can, until she disappears into the crowd.

After the last cell has been called, I feel the wind begin to die down, as if on cue. Then, the image in my viewfinder and on all the screens all around us cuts to a close-up angle of the balcony of Primitus Castle, which is hundreds of yards in the distance. The leader of Primitus, a man named Shamus, appears on screen, mulling about the large opulent balcony, pacing back and forth. His white hair and gaunt face appear haggard and worn, as usual, his red and gold military jacket gleaming in the sun.

Two men and two women stand behind him, all of them with their arms crossed. Shamus's official title is King of Kings, and assembled behind him is his High Council, his top advisors. A shadowy group which consists of one Warrior Soul, an imposing woman named Kali, dressed in black, one Guardian Soul, a tall slim man named Claudius, dressed in white, and two King Souls, a woman named Druscilla and a man named Bael, both of whom are well-groomed very good-looking, and dressed in red, clothes like my own, only more glamorous, statelier. Red is the color of Kings, according to The Word, and Druscilla, Bael and Shamus are draped in it from head to toe, while the rest of us wear just a small red arm band.

"These are dangerous times," he starts in a grave tone. "Dangerous," he repeats, his face gradually filling more and more of the screen. "Perilous, desperate, and dangerous." After a dramatic beat, the camera focused tightly on his pensive look, he goes on. "The Word is the only thing that can save us. We must cling to it, adhering to its commands as strictly as humanly possible, *fanatically*, each and every one of us, for our own survival and the survival of humanity," he says. Then, clenching his jaw, he begins to grow angry. "Unordered soul assimilation is forbidden!" he screams. "In accordance with The Word and in accordance with God!" he yells, spit flying out of his mouth, veins bulging in his neck. He straightens up and smooths his hair. In a voice of controlled calm, "It is impossible to understand what Karl Alastair is thinking, tearing up The Aurora Treaty, why he would choose such a blasphemous, provocative, and reckless course of action. When he knows new souls outnumber old, that we outnumber them five hundred to one!" he yells, and the crowd roars.

Shamus begins to pace about the balcony, the camera following his every move.

"His actions are against the will of God!" he concludes. "We are dealing with a dangerous, sadistic man, a man who lacks not only righteousness but sanity. A man who does not want humanity to survive." Shamus shakes his head disapprovingly as the image on the screens dissolves from his face to the small, blonde-haired, blue-eyed woman at the center of The Aurora Treaty, Val. The only pregnant woman on Earth. A new soul, currently being held captive in Antiquus, the enclave of old souls.

"*She* is one of *us*! She is a *new* soul. She belongs *here*!" he shouts, veins visible in his neck and forehead, and the crowd begins to cheer. "We will storm the gates of Antiquus, and we will bring her home!" he promises. The sea of King Souls erupts, roaring in agreement. "Antiquus will fall, and the old souls will die for the actions of their leader. It is what God has ordained. We are now at war, make no mistake about it. But God is on our side."

The Status Office is a small government tent on the edge of the center square. It's where Keepers go to register their girls. To update their status to Servus once they are of use to The Cause. From that day on, the girl's body is no longer hers, legally. Her body and all of its parts are property of the state under the guardianship of her Keeper.

I put my head down and increase my pace towards the mountains in the distance. I'm trying to put as much space between me and the Status Office as quickly as possible, when I hear someone behind me.

"Hey!" a voice shouts in my direction. My heart leaps up. I know I should stop and turn around, but I keep walking, even quicker now.

"*Hey!*" the booming voice shouts again.

Thinking of all the weapons that are likely pointing at me and thinking of Iris being placed with another Keeper, I stop. Turning around, slowly, I start raising my hands in the air.

"What the fuck are you doing?" Cicero asks of my arms above my head as he jogs towards me smirking.

I exhale, a sigh of relief.

"Hunting," I tell him trying to slow the pounding in my chest.

"Well you look like your being hunt-*ed*," he quips.

"Aren't we all?" I say.

He nods, then, "Caught anything lately?" he asks. He's outfitted for a hunt with his crossbow and game bag, just like I am.

"No. Not a thing," I admit, finally breathing normally again.

"Last I got was a fox, four weeks ago," he says.

"Coyote, same, four weeks ago," I tell him.

"Honestly, I'm starting to wonder if there's anything left out there to hunt," he says.

King Souls hunt, scouring the mountains, and return with nothing, day after day after day. I once said this same thing to a King Soul I passed as we both trudged in empty-handed. He looked at me a minute, his head cocked to one side, then he punched me in the face.

"I've been wondering the same thing," I reveal, beyond amazed to see that there really is someone else who thinks like I do.

"You always hunt alone," he says, more observation than question.

"Yeah," I say.

"Me too," he tells me. After a beat of quiet, "I thought we

might have better luck if we try teaming up," he suggests.

King Souls often team up for hunting, though if anything is caught, one always ends up killing the other.

"All right," I say, trying to size him up without him noticing, and catch him doing the same. Both of us trying to determine who may end up killing whom if we happen to catch anything.

"You're Roman, right?" he asks as we head towards the mountains.

"How'd you know that?"

"Lucky guess," he says.

I look over at him, knowing that's not something a person just guesses.

"Only kidding," he whacks me in the chest with a laugh. "Your girl, she talks an awful lot. According to my girl," he says.

"Iris," I tell him her name. "And yes, she does," I agree, and we both smile, then put our heads down and walk.

I start to worry about Iris, about where she is and what she's seeing. And I especially worry about her trying to keep so many secrets.

We arrive in the foothills at the edge of the rugged mountains where there are two paths. One goes to the eastern ridges and one to the western. Cicero and I stand at the fork.

"I've been hunting in the east for weeks," he says.

"Me too," I remark.

"They say there's no more wildlife to the west," he says, and I nod.

We stand there, quietly, both of us nodding. Both of us looking towards the west. At the same moment we look at each other, and then both head down the path to the west.

After just a few minutes of walking up the foothills, the deep sand gives way to rocks and packed dirt beneath our feet.

"You were right," I say, "about The Aurora Treaty."

""I've noticed a pattern to the chaos. It's about one thing, war," he says and I nod agreeing.

"When he said today that now we were at war I was like, oh *now* we're at war? I mean, when have we *not* been at war?"

"Exactly, it's like the entire goal is to keep it going, war," he sighs, when suddenly, a streak of white catches the corner of my eye.

I put my hand up in a fist, and we both stop walking.

"Did you see that," I whisper, readying my crossbow, and Cicero nods, readying his. We continue ahead at a slower pace, keeping as quiet as we can. Then, a hundred yards up I see a flash of white again. It streaks across the path, and then disappears behind the brush.

"Rabbit," Cicero comments, and I nod.

"I think so," I say, remembering Iris's request and wondering if I could really get this lucky, and so quickly. If this could possibly be real. "Two people can't see the same mirage, right?" I wonder.

"I don't think so. Come on," he says, and we pick up our pace heading towards whatever small white animal keeps catching our eye. There are no trees, just bare mountain ridges as far as we can see, littered with boulders of all shapes and sizes and scorched underbrush. Not too many places for a rabbit to hide.

I spot movement in the distance, farther up ahead.

"What's that?" I point out over the next ridge. Cicero squints, trying to see what I'm talking about. "Almost looks like… figures, black clothes. Warrior Souls maybe?"

"Can't be," he scoffs, only King Souls are permitted to hunt. "Drones would have got them by now for being all the way out here."

He stares, rubs his eyes and stares some more.

"I don't see anything," he says finally.

Whatever I saw now was gone. "Maybe it was nothing," I say, feeling uncertain. "Had to be a mirage, I guess."

"You know how the desert is," he remarks, "how it plays tricks on your mind."

I nod, and we keep walking.

"So, you definitely think we're being lied to about the treaty, huh?" I ask.

"You don't?" he asks, turning his head to look at me.

"No," I say, "I think we're being lied to about *everything*. Everything in this whole entire world."

Then, as if it appearing out of thin air, a large, scraggy bush of wild licorice sits in the middle of the path just a few feet ahead.

"All right, am I imagining that?" I ask

"Nope, I see it too," he says as we approach it.

"What are the chances?" I wonder. "Actually, don't tell me. I don't even want to know. Let's just get some and find that white rabbit and get back," he says.

"What makes you think it's a rabbit?" he asks as we take our hunting bags off, set our crossbows at our feet, and start gathering up a few handfuls each of the coveted herb.

"Do you hear that?" I ask, picking up a faint pounding.

He stops to listen, "I don't hear anything," he reports and then continues gathering.

"Shhhh," I tell him and stare off in the direction of the subtle noise. Then, about a hundred yards ahead, the figures dressed in black reappear, much closer than before. A group of six charging at us.

"I don't think that's a mirage," I say, hitting Cicero on the chest with the back of my hand before grabbing my crossbow. Cicero looks up from the bush, eyes wide.

"Dragon Souls," he says, his voice drenched in terror, as the same words appear in my Oculum. A flashing red warning: DRAGON SOULS, APPROACHING AT 9.8 MILES PER HOUR. BE COMBAT READY. YOUR ENEMY WILL ARRIVE IN 10, 9, 8, 7, 6…

EVE

SEVEN

—— ✹ ——

It's all too much, she thinks, her head swirling.

This new discomfort in her stomach, so painful and unfamiliar. The fact that she agreed not to be registered, an insane decision, one that's now making her feel nauseous. Her own Keeper admitting he doesn't believe in The Destruction Story, the very ruins of which she's about to see with her own eyes for the first time. It's all just too much. All the secrets and the lies, the fear, the pain, and the discomfort, she thinks, that's what's making her feel like she's about to vomit. I sit beside her, stroking her hair and trying to calm her, though of course, she doesn't know I'm here.

For the long round trip, out to the ruins and then back to Primitus, each girl was given a little white bag. Iris clutches hers in her sweaty fist. Her other hand mashes against her clammy forehead, her eyes closed, trying to stop the world from spinning. She doesn't know how much more she can take of the retching sounds echoing off the tall metallic walls and high ceiling of the cavernous military cargo plane, the putrid smell all around her, the sour sting of stomach acid pooling in the back of her throat, the way her bones mash into the hard, dusty flood where she sits. She can't take any of it any longer.

Putting the bag to her mouth just in time, she heaves, throwing up the entire contents of her already empty stomach, a thick, warm, yellow liquid and macerated remnants of a few bush berries.

Her body convulses, which sends a throbbing down her arm. She wonders if the infection is worse than Roman thought. Maybe it's so bad it's making her sick. She looks down at the red enflamed skin beneath the new King Soul tattoo she was so excited to get, and her stomach tumbles again. She feels herself turn green.

It's just motion sickness, she reassures herself, as the cargo plane sways and rocks back and forth, carrying her and the hundreds of other eleven-year-old girls from cell ten lumbering through the blinding white sky. Roman had warned her to expect this very feeling. He told her how the crosswinds over the desert at five thousand feet in this enormous flying beast would be nauseating.

"I hate this," Iris says abruptly to the girl next to her. A girl she doesn't know well, but who she's usually seated near in class, who's also getting sick. Her flat brown eyes stare back at Iris, emotionless, the rest of her face obscured by her bag.

The girl cocks her head, then removes the bag from her face. With the back of her hand, she wipes the vomit from her mouth.

Iris, heart racing, "I mean, I hate throwing up," she tries to clarify, but now she worries that the girl knows exactly what she really means. That this whole thing is awful, from the motion sickness to where they are going to and why.

The girl's silence unnerving. "I mean, I just, you know my stomach hurts, and..." Iris rambles, feeling sweat forming on the back of her neck and on the palms of her hands as the girl stares blankly at her another uncomfortable moment.

Then, like a robot, the girl stands up.

"No," Iris whispers

She watches, helplessly, as she marches over to Ms. Medea. I wrap my arms around her shoulders, trying to help her stay calm. I hear her heart racing and feel a wave of heat, the adrenaline surging through her.

Ms. Medea bends down listening to the girl, who points in Iris's direction. After they're done talking, the teacher directs her to another spot to sit on the other side, then disappears to the front of the plane.

A few moments later, walking up the center aisle, "All right girls, it's time," Ms. Medea proclaims, intensity and excitement in her voice.

Iris watches in wonder as all the girls around her perk up, smiling and wide-eyed. If Iris remembered what dolls were, she'd know that's exactly what they look like. Programmed robotic dolls.

"On your feet," their teacher commands, and everyone jumps to their feet, dusting themselves off and crowding towards her eagerly. Iris, filled with dread instead of excitement, feels like a sudden outsider. "Now, before I open the cargo bay door revealing the incredible terror below, a window into everything you've ever learned, I want you to understand one last thing." Her eyes sweep over the hundreds of faces until she finds Iris's. "Unbelievers will die," she reminds them, something she says all the time, something Iris never thinks much of. But now, as Ms. Medea stares at her, the words take on new meaning.

"Unbelievers won't be the ones who are left when the work of the faithful bears its fruit. When we are all saved, all the ones who believed. And not only will they never see paradise, but they will all die horrible deaths here in this world. As they should. Even one unbeliever makes us all less safe and the world even more dangerous."

Iris swallows hard, her tiny body trembling.

"Open the door," Ms. Medea yells, and the massive door begins going down, as if half the floor of the plane is dropping out.

A thick yellow line marks the spot on the floor which they've been told they can't go past or they'll be swept out by the draft. In a tight pack, the girls all huddle near the center of the plane, the opening so enormous they don't need to go anywhere near the yellow line to see what's below. And though all her books at school are filled with pictures of this very site, none of them capture what Iris now sees.

Mountain after mountain of decomposing corpses, billions of people, rotting in mountainous piles, along with all the rubble of every sky scraper, every building, everything man had ever created. The Grand Canyon all but filled in with nothing but death and destruction.

"Incredible, isn't it?" Ms. Medea remarks in breathless wonder. "Terrifying, frightening ... what just one girl can do," she says, then sets her sights on Iris.

Walking towards her, "Iris said she hated this," she charges, loud enough for everyone to hear. All the girls around her move away. Suddenly she's standing as alone as she feels.

"No, I said, I was getting sick and I—" Iris tries, voice

trembling, but Ms. Medea cuts her off.

"Many of the people down there were sick. Did you forget somehow that many of those who weren't drowned or bludgeoned or crushed or starved to death died because they were sick? Did you forget about The Events and The Unthinkable, the wicked acts that caused the destruction of all the world and most of humanity? Did you forget about the plague that killed millions?"

"I didn't forget," Iris whispers, tears streaking down her cheeks.

"Well, if you didn't forget all that, and you didn't forget what she did to the world ... then you just don't believe," she assesses.

The sound of gasping all around her, "No, I believe! I believe," Iris scrambles to rebut the accusation. "I believe completely. I always have!"

"I can't really see any other reason why you'd say such a thing. Why you would hate anything at all about being granted, so generously, the opportunity, *the privilege,* to come here and to see this. Do you see any Guardian Souls or Warrior Souls or Gypsy Souls given pilgrimage?"

"No, ma'am," she answers.

"No, of course not. So, why then, why would you say such a horrible blasphemous thing?"

Iris is stunned silent, her mind racing, scrambling, and

all at once blank. Ms. Medea and everyone else staring at her.

"Unbeliever," her teacher charges, then grabs Iris by the arm violently and drags her towards the opening.

"No!" Iris begs, the wind whipping harder the closer they get. She reaches out grasping for the other girls, for someone to take her hand to help her, but they either turn away or look at her in disgust.

I stand at the edge of the opening like a brick wall.

Iris weeps, throwing all her weight towards the ground, her teacher dragging her towards her death.

"We are the faithful, the righteous!" she proclaims.

"No, please," Iris begs.

"And you make all of us less safe," she charges. And with that, she pushes Iris beyond the yellow line towards the abyss.

Iris goes stumbling towards the opening, well beyond the yellow line, the whirling draft sending her clothes and hair into a whipping frenzy. She should have been swept up immediately, but I'm holding her down, making her feet appear glued firmly to the floor. Iris peeks over her shoulder, getting an even closer glimpse of the mass grave and staggering carnage below, then turns back.

Ms. Medea looks on angrily. She waits another moment to see if she'll be swept out of the plane and watches as Iris stands firm. The rest of the class looks to the teacher.

Ms. Medea weighs her options.

"Go on out and push her, Maggie," she tells the girl who ratted Iris out in the first place. But Maggie, whose eyes were so flat and deadened doesn't appear emotionless anymore. She looks at the teacher, eyes now wide and desperate, body frozen in place.

Frustration mounting, "Who will do it? Who will protect the rest of us from this threat?" They all watch in wonder as Iris stands far beyond the yellow line, defying the wind. They don't know how she's doing it. No one moves. Until finally, one girl raises her hand, both smugness and fear on her face.

"Thank you, Penny, I can always count on you," the teacher praises as Penny sets her sights on Iris.

As if coaching Penny, "Iris is trying to destroy everything," Ms. Medea proclaims. "She is a threat to everything we are working so hard and sacrificing to accomplish. She must be eliminated," she commands. On that, Penny steps out of the pack and moves towards the yellow line, inching ever closer. Her first foot barely crossing it, she goes whipping out like a paper doll. Her body slams into the metal ceiling before being sucked out. Iris watches over her shoulder as Penny disappears. She turns back to a sea of shocked faces.

Teetering between anger and fear, Ms. Medea knows if she wants it done, she'll have to be the one to do it.

Weighing the risks.

"Close the damn door!" she commands, her eyes trained on Iris.

EIGHT

—— ✠ ——

Iris has never seen the inside of Primitus Castle and never dreamed she would. Then again, she never imagined her teacher would try to kill her and that she'd actually survive to tell the tale.

Dragging stumbling Iris behind her, Ms. Medea storms through the slim halls and dark winding corridors as fast as her long legs will carry her.

"You've really done it," her teacher warns. "Summoned by the High Council and King of Kings for your dissent," she chides.

Though she's shell-shocked and barely able to stay on her feet, Iris still cranes her neck, fluttering her eyes at everything they pass, trying in vain to see it all. Sounds are the same way. She can't make out the words her teacher is mumbling to herself except on occasion, here and there, when one bursts out louder than the rest.

"Grumble mumble, *TRAITOR!* Grumble, mumble, *UNBELIEVER!* Grumble mumble, *THREAT!*" Ms. Medea fumes, the words Iris can't understand concerning her even more than the alarming ones she can.

Baffled and even more humiliated, Ms. Medea is eager to see that Iris is dealt with—and swiftly. The harsher the better. She turns a sharp corner and abruptly stops.

Iris finds herself staring at a large iron door. She sways on her feet, her arms light and tingly, ears ringing. Ms. Medea bends down and gets right in her face.

"This is going to make for quite a lesson … for all the other girls that is. A cautionary tale about what happens to unbelievers," she says, her voice shaking with anger and nerves, Iris wondering what Ms. Medea is so afraid of.

Ms. Medea pushes against the heavy door. It slowly swings open, creaking as it goes, and Iris finds herself standing at the back of a cavernous room. Dark and foreboding, draped in heavy fabrics, with a stark white throne at the other end made of hand-carved ivory and lit with piercing white light. She recognizes Shamus, the leader of Primitus, sitting upon the throne, and his High Council standing around him.

"Come in, come in!" Shamus shouts to her, sounding gleeful.

Iris is frozen in place.

"You must be Iris," he says.

Iris looks up at her teacher who pushes her forward.

"Go on!" her teacher commands her through clenched teeth, shoving her once more. Iris starts the long agonizing walk.

"The last of our little party to arrive," Shamus declares. "We've much to discuss. It's been a *very* eventful day!" Shamus exclaims. "Ms. Medea, you'll join us as well," he orders, and Iris hears her teacher's footsteps behind her.

As she nears the front of the imposing room, Iris is stunned to see that Roman is also there. He's standing off to the side, facing the throne, head down. No weapons on him as far as Iris can see, hunting bag at his feet.

Iris casts her gaze at the ground, like Roman is doing, fear coursing through her body.

"You're just in time for the show," Shamus informs Iris and Ms. Medea. The enormous walls in the all flick to life. Iris and everyone else watch Roman on the screen, seen through the view of Cicero's Oculum. They're out in the mountains standing over the licorice bush gathering up a few handfuls each of the scraggly herb.

"Do you hear that?" Roman asks.

Cicero stops to listen, "I don't hear anything," he reports and continues gathering.

Roman stares off into the distance.

"I don't think that's a mirage," he says, hitting Cicero on the chest with the back of his hand before grabbing his crossbow. Cicero looks up to see figures dressed in black, a group of six charging at them.

"Dragon Souls," Cicero says in wonder, as the same words appears on his Oculum screen. On the side of his view calculates how fast the enemy is approaching, 9.8 MILES PER HOUR. Then the words, BE COMBAT READY blink, a final warning. Then, YOUR ENEMY WILL ARRIVE IN 10, 9, 8, 7, 6, 5, 4....

They hear Cicero's breath shaking as a murderous-looking Dragon Soul closes in. They seem to collide as the camera angle whirls to the ground then focuses in on Roman, who's fighting off three Dragon Souls, his own Oculum flung off into the sand. We see two Dragon Souls already lying dead, one five feet away from Roman, the other ten feet away, both struck with arrows. The Dragon Soul who collided with Cicero walks towards Roman as well, almost curiously, watching as Roman overwhelms several Dragon Souls all coming at him at once. He kicks one in the gut, sending him sailing several feet, then grabs an arrow from his back, holding it near the tip like a dagger as another Dragon Soul charges him. When he's two feet away, Roman slings his bow over the Dragon Soul's head, spins him, pulls him in to his chest, and stabs him in the neck with the arrow. As the man drops to the ground, Roman lifts his shirt and grabs his hunting knife from his waistband, whirls around and slashes clean through the midsection of another Dragon Soul who'd come up behind him, sword drawn overhead. Roman sets his sights on the only one left standing, who cocks his head then charges at Roman. They go tumbling to the ground, the man punches Roman in the face, Roman lying there, appearing to almost let him. To see what he's got. After a couple of punches, Roman rolls him over, sits atop the man's chest, and starts punching him. Cicero gets up and walks over. We see Roman from above, whaling on the man until he stops moving.

Cicero looks around at the six Dragon Souls splayed out around them, the one Roman kicked, the only one still moving. Cicero walks over and launches an arrow into the man at point blank range. Then turns to Roman, who's still breathing heavily.

"Thanks for the help." Roman smiles.

Cicero walks back towards Roman.

"How in the world … Roman, what the hell was that?"

"What?" Roman asks.

Shamus starts to laugh and the screen freezes.

"That's my favorite part, right there," he points to one

of the screens surrounding all of us, *"What?"* he mimics Roman as he walks over to him.

Then, staring at Roman face to face, Shamus cocks his head curiously to one side.

"Oh, come on. You must realize?" Shamus wonders, almost to himself. He shakes his head. "You're not normal," he informs Roman. "There is something about you," he says, "both of you now, apparently." He includes Iris. "You're different," he says. "You're not ... typical," he informs them. "Particularly this one," he points to Roman. "You see, a typical Keeper would have registered his girl ... he would have followed The Word," he says looking to Iris. "As you knew he planned not to ... and yet, you said nothing to anyone, making you odd as well, I'm afraid," he says to Iris.

Shamus turns around. "The first King Soul in history to break this law," he announces to the entire room. Then he turns back, "You're also the first King Soul to stop wearing your Oculum when you sleep ... which you stopped doing months ago. Then, because you stopped wearing yours, she stops wearing hers," Shamus motions to Iris, "now the two of you don't wear them at all unless you're going outside. It's like you don't care what's going on in this doomed world. You question just about everything ... don't you? So, of course, we didn't expect you to register her," he says to Roman. "But it was still shocking to watch."

"And you," he moves on to Iris, "we're *very* concerned about you, Iris. Not only are we concerned about your soul, of course," he raises his eyebrows, "and how quickly it can be corrupted, but we're not entirely sure what to make of this," he says, and on his words the screens all around the room flick to life again, and the footage from the cargo plane plays.

Iris studies the footage of herself, mystified at how she managed to stand firm in the powerful vortex. How she didn't go flying out despite the sweeping tornado all around her. Especially when Penny, who was much bigger than Iris, comes briefly into frame only to get instantly sucked away.

"It defies logic," Shamus concludes, staring at Iris. "Wouldn't you say, Bael?" Shamus asks.

"I would. If I didn't know better, I'd say it looks almost … demonic," Bael assesses.

"Yes, I'd say you're right," Shamus concurs. "What would you say, Druscilla?" he asks.

"It definitely defies logic, to say nothing of the laws of gravity," says the tall curvy woman draped in an opulent red garb. Then she saunters towards Iris. "As far as being demonic," she goes on, studying Iris. "Yes, either she is a demon, or she was being helped by one," she concludes. Iris swallows hard. "What do you think Ms. Medea?"

"Having seen it with my own eyes, I can tell you without a doubt, it's unholy, whatever it is. A disease that needs to be cut out before it spreads," she says, looking at Iris spitefully.

Druscilla walks towards Ms. Medea, nodding her head and seeming to listen. Then she pulls out a knife, grabs the back of Ms. Medea's head and slices her throat. She drops Iris's teacher to the ground, then walks casually back to where she was standing.

"She's seen too much," she says. "Roman, as I have no doubt you've now realized," Druscilla says, "we've been watching you, listening to every word you say. Everyone is watched and listened to, of course, but well, you've captured our attention. Like Cicero here." Cicero is dragged in by a couple guards, half a white rabbit in his hand. "He began to say strange things, to wonder strange things, we knew it was only a matter of time before the two of you found each other. But you, Roman, you not only say strange things and wonder strange things, but you do strange things as well, like sharing a rabbit, despite that no other King Soul in these dire times has ever done that. After you defeated the entire insurgency single-handedly and didn't kill Cicero for the rabbit, when it was clear you could have easily, our decision became final."

"What decision?" Roman asks.

"Roman, you've been selected to lead a military operation," Druscilla starts, "a very special one. As you know, according to The Word, Val belongs here in Primitus. And you are going to go to Antiquus and bring her back. Bael and Kali will accompany you, along with Cicero and two Guardian Souls who'll serve as nurses to care for her *condition*. Iris will be held here, as collateral since you clearly care about her, until Val's safe return. Should you not return for any reason or return with Val in any condition other than perfect, Iris's change of status will be immediately processed, and she will be given to another male Keeper. The Cause continues, of course." Druscilla then walks over to Roman and unbuttons the first two buttons on his shirt.

"You won't be taking this with you, however." She takes the key from off his chest and lifts it over his head.

She turns it over in her hands, then eyes Roman.

"You say you don't know what it opens?" she asks, hinting at all the other things he's said about it.

"No, I don't know what it opens," he answers her. "If anything," he adds. She stares at him silently.

"For the record ... I don't believe you," she says, then leans in close. "Regardless, it's unregistered, so it's government property anyway."

She tosses it to Shamus, who puts it around his own neck.

"And when what it opens can be determined, whatever that is will be government property as well," she finishes. Roman says nothing. Iris looks at him, tears running down her cheeks.

"I hope it's not some kind of good luck charm," Shamus says to him as he looks the key over, now hanging around his own neck. "Because you're going to need all the luck you can get," he remarks. "They do know you're coming, of course, just like we knew the Dragon scouts were coming, and soon the full insurgency."

"But … if they know we're coming, then what is the point?" Roman says. "They're not going to just let us leave with her."

"Or maybe they will," Shamus states, "Just like we are watching you and every move you make, we're watching Antiquus and they are watching us. There is no element of surprise anyway, and since our goals are essentially the same—war—and we both want a war our people will fight, all these things are highly coordinated," Shamus says.

"So, it's not real then? The mission, any of it?" Roman asks.

"Define real. I mean, the bombs are real, the war will be real, the deaths are real … but also theater. The theater of war, it just keeps everyone dug in, committed. Patriotic. You think Karl Alastair just decided to tear up The Aurora Treaty all on his own?" Shamus laughs.

"Why would you want war?" Iris asks to everyone's surprise.

"We want war, sweetie, because we believe we can win," Shamus condescends to her. "We believe the new souls are supposed to win, that only when the world is rid of all old souls will paradise return."

"Then why are you coordinating with them?" Roman asks.

"Because they want war too, for the very same reason," Shamus remarks sounding at a loss. "I'm sorry, am I speaking gibberish here? This is how war works. How do people not know this?" he asks, flinging his question out to everyone and no one all at once. "The future belongs to the new souls, my beautiful new souls. The old souls think it belongs to them," Shamus laughs. "But we know it belongs to us because five hundred times more new souls survived the plague."

"Who says it belongs to either?" Iris chimes in boldly.

"Do you see?" Shamus asks. "Do you see how questioning one's beliefs weakens resolve? Threatening us all? This is precisely why beliefs need to be stoked."

Shamus nods to a guard who grabs Iris and drags her off.

"Don't worry, she'll be here when you get back, *if* you get back," he says to Roman, as several guards work to hold him back.

With cameras and lights everywhere, against a fake backdrop that looks identical to the desert outside, Shamus films war propaganda, staring Roman.

"This is the most important military operation of our lifetime," Shamus tells every new soul receiving the stream instantly to their Oculum, his voice ominous. "He will leave Primitus on foot," he says, as the camera pulls back to reveal Roman, showered, groomed, and outfitted in fresh clothes. He's taller than Shamus, and with his tan skin, sharp jawline, and a wavy lock of his sun-lightened, unruly brown hair falling near his brilliant green eyes, he has just the kind of movie star good looks that make the best propaganda. That somehow makes people want to believe in things.

"We can't send just anyone. It has to be him, and only him. This mission is too important. Val is the hope of humanity."

ROMAN

NINE

___ ❈ ___

We set out heading north, the six of us, lumbering along in a single-file line like a caravan of pack mules. We're loaded down with weapons and supplies, and it's slow going, slower than I'm used to. The blistering sun bakes down on us, the whistling of the wind the only sound in our ears.

After trekking for hours, through miles of deep sand, Primitus begins disappearing behind us. High-peaked rocky mountains are visible in the distance ahead; a mysterious-looking range, one I'd never ventured to before. One I didn't even know existed. The western and eastern ranges, which straddle Primitus, are the only mountains I knew of that surrounded us. The only ones we're told about, and the ones close enough to reach, hunt, and return in a half days' time. But now, as I stare ahead at the sharp peaks, taller than any I think I've ever seen, what I thought

I knew about the world around me begins to shift.

Since Bael knows the route, he leads the pack for now. I'll take the lead once we leave the armory.

I haven't figured Bael out yet. He hasn't said more than four sentences since we left Primitus. I walk directly behind him, followed by Cicero. Behind Cicero are the two Guardian Souls who'll serve as nurses for Val once we've "rescued" her. Their names are Payge and Ruby, and they were hand-selected by Claudius out of the millions of other Guardian Souls. They both seem to be somewhere around my own age, clothed in small white garments shredded by wear and sun, their legs, arms and stomachs exposed. I haven't figured it out yet, but something about them both is strangely familiar.

Because of their place as lower souls within the society of Primitus, they averted their eyes towards the ground when Cicero and I were introduced, as if we were some kind of Gods. Neither Cicero nor I had ever met a Guardian Soul, so the whole thing was remarkably awkward. The blonde-haired one, Ruby, glanced up at me briefly before returning her gaze to the dust and rubble at her feet. I met her mysterious eyes with surprise. After she looked away, Cicero and I exchanged a look.

In Primitus, we're told a great deal about the other soul types, all their negative qualities, how they drain the resources and pose a threat to us. We never intermingle with souls outside our own sector. So, none of us knows how to act around each other.

I stared at her while she wasn't looking, and wondered what she was thinking, what she'd been through. What she knows. How her story might fill in the gaps in mine.

But no one asks questions like that, so instead of voicing any of the real things in my mind, I kept my queries practical. I worried aloud about how their footwear would fare on the long journey; thin-bottomed sandals, fastened with ties that wound up their legs all the way to their knees.

"Seriously?" I asked Bael of their flimsy, pathetic excuse for shoes and scant clothes before we set out.

As a King Soul, and as High Council member, Bael outranks us all. Even though I'm supposed to be "leading" the mission, I'm not quite sure yet what that means.

Bael never acknowledged my concerns. He just looked at me, then looked at Ruby and Payge, and then walked away, assuming his place at the head of the expedition.

Kali, a brutish woman at least my own size, maybe larger, brings up the rear of the pack, behind Payge. Both she and Bael are members of Shamus's High Council, and between the two of them, we are surrounded, with Bael at the front and Kali at the back. The other two High Council members, Druscilla and Claudius, stayed behind with

Shamus. After witnessing the inner workings of Primitus castle, I'm not sure who's in charge, him or them. All I know is that I don't trust any of them, and that I need to get back to Iris as quickly as possible.

As we approach the northern mountains, I start to understand what Bael meant when he told us we won't be going over them. Just ahead of us, there's a pass between the highest two peaks, a slim corridor that's unnoticeable from a distance. It looks like it was *created* somehow, blasted out perhaps, but I don't ask. I just walk, following behind Bael, forward through the pass, towering mountain walls rising to peaks that seem to pierce the sky on both sides of us.

Finally, we stop to make camp. Bael informs us that tomorrow we'll come to a spot at the edge of the northern mountains.

"Where the world ... opens up," he says. We all look at him curiously. "The dead zone," he clarifies. "Between Primitus and Antiquus there are some ... anomalies in the environment, more products of The Destruction. The dead zone is filled with anomalies."

"The *dead* zone?" Ruby asks.

"Yes," Kali says.

"I can't imagine anything deader than Primitus and the wasteland that surrounds it," I say, to which Bael just stares at me blankly for a moment until finally going on.

"We have to cross the dead zone to get to the military armory," he asserts. "That's where we'll be outfitted with the vehicles, more weapons, and provisions we'll need for the mission."

While setting up camp a few minutes later, as Bael and I assemble one of the two large tents we have, I ask a question that's been plaguing me.

"I would have thought that the bulk of our military supplies were kept in Primitus." I say, a statement more of a question, one he immediately seems annoyed I'm asking.

"They're not," Bael answers, throwing me a rope to stake off.

"How can a state be expected to defend itself when..." I start. He glares at me, and I go quiet, drawing a conclusion to my question.

Maybe they're not. Maybe someone else in control, someone other than the faces we see, someone else managing and overseeing what really happens. Directing the theater of war.

We quickly eat our dried meat and stale bread and retreat into the tents. Bael divides me, Ruby, and himself into one tent. Cicero and Payge and Kali into another.

Sleeping is impossible, for me at least. The heat inside the tent is unbearable, worse than the mud-brick hut. I stare up at the top of the tent, the sun blaring through the thin fabric. My thoughts turn to Iris.

Bael stares up at the tent ceiling for a few minutes, then gets up and goes outside.

I look over at Ruby.

"I guess he's not going to sleep," I comment to break the silence.

She's curled in a ball on her side, her eyes open and staring at the tent wall in front of her as it billows in and out from the gentle breeze.

"Do you think what we're doing is important?" she asks.

"I guess. Do you?" I ask her.

"Yes," she says.

"Why?" I ask.

"Because Val is a new soul and she belongs in Primitus. Unordered soul assimilation displeases God," she states.

I nod.

"Why do *you* think it's important?" she asks, after a moment.

"I don't know really. The only reason it's important to me is because it's what I have to do to get back to Iris."

She looks confused a moment, then she smiles, her eyes twinkling. She props herself up onto her elbows.

"You're very sweet," she says.

A strange feeling comes over me. It's as if I recognize her somehow.

TEN

—— ⊗ ——

After another half-day of walking, the rocky mountain scenery on both sides unchanged, something odd starts to appear ahead. A glowing line of blue along the horizon out before us.

"What is that?" I ask Bael.

"The dead zone," he remarks without turning around.

Another few hours of walking, and what was a line of blue is now half the sky from the ground up. The other half is the baked bone white I'm used to.

"What is happening to the sky?" Cicero whispers from behind me.

I shrug, "I do not know," I tell him, staring at it.

"And where's the wind?" he asks. "It should be kicking up by now," he remarks.

"I know," I turn and say.

Finally, at the spot at the edge of the mountain, I see it. The spot where "the world opens up." This is a perfect description. Entering the dead zone feels like leaving one world and entering another. Behind us is a flat white sky over a scorched world. Out before us is a world of colors: deep blue sky stretched out from end to end, rolling land of green and brown. Even the searing heat gives way to comfortable cool air. But perhaps the most remarkable thing is the smell—clean, pure, fresh, sweet, dewy, invigorating.

"How could *this* be the dead zone?" I ask, words directed at no one in particular. Cicero, Ruby, Payge and I stare out in wonder. Cicero glances at me with an uneasy look on his face.

"This way," Bael directs us, leading us onward into the dead zone.

The moment I step into this new place, as my feet go from the rocky gravel to the soft textured ground of this new place, I start to feel different. My body feels light, my head clear.

I reach down and run my hand over the soft green ground covering beneath our feet.

"Grass," Bael tells me, a word that, as he says it, feels like a lightning bolt striking somewhere in a dusty corner of my mind. Not only am I mystified by the mossy green softness and the fresh dewy smell, I'm convinced that I absolutely *remember* grass.

As we get on our way, instead of falling into the formation we've kept the entire time, I find myself walking next to Cicero. Behind us, I notice Ruby and Payge are walking alongside one another. Bael is still in front and Kali in back. And I wonder, briefly, why we'd been walking single file until now. And why now, suddenly, we're not.

"After we've seen this, you really think they're going to let us go back to Primitus?" I comment under my breath to Cicero. "And risk us telling the others."

"We have to bring Val back, don't we?" Cicero says.

"Do we?" I ask, glaring at him. "They said they needed our help to capture her, not to bring her back."

Kali, who's kept completely quiet up until now, comes up on us.

"Keep your wits about you, boys. This is where things can get a little … weird," she tells us just as something large and white streaks through the sky behind her.

"What was that?" I ask. She half turns to look.

"No telling. The dead zone is a thin place," she informs us.

"A thin place?" I ask, still craning around her trying to see what it was, finding nothing.

"Yes. Very dangerous, make no mistake. It's completely unpredictable. It shouldn't even exist," she tells us, loud enough for the whole group to hear. Then she lowers her voice, leaning in close to me and Cicero. "Dead zones are transitional," she whispers, speaking rapidly. "What you don't know, what no one will tell you, is that something is ending and something else is beginning. And dead zones like this one are places where what is beginning has won out over what is ending. That also makes them battle grounds between the two worlds." She glares at us, then walks ahead towards Bael.

Cicero and I walk behind Kali and Bael, stepping cautiously, and look all around.

Both Bael and Kali draw their swords and keep walking.

I start to notice that the blue sky moves as if there are things behind it and that the ground in certain places out ahead, much like the sky, rolls and forms as if there's something moving beneath it.

"What in the world…" I say, tilting my head.

"What the hell?" Cicero says, both of us readying our crossbows.

"Come here," I tell Payge and Ruby, who come up quickly from behind us, putting themselves in the middle of me and Cicero.

"What is that?" Ruby asks, pointing towards the sky. It looks like arms and elbows pushing against a canvas from behind.

"Something that wants in," Cicero comments as we all stare.

Ruby turns to me.

"Is that true?" she asks. "Is that what Kali told you?"

There's something about Ruby's eyes. Something haunting. I hadn't realized it until now.

"Well, in not so many words, but … yes," I say, not wanting to scare her.

Ruby and Payge step closer to one another, Cicero and I flanking them, moving in tighter.

All six of us stalk forward on high alert.

Several slow, cautious miles later, everything is quiet, remarkably quiet. Eerily quiet. We're surrounded by *trees,* something we'd only heard about in The Word. Something we are told doesn't exist anymore. The trees, which at first are flickering in and out, then begin thickening gradually, growing denser the more solid in reality they appear. Larger too, like giants.

Around a bend we come upon a lagoon of crystal-clear water.

"Let's stop here to rest," Kali suggests, dropping some of her supplies and beginning to unstrap the others.

"No. No let's keep going, let's push on," Bael insists without so much as stopping his long stride.

Kali starts unstrapping her shoes.

"We're going to rest here, Bael," she asserts.

Ruby, Payge, Cicero, and I stand near Kali, looking to Bael.

"Roman?" Kali asks, as if I should be the one to decide. And now everyone looks at me.

"I—I agree. We haven't taken a single break. Seems like a good spot," I assess.

Everyone, except for Bael, immediately begins setting down their bags and gear, as if my word is the final decision.

Bael watches me as I set down my gear. Then he looks at Kali, who just stands up and peels her clothes off. Soon her black pants and shirt are in a heap on the mossy bank of the lagoon. She wades in completely naked, utterly unconcerned that all of us are watching her.

"It's just water," she tells us, and Ruby and Payge begin peeling off their clothes.

ELEVEN

—— ❈ ——

Me, Bael, and Cicero sit on the bank, keeping watch while Ruby, Payge and Kali swim and wade in what looks like cool liquid sky.

Payge sits in the shallows, water to her waist. Kali swims fearlessly out to the center of the lagoon, her gliding strokes propelling her through the water. Ruby stands in about four feet of water, facing away from us. She's dipping in and out, standing up and then crouching down. She goes all the way under, her golden hair the last thing to submerge above her in a circular gulp. She quickly resurfaces and stands. Her head looking downward, she seems to be watching the water trail down the front of herself, then wringing her long blonde hair with a twist. The reflective shimmer off the surface of the still blue lagoon all around her is almost as transfixing as watching the glistening water trail down the never-ending curve of her sun-browned back.

She turns towards us, unexpectedly, her eyes sparkling.

"You've got to come in!" she beams, her voice filled with wonder and excitement. Happiness, I think, looking at her contagious smile. *I remember happiness...*

After a moment I realize that Cicero, Bael, and I are staring at her in silence. Just gawking. Her beauty is transfixing, magnetic.

What is it about her?

"Come on!" she calls over to us.

"You know she's talking to you, right?" Cicero leans towards me and says under his breath. I look at him, his eyebrows raised. "What are you waiting for?" he asks me.

I swallow nervously.

"How is it?" I call back to Ruby, "... the water," I clarify, and because I don't know what else to say. Cicero rolls his eyes.

"You're an idiot," he whispers, "a fucking amateur idiot."

"How do you think it is?" Ruby calls back with a laugh.

Again, we only stare at her in silence, the three of us paralyzed by her. By her alluring beauty, calling to me like a siren's song, entrancing, but also frightening. Something in the way back of my mind tells me it's even deadly.

Cicero leans towards me again.

"You're a fucking fool, you know that?" he whispers.

"Yeah," I tell him, "I know that." I'm unable to take my eyes off her. It's like she's from some other place, a place I've been, a place where I could feel good, even be ... happy.

"Come on! Get in! It's unbelievable!" She dips herself back down into the water. "I don't think anything's ever felt so good," she says, her voice oozing with pleasure, practically moaning, almost a glowing light around her.

Just then, Kali starts swimming back towards the shore. Her arms move quickly, her kicks sending water splashing several feet above the surface. Ruby turns to look at her.

"Out!" Kali shouts. "Out of the water!" she yells at Ruby and Payge.

Payge leaps up and dashes onto the shore, grabbing her clothes from the mossy ground and clutching them against her chest before Ruby even moves. She seems frozen in place.

"Ruby, come on!" I stand up and say, having no idea what Kali is swimming from, but knowing that if it's frightening Kali, Ruby is certainly no match for whatever it is.

"What is it?" Bael stands up and shouts to Kali.

Kali gives Bael an ominous look as she keeps swimming towards the shore as quickly as she can, right towards Ruby.

When she's close enough, she hooks her arm around Ruby's and starts dragging her out of the water, but something gets ahold of Ruby's leg at the same time. Something unseen. Something strong. It rips Ruby away from Kali and pulls her under in one violent splashing gulp.

I tear my shirt off and grab my sword. I run past Kali who's standing now in the shallows, panting, just looking at the water in shock.

"What is it?!" I scream. "What's got her? What's down there?" I demand to know.

Kali just shakes her head, staring vacantly at the little ripples that are left on the surface.

"There's nothing we can do," she says absently.

"We're just going to let her drown!?" I scream, then turn Kali towards me, grabbing her by the arms, shaking her, shocking her awake. Her eyes focus intently on mine.

"She's gone, Roman," she assures me, staring into my eyes.

Then she breaks out of my grip and heads for the shore in long splashing strides.

I head in the opposite direction, farther into the lagoon. Maybe it's instinct, or the feeling that I'm the leader and everyone here is ultimately my responsibility, or maybe it's something else altogether, but as I dive head first into the water, my only thoughts are of saving her life.

I swim down through the clear blue, descending as quickly as I can, kicking hard, sword pointed out in front of me. The rocky white sand bottom is twenty feet below me, scattered with giant boulders I can't see around or behind. A skinny trail of air bubbles a few feet ahead catch my eye, right near the mouth of an underwater cave. I quickly ascend back to the surface, kicking as hard as I can. I take in as much air as my lungs will hold, then submerge again. The bubbles are gone, but I head there anyway, swimming down as fast as I can.

I come to the mouth of the cave. Once inside, the daylight dims. Ten feet or so in front of me I see a trail of white air bubbles floating upward again. Beyond that, there's a shaft of light as bright as the sun. Swimming forward, my lungs starting to burn, the low light unnerving me. I see what looks to be a tail. Like a lizard, a very large one. Any lizard a tail that size might be attached to would have to be my own size, at least. Then, above the tail appear two glowing yellowish-gold orbs with long black centers—eyes. The eyes stare at me a moment and then disappear.

I take off after them, no thoughts of turning back. Soon I'm swimming past where the eyes were just seconds ago, the shaft of light only a few arms lengths away.

I reach the light and look up through a circular hole in the rock overhead. I ascend towards the light, breaking the surface slowly, trying to catch my breath while I look around, but also trying not to disturb the water or make any noise.

The rock walls extend high overhead, fifty feet or so. It's a massive cave. A tiny hole in the center of the ceiling casts a faint yellow light into the large grotto.

I pull myself out of the water onto the rocky ledge as quietly as I can and look around, slick slimy stone beneath my feet. In the distance up ahead, the glimmer of faint silver light draws me away from the water and deeper into the mysterious cave. I stalk forward slowly, controlling my breath as best I can, listening for the slightest noise. My whole body is on high alert.

I hear the muffled sound of choking.

EVE

TWELVE

— ✦ —

In all my life, my blood has been drawn exactly three times.

The first time was for my original Animus test, the results of which Payge destroyed. Then it was drawn again for my second Animus test, after Ruby went to Dr. Alastair with what she knew about me, and I was dragged back in for another test—the test that would change everything. And it was drawn a third and final time when I gave three pints to Shamus. I thought that things between us had been healed. I was wrong.

Growing up, Cian was always very... *protective* of my blood. He never allowed it to be drawn under any circumstances. No doctors, no physicals, nothing like that. Shamus had things like this from time to time, but not me. Nothing and no one came near my blood. Cuts and even minor scrapes, which I accumulated my fair share of growing up, were promptly treated and bandaged, always by Cian himself. And then re-bandaged a day or two later. He closely monitored any broken skin until it was fully healed. It had been this way all my life, so far as I can remember. I never thought to question it.

Then one day, when I was seven, I discovered Cian burning what he'd just used to clean and cover one of my abrasions. We were staying in a small farming town in upstate New York, and I'd gotten a nasty patch of road rash across my thigh when I'd fallen from a moving bicycle to static asphalt. Shamus had come along and pushed me, then he smiled back with his most sinister grin as he jogged away, leaving me lying in the middle of the road.

Less than a minute later, Cian was right there scooping me up and carrying me back to the cottage. He sat me on the tiled kitchen counter to have a look, and that's when Shamus came skulking in. As Cian treated my cuts, carefully and gently, Shamus hovered over us, his dark eyes glaring at me. A volatile and menacing twenty-five-year-old man, it wasn't hard for Shamus to intimidate a small seven-year-old girl into keeping quiet.

But my fear of Shamus was never quite what he wanted it to be. He could never really silence me, hard as he tried. Even at seven I knew how and when to use the truth, and I also knew when it was best to wait for the right moment.

Once my cuts were cleaned and we all went our separate ways, Cian retreated to find some peace and quiet, Shamus stumbled back to the local bar, and I walked into Cian's room with the intent to tell him the truth about what had happened. His door, which was usually closed, was partially open, as if he knew I was coming. I saw him standing near his bed facing the other way. I gave a little tap of my knuckles as I passed through the open door and let myself in. Then he turned, as if to show me, that everything he'd just used to clean my still-stinging bloody scrape was burning in the white abalone shell he used for smudging sage. Right there, in the pearlescent white bowl sitting in his rounded palms, I saw the gauze and everything else that had my blood on it. And he was incinerating every last bit of it.

"Why are you doing that?" I asked, staring up at him.

He sat down on his bed and patted the spot next to him.

"Come, sit," he said, and I sat down next to him. "The time has come for me to tell you about your blood. There is something about your blood, Eve. Something very important ... but also dangerous," he informed me, eyebrows raised.

"What is it?" I asked, utterly fascinated.

"First tell me this," he said. "Are you afraid?"

"No," I said boldly, "not at all." I was more curious than anything.

Cian nodded, and then he went on to explain what I would later come to understand was essentially ... *everything*. The holy grail, the philosopher's stone, the ark of the covenant—everything that man had always searched for, Cian revealed to me when I was seven years old.

"At the root of all fear is death. Nonexistence," he said, then blew gently on the smoldering remnants, causing the embers to reignite into the bright orange and yellow flames, waking them up, reminding them to devour everything. "Naturally, the idea of nonexistence scares us," he went on. "But, also at the root of all fear, sitting right next to death, is life. Because life is indestructible, immortal, we know it deep inside. And that also scares us, Eve," he said, looking over at me, the bright orange flame between us dancing in his liquid blue eyes.

"Almost as if life and death are ... the same ... or equal," I said.

"Indeed, they are equal. Equal partners, in fact. When life and death are truly understood, honored, and embraced for what they are, and when they are working together, each to their own strength, humans transcend all limitations. They cross dimensions. Time dissolves, and they exert the power of creation over their experience, the same way a man and a woman do when together they bring a child into the world. This is a difficult thing to figure out in the span of just eighty to a hundred years," he said, and I nodded in agreement.

"And then, poof, everything you've learned is forgotten again," I said.

"Yes, exactly. And on and on it goes," he trailed off, wistfully.

"But ... well, what does that have to do with my blood?" I asked.

Cian looked me square in the eyes.

"Your blood is both, Eve. It is death, capable of destroying worlds, and it is also life, indestructible, inextinguishable. Life in a whole new way—a way that can no longer be hidden."

"How is that dangerous though?"

"Your blood is the truth." The gravity in his tone startled me.

"But that's good, right? I mean, the truth is good..." I suggested, clinging to hopefulness around words like death and nonexistence.

"No, Eve," he said, emphatically. "The truth, in and of itself, is merely *powerful*. Just as the knowledge contained in your blood is very powerful, as it is the truth. But you see, the power of the truth can be used *by humanity*, in which case it is good. It is the elixir of life. Or it can be used *against them,* and then it is bad. The truth is the most powerful weapon in the universe, and like any weapon it can be used to liberate people or to enslave them, and that, my dear Eve, depends merely on which purpose it is used for."

"How is humanity to know the difference?"

"It's quite simple, actually. When powerful information is used to control people, it is of the old world—enslavement—and when powerful information is used to set them free, to liberate and enlighten, it is of the new world, the new Earth.

"What is the new Earth?" I asked, having never heard Cian use those words before.

"The new Earth is a place that already exists, called Aquarius. And when the power of the truth is finally used for the complete liberation of humanity, the old world will simply fall away around us. And we will understand that it was always there, we could have created the paradise anytime, but we just didn't know because we were enslaved."

"I don't understand. What's the problem? If this Aquarius exists and it's better as you say, why don't we just … get there. Just tell them the truth. Tell them about my blood."

"Well, humanity has a long history of not being crazy about the truth and not being ready for it to liberate them, though deep down it's what they want. Deep down they know their truth, that they are free, sovereign beings, that the world is telling them lies. All while buried inside their hearts is the yearning for enlightenment, for their liberation. For now, the stakes are too high. The stakes of the old world will one day become higher, high enough for humanity to choose to walk through the fire of resurrection, allowing the old control world to burn down around them and revealing the new Earth."

As I rolled this over in my seven-year-old mind, I thought of Shamus, and how much he preferred lies to the truth. How he feared the truth for what it would make him have to see about himself.

Feeling disappointed, I asked, "Is it going to be impossible?".

"I don't know," he said, never one to sugarcoat things for me. "Only one thing is certain though. Your blood will change everything." He looked from my eyes back down into the shell. And when he did, so did I. Now there was nothing left but a small pile of light gray ash.

I sat there next to him on his tiny, neatly made bed, staring into the shell, seeing myself in the smoldering pile of nothingness. Seeing myself burning down the world. Seeing not simple ash in the bowl but gun powder, death, and destruction.

"But I don't want my blood to hurt people. I don't want it to be used to enslave them. Will I have a choice?"

Cian thought a few moments, considering his words carefully, and I worried as I waited for him to answer.

"Sometimes when people think they're being hurt, maybe they're even dying or believe that they are, or that whatever they're enduring will kill them, but what's actually happening is that they're being transformed, reborn. You see, death is necessary for the transformation from being unenlightened to enlightened. Death is the only thing that gives birth to life. Enlightenment is a destructive process. The blood of death *is* the blood of life," he told me. I found it a surprising and unsettling statement, one I could hardly believe he'd say. One I couldn't, not yet.

And I wouldn't understand it until one year later while we were traveling through western Bolivia, when I would finally see just how true all this was.

We were in a small Andean village perched at thirteen thousand feet near the ruins of Tiwanaku, when what started as a pounding headache quickly spiraled into something much more serious, something that's usually fatal.

"Meningitis," Cian said with certainty once the extreme sensitivity to light began. I was sluggish and uninterested in food the entire day before. His intuition had always been otherworldly. He immediately began to suspect the deadly bacteria was in my brain and spine. Then, when I began crying out in agony and hiding my face from the light, he was certain.

When the high fever, wild hallucinations, mental confusion, and altered states of consciousness began, Cian went to some of the villagers for help. He was having trouble keeping me hydrated and was hoping to find some ice to cool me down. The local shaman and half the village came to see me, against Cian's wishes. The shaman agreed that it was likely meningitis. Though, he warned, there was also the possibility that I'd been possessed by a demon. They would need to perform an exorcism just to be sure, unless we could provide proof that meningitis was the cause of my illness by means of a simple blood test.

Cian flat-out refused to allow my blood to be drawn, even throwing his body over mine as the village physician approached with a needle, trying to explain to Cian that an exorcism, in their ancient tradition, was not something he wanted me to be put through if it wasn't absolutely necessary.

"We'll do the exorcism," I remember Cian saying, through the haze of my mental delirium.

That's when the elders were called in.

I could only make out the feathers on their headdresses, and as I slipped in and out of hallucination, I imaged them a swarm of plumed serpents floating into my room in our primitive cottage on the village outskirts. Not surprisingly, Cian gave them the same answer he'd given the shaman and the physician, a resounding no. The elders decided that if he wouldn't allow it to be proven by blood, an exorcism would have to be performed, just to be safe. We were too close, they said, to the sacred site, to take any chances. The ruins of the ancient city of Tiwanaku was considered the gateway of the sun, deeply connected with life and creation. If any demons could come in through the portal of this ancient place, the darkness would spread unstopped over the whole of the earth. The people of Tiwanaku considered themselves the gatekeepers.

Knowing, as Cian did, that my blood was life and, as such, my body could heal itself of anything, even deadly spinal meningitis, rather than hand over an entire vile of my blood, Cian agreed to the exorcism.

First, I was prayed over by The Seven Shaman of the Andes, who'd all been summoned hours earlier as events began to escalate. Then my aura was cleansed and purified with heavy plumes of thick Palo Santo smoke. After that, The God of the Feathered Serpent was properly invoked in a ritual of shamanic drumming and chanting during which I felt myself slipping away from my body.

Finally, they brought me to their most sacred temple, an ancient site called The Stone at the Center of the World.

It's an enormous square monolith with a rectangular, door-shaped archway in the center. I was laid beneath the archway, in what they called The Gate of Worlds. That's when the figure carved at the top of the stone, a human-like being with wings and a curled-up tail became the main subject of my ongoing hallucinations, which had only increased steadily.

For thirteen hours, under the dark of night, my body sweat, thrashed, and seized, coming to the very brink of death before beginning to overpower the ravenous bacteria. That's what Cian would later report. During that same time, however, I was busy traveling the cosmos with this winged otherworldly being. I called him simply Weeping God. We spoke to one another without words. He wore the sun as a crown and an odd rectangular helmet on his head. Most fascinating of all, carved into his stone cheeks were a thick line of tears streaming down his face, like elongated rectangular boxes of falling rain.

We explored the furthest reaches of the universe aboard his golden flying craft, one part motorcycle one part rocket, the two stone lightning bolts from his hands set at his feet as he drove.

First, we flew beyond what appeared to be a spiraled scarlet rose.

Two interacting galaxies, he explained, *pulled together into the miraculous shape of a rose on a stem. The bright blue points across the top her young star clusters.* I stared at the hot blue stars hovering above, adorning the flower in ultraviolet light.

I think that's the most beautiful thing I've ever seen, I told him.

Time being nonexistent, we were suddenly not near the rose galaxy anymore, but flying past clouds of glowing purple and ice blue stellar dust.

A star nursery, he said, *about to burst to life.*

Then suddenly, we were through a burning white nebula that stretched upward over millions of miles.

We stopped at Orion, the archer in the sky, the hunter, set out against the black canvas of deep space.

Orion, The Gate of Man, Weeping God said of the shining silver figure. On his words, the archer came to life, dropping his arms down to his sides, turning his face towards me. The sadness in his eyes was overwhelming. A flood of tears poured instantly down my cheeks.

He's heartbroken, I said, noticing that I was weeping, feeling the sadness pouring out of me from some mysterious place in the deepest depths of my soul. It was as if he was me and I was him. Like I was looking in a mirror or staring at another side of myself.

His heart is not broken, dear one, it is exhausted, Weeping God clarified.

Why? I asked.

From being incomplete, he started, staring deeply into Orion's eyes as he spoke. *At first it was invigorating. There was so much to be learned by manifesting this way, as man without knowledge of God also inside him. Simply human, or so he wanted himself to believe, man ruling the world with God placed somewhere else, somewhere outside himself. He wanted to see what it would be like, how far he could go? What could he accomplish without the knowledge of his divinity and without his other half, woman, square at his side, where she truly is in the truth of the universe. For a very long time it was as if his desire to grow and to experience life in this way would never end. But while he was soaring to new heights, amazing himself in his accomplishments, he was also descending to new lows, discovering new pits and recesses inside the deepest parts of his being. Depths he never imagined he could reach. Sorrow he could feel and create that he never imaged existed in this universe. The consequences were suffering, more and more of it. And finally, at his most disconnected point, he successfully convinced the world that there was not enough love in it for everyone. He had found the bottom, though he didn't know it yet. Then he lost himself way down there in the empty hallows of his shadow self. He became addicted to war, to objects, to sex, to food, to control, to money, to power, all in place of the love that was inside himself all along. Love that he convinced himself there was somehow not enough of in the world for everyone, a delusion that caused him to hoard things in its place, to fill the emptiness he wrongly perceived in himself in others and in the world. He had found hell. And it wasn't a place, it was a state of being.*

I nodded, knowing as I did, even at eight that hell was not a place but a condition. We sat there in silence, watching Orion. My heart drowning in a river of tears being cried by my soul.

Finally, he has seen all that there is to see here in this way. The Mayans foretold when this would happen, giving the very date the shift inside man would occur. Other ancient civilizations mapped it out in the sky and placed reminders, monuments, and towers, all over the earth. On December 21, 2012, this world he created ends.

My thirteenth birthday, I told him.

Yes, I know. He smiled.

I felt that I had to help Orion. It was the strangest thing. I knew I was supposed to help him. I felt it coursing through my veins, beating in my heart. But I didn't know what to say or do or where to even begin.

Man is ready to move on, to come into perfect union for the first time ever. Man, woman, human and divine, God-made flesh in both he and his co-creator, woman. He's ready to merge, but the confusion that's been spun isn't proving easy to awaken from. He's ready to get on with it, but part of him is holding back. All of mankind must awaken for this to happen, and there is some part of him that's still holding back, attached and clinging, despite that something far better awaits. The longer it takes, the wearier and more worn out he becomes," Weeping God said.

That's awful, I wept, feeling helpless. *I wish he could just move on.*

It gets worse. There is a point of no return. If he passes it before he merges, he'll have to destroy himself again … and all of mankind, all that's been created here in this way. Everything that's been learned will just be … lost. And he doesn't want to do that. Not this time. He's discovered so much, and he's come so far, and he wants to bring all of that knowledge forward into the next place. He does not want to start over again, he never wants to start over again, Weeping God said with the saddest look on his face, his gaze locked on Orion.

What does he need to move on? I asked.

On my question, Weeping God nodded to Orion, who began moving his arrow, lifting it upward.

His co-creator is on the other side of the galaxy. He needs to merge with her as well as with his higher self. Orion's co-creator, his soul's eternal mate, is Ophiuchus.

How can he get to her if she's all the way on the opposite side of the galaxy? I asked, feeling anxious for Orion. *It sounds impossible.*

You. Your blood. Cian was right. Your blood has the power to change everything, he said, just as the gleaming metal tip of Orion's arrow appeared before me.

My instinct was to reach out and touch it, like Sleeping Beauty pricking her finger on the spindle. Uncertain, I looked to Weeping God.

Go on, he encouraged me.

My hand was steady, but my heart was pounding as I reached out my finger. The silver tip seemed to move towards my flesh in exaggerated slow motion. The second I touched the razor-sharp arrow, I felt it pierce my skin. Orion appeared filled with gratitude and relief. Then he slowly pulled the arrow towards his bow, balancing a large round drop of my crimson blood on the shining silver tip.

The day will come when you are asked for your blood, when Cian's work is done and he's no longer at your side. You must give it. Your blood is Orion's arrow, he says. On his words Orion shot the arrow from his bow and it goes soaring straight across the galaxy, towards the heart of the constellation Ophiuchus, on the direct opposite side of the galaxy.

We zoomed off after it, chasing the arrow at warp speed. As we careened through deep space, we were barely able to keep the arrow in our sights. I turned to look back at Orion, but he had already disappeared in the distance behind us.

Then, suddenly we were stopped. The figure of the serpent bearer stood out against the dark of space the same way Orion had.

Ophiuchus, Weeping God announced.

The first thing I noticed were the Seven Sisters of Ophiuchus shining before us, luminous hot blue pulsing stars. They appeared close enough to touch, and they danced as they shimmered like long-lost ancient sapphires rising out of a bowl of black ink, adorned with pin-sized white diamonds all around them.

It will take your blood several Earth years to arrive here, he said.

Am I Ophiuchus? I asked, out of instinct and intuition.

Yes, but you are just half of her, the other half is also you but in another female human form. She is on Earth now as well. You've yet to meet her, but when you do, you'll know it.

How?

Your souls are quite literally opposing gravitational forces, and they will be drawn together like magnets, each helping the other one to ... evolve, he put it, choosing the word carefully. *When the end comes, there will be four from the four corners of the earth, Russia, Africa, North America, and New Zealand, two males of Orion and two females of Ophiuchus; shadow and light. In what transpires amongst the four, the fate of humanity will be decided,* he warned.

I was feeling suddenly overwhelmed.

Then Weeping God took my hand. His eyes locked on mine, he turned my hand over palm facing up. There was another drop of blood sitting on the tip of my finger. He pinched the air just above it and pulled upward. My DNA spiraled up two feet off my fingertip, spinning between us like a hologram image. It pulsed hot blue, the very same vibrant glow as the Seven Sisters burning before us.

Here, let me show you something. You see? There are thirteen stands, he said of the twirling structure rising out of my blood.

I counted them, the strands of my own DNA. He was right.

Humans only have twelve strands of DNA, I said nervously, something I already knew well, even at eight.

Yes ... when incomplete or when non-human. There are non-humans on earth, their DNA is twelve strands. Humans have twelve visible strands. The thirteenth is there, but it is not activated, therefore invisible. Yours cannot be deactivated, it cannot be made invisible. It is the new consciousness, the fullness of humanity, Earth and stars, Ophiuchus and Orion, all together and balanced, finally—perfect yin and yang. You are the final evolution of the human race, and the human race is the highest evolution of all beings, the pearl of the universe.

I thought it all over, everything he was telling me.

So, Orion will merge with Ophiuchus? I asked, but I don't remember him answering.

I sat up beneath the archway and opened my eyes, Cian's face only a few inches from mine, a radiant golden sunset burning behind him.

That's why I was nervous as the first vial I'd ever given was drawn. When, like everyone else in Rugby, my blood was extracted for Animus testing I was afraid, but I thought this must be it. It must be time for what Weeping God had told me. But then, after what Animus became, I wasn't so sure I'd done the right thing.

Then later, I suspected it again, that the right time had come, the time I gave an even larger quantity to Shamus. I did it because of my heart, how it was opening, how it yearned to show Shamus love, unaware of how impossible it still was for him to receive it. Not knowing that all of it was a trick. Just another part of Ansel's plan to stop me.

Now, I stand unnoticed in the enormous laboratory next to the armory. Where unending rows of vials are being born out of machines so sophisticated no one would believe any of it exists or that something this destructive is really going on at such a desperate time for humanity. That these miles of machines are filled with a synthetic copy of my blood, the blood that can do anything, including raise the dead. The blood that can be used *by humanity* or *against them*. Either to liberate or to enslave, depending on why it is used; whether it's to control people or to set them free. And that it's being churned out with blinding speed and efficiency by Ansel, who in my absence from this plane is now at the helm of Aurora, the shadow leader who operates under a tight veil of secrecy. Doing everything he can to prevent humanity from waking up.

PART TWO

SMOKE AND MIRRORS

ROMAN

THIRTEEN

———— ✠ ————

I stand in the cover of shadows, watching it. The way it moves, slinking through the darkness. It's not human. I don't know what it is.

A scaly skinned, half-lizard and half-man, yellow-eyed … thing. His spine protrudes like overgrown roots beneath his skin. It starts right behind his head, goes down the entire length of his long, hunched back, and extends several feet behind him. His small downturned mouth and tiny nose are all but nonexistent compared to the large disk-like eyes that take up half his angular face. Even slouched over as he is, he's taller than me by perhaps more than a foot.

Ruby continues coughing up water in fits here and there, but she seems to be getting air back in her lungs, albeit in short, panicked gasps.

I know I must wait for the right moment to make my presence known. I'm not sure what this monster is capable of, and I want both Ruby and I to make it out of this cave alive. I glance behind myself, then look all around, trying to see in near pitch black. I begin to feel there are more of … whatever he is, lurking somewhere nearby. I can feel it. Of course, a creature like this would travel in packs. Though this thing, now pacing about in front of Ruby, is no animal, that's clear. It's some kind of human-like underworld being. The kind of weird wonders and strange anomalies that Kali told us occupy the dead zone.

He appears more fascinated by Ruby than anything. Marveling, as he takes her in, studying her naked body.

She squirms and flinches at his every move. Laid out on a stone altar cut into the wall of the cavern, she's displayed like a human sacrifice. Though she's not restrained, she simply stays put out of fear for her life, shaking like a leaf as he skulks around her, whimpering as he examines her. Incredible anger rushes through my veins watching him look her over like a piece of meat. My back teeth grind together. How cowardly of a creature like this, who's so much bigger and stronger, delighting in her helplessness. How vile the way he sexualizes her just because she's beautiful. What a revolting pathetic monster. A dark blinding rage rises in me as I begin to calculate my next move.

Then another emerges from around the corner, behind the altar. And another, followed by several more, until there are eight of these nightmarish scaled predators surrounding her in a tight circle. The last one to enter is the largest. He walks more upright and seems to be the leader as they all assemble with him at the center.

I can't see Ruby now, only that all of the creatures' arms are at their sides, so I know no one is touching her. Her whimpers turn to sobs as she no doubt begins to imagine what they plan to do next. She has no idea that I'm here, and that I am not going to let anything happen to her.

"How many hideous lizards does it take to torment one frightened defenseless girl?" I ask, stepping out of the shadows.

"You'd be surprised," one of the lizard men hisses.

None of them even bother turning to look at me.

"Did you think we didn't know you were there?" the leader asks me, never taking his eyes off Ruby.

"Filthy human," says another, "we could smell you before you even jumped in the water."

"Keep your distance, vile creature," commands the leader.

"But I'm, I'm human too…" Ruby bargains, desperately.

"Yes, but you are *female*," the leader corrects her.

"But we're both human. We're the same exact thing," she pleads.

"Is that what you've been told?" The leader asks, heavy sarcasm in his raspy voice. A cacophony of rapturous noises echoes off the cave walls. It's the laughter of underworld monsters, and it's dark and unsettling.

"The female earth dweller has been so deceived," the leader informs Ruby. "The most enchanted *and* the most enslaved being in all the universe and across all galaxies … because you have always been so feared … by man," he says, caressing her hair.

Feeling like I sometimes do in dreams, it's as if my boots are suddenly glued to the rocks beneath them, but my body is buzzing—I don't feel real. There's something about what he's saying. I'm overcome with a bizarre feeling, like I'm staring out from inside myself with what can only be described as my bare soul.

"This has been since the very beginning," he explains, and I'm overcome again. This time by a stinging in my heart, as though his very words are piercing through my chest like the razor-sharp end of a long dagger. A dagger bearing the name of my soul.

"The female earth dweller has never been told what she is. She has never been allowed to know. You were never taught the truth of what you are…"

"*What*, what am I?" Ruby asks, voice shaking and weak, sounding terrified at what he might say.

"You are a reservoir of the energy," he says, like this should mean something to her.

"What energy?" she asks.

After a long pause, "*The* energy," he repeats.

She sits in her unknowing, weeping quietly.

"The energy of pure life. The most coveted force in the universe," he explains. "And you," he says breathing in, smelling her, "you are *extraordinary*. Almost ... the very essence of it." He breathes her in again. "The source of the energy itself," he says, sounding mystified by her. "Do you know what the energy does," he asks her, "what it's used for?"

"No, I don't," I hear her say, and though I can't see her, I can tell by her voice that she's beginning to cry.

"It gives the possessor manifesting power, inexhaustible and unlimited. The energy is the most precious natural resource in the universe, and female humans are made of it, through and through. As you grow in your mother's womb, it's infusing into your body. It's in your bones, in your hair, your skin. The moment you're born, it's just pouring out of your soul into the world, out of your *female* spirit," he hisses out, sounding vile and hungry.

I'm still frozen inside myself, transfixed by what he's telling her. His voice echoes off the cave walls, filling all the space around me. His words vibrate through me.

"Your spirit is the best place to drain it from, your body a close second. You see, the energy has always been stolen from you, all your life. Syphoned off you, like oil being pumped out of the ground, and you don't even know it. You've never known it. Though somewhere deep down you do know, because you're also *very smart*—female Earth dwellers. That's what terrifies everyone the most about you, that one day you will realize what's going on. And on that day, the world as we know it will shatter like glass, and the universe will contract with a howling shriek, followed by a monstrous roar that will echo through the galaxy. Then everything and everyone that's ever harmed you will be consumed by your rage. That's why the knowledge of the energy that you are is so forbidden, why it's never spoken of, and why you're lied to, because if you knew what you were, this world would end. Best you have no idea of the power inside you, how it works, or that it's yours to use. Best it be used by man for his gain. Better that he uses your own power against you ... or so he thinks. You see, what man never realizes," he laughs wickedly, "is that when he weakens you, when he thinks he's enslaving you, he's really enslaving himself." He turns his head and speaks in my direction.

I feel the energy in the cave suddenly shift.

"The only thing that can be done about man is to

destroy him," he says like a command. Then, as though they're operating as a single organism, the other seven creatures turn their scaly bodies to face me at the same moment, their backs now to Ruby.

My body awakens with a surge of adrenaline. I steady my sword pointed in their direction. Then I see Ruby behind them standing on the alter, a large rock raised over her head and a look of grit and anger on her face. A look of unbound rage. In one ferocious move, she brings the rock down, slamming it on the head of the leader. His eyes two burning yellow disks are round with shock, his gaping mouth hanging open in surprise. Suddenly, the bright golden color of his pupils drains to black. Then he crumples to the ground. The eyes of the other seven go from glowing gold to black, and they fall to the ground all at once.

The sound of sizzling begins to rise off them, followed by thick white smoke, and then a noxious vapor.

"Don't breathe it in," I say through the putrid stench, lifting my hand to my face.

Ruby buries her mouth and nose in the crook of her elbow as the creature's bodies burn from the inside out and melt into the rock bed.

Once the smoke and vapor clears, I walk over what remains of them, a wet slick of tarry, black oil. I step slowly towards Ruby, who's still standing on the altar with a blank look on her face. Shocked by what she's just accomplished. Her body is stiff, the blood-splattered rock still in her hands. She stares into my eyes, her mouth gaping, shaking her head ever so slightly, shuttered up in her shock. Then, all at once, a flood of tears fills her piercing blue eyes, and the rock falls out of her hands with a crash. She crumples back down onto the long slab of stone, weeping.

At the sight of her sobbing so hard, her body rocking violently, cold and wet and terrified, bared naked on a sacrificial altar like a slab of meat, stripped of her humanity, I drop my sword and am overcome with sorrow so blinding that everything inside me, my very soul, seems to plummet down through the earth.

"I am so sorry," I say to her, my voice breaking off from all the emotion, from trying to express in words something from the very pit of my being, from the deepest depths, a place I don't even recognize. How to put into words such profound sorrow? It feels impossible.

"I am so sorry," I say again, not knowing exactly what it is I am sorry about.

This time she looks at me. Looking back at her through the tunnel of our eyes, it becomes even more difficult to locate the exact source of my sympathy. Whether it's because I wasn't the one who saved her, or because of what she's just been through. Maybe it's because of all the things the creature just said. I'm not sure it really matters.

"I am so sorry," I say again, clearly this time, and firm, standing right in front of her.

She begins to weep again, this time even harder, but silently. Her body convulsing, consumed by sorrow, her hands shoulders, feet, every part of her trembling.

I quickly remove my shirt and drape it over her, wrapping it and my arms around her shoulders, covering and comforting her. I feel her start to relax beneath me, the tension of fear collapsing underneath the weight of my embrace.

"I'm here, Ruby. I've got you," I tell her.

"Thank you," she whispers through her tears, "Thank you for coming for me … for not leaving me," she continues, crying in fits and starts, her whole body shaking like a leaf.

"Shhh," I whisper, feeling my throat tighten and tears welling in my own eyes. "It's ok, shhh," I tell her. "Of course I wasn't going to leave you," I say, tears streaking down my face. "Shhh, it's ok," I repeat again, nose sniffling.

She looks up at me, studying me and my emotion, my teary eyes and face, my chest, my shoulders, my arms, everything about me. Like she's seeing me for the first time. I take in her tear-soaked face and matted black lashes. Then her crystal blue eyes zero in on mine. Our faces a few inches apart,

I feel her warm breath. My heart pounds inside my chest.

She starts to lean in slowly, cautiously, a millimeter at a time, until finally our lips touch and she's kissing me.

My arms already wrapped around her, I pull her into me even closer. Then, wanting to hold onto the kiss, I move my hands gently to her soft face. Holding onto her warm tear-soaked cheeks, not wanting to let go. It's as if time has stopped, and the entire world outside this cave has disappeared. My mouth moves slow, deeply, with hers.

She ends the kiss by pulling back to look up at me. The small shy smile on her swollen pink lips morphing slowly into a wider one.

We both laugh nervously. She looks at the ground.

"I never noticed your dimples," I say, seeing the tiny little indents in her rosy round cheeks on both sides of her smiling mouth.

"I don't usually smile," she replies.

"Right," I remember. Primitus, war, famine, The Cause ... and for the first time, I start to wonder about the ways in which our life is the same. If she has a Keeper. If she's someone's girl like Iris is mine. I wonder what he's like, if he's nice to her, and how old he is. I wonder if The Cause is the same for Guardian Soul women ... and men ... as it is for King Souls. Then, thinking of The Cause, about Iris and her status, I start to feel angry.

Knowing my anger isn't going to help me, not right now anyway, I take a deep breath and shift my focus to getting out of this cave.

"I guess we need to go back out the same way we came in," I say, motioning towards where the tunnel leads to the water. "We'll have to swim down—"

"I can't swim," she says, stopping me in my tracks. And I remember how the creature had dragged her through the water all the way here. That she didn't swim to get here, not the way I did.

"Is that why you were only half in the water when we were on the shore?" I ask her.

"Well, yeah ... *sort of*," she says, smiling again. Her eyes shine as she hops down and buttons my shirt up the front of herself, watching me watch her.

I swallow nervously at the thought of her knowing how transfixed I was on the shore, how transfixed I am right now by her, how helplessly mesmerized. The thought of Ruby wielding the power of her beauty and every other mysterious and unknowable thing that she is, channeling all *the energy* inside her—it terrifies me.

"Are you ok?" she asks, placing her warm hand on my cheek.

Her steady eyes, tender and filled with confidence, steady mine.

Feeling the magic in her touch, I realize that nothing could be more fulfilling to watch her grow into all the power within her. That nothing could be more beautiful to witness.

"*I am*, thanks," I tell her, and she nods. Then we both start looking around, trying to find a way out of here.

I glance in the direction that leads to the water.

I wonder if I can do it. If I can get us out of here through the water.

But then I remember how hard it was and worry that if I try pulling her behind me, we may get into trouble in the long stretch of open water once we're out of the cave.

The others may no longer be on the shore. Picturing the rocks and soft grass at the edge of the water empty, I see her drowning in my mind. Me, watching from a few feet away trying to grab onto her without her pulling us both down, helpless to save her. Then, her staring at me, face frozen in shock, floating away into the deep.

I shake the terrible thought from my mind.

"There has to be another way out of here," I say, and we both look towards the altar.

"Where do you think it leads?" she asks.

"I don't know, but maybe out," I say, "I don't think we've got another option."

"What if there are more of them?" she asks. "Or something even worse?"

I pick up my sword where I'd dropped it.

"We'll just deal with whatever comes our way," I shrug. "Grab the rock," I tell her with a smile.

She hefts up the large jagged rock she used to kill the creatures.

"Nicely done, by the way," I marvel of the bloodied rock back in her infamously deadly hands. Her eyes light up.

"You like that?" She jokes, smiling, pure light beaming out of her. She turns serious.

"You know, I'm actually *pretty* proud of myself," she admits emphatically.

"You should be," I tell her. "You should be *very* proud. It was brave, incredibly so. But also ... smart, so smart. Absolutely *cunning*. You likely saved my life," I admit freely, wondering if I could have killed all of them. Then, I think of the last thing the creature said, about what man never realizes. When he deceives the female about her power that he's really killing himself.

"I *did* save your life," she tells me boldly now, amazed at herself.

"You really did," I tell her.

"But if you would have died, I'd have been dead for sure," she points out. "You were my lifeline," she says, words that cast a strange knowing over both of us. A bone-deep, familiar feeling.

"And you were mine," I say, mystified by the undeniable link between our lives, blanketed by a knowing I can't fully grasp.

"It's what I do," she jokes of the heavy rock she's resting on her hip, breaking the eeriness of the moment.

"How did you know that if you killed the one they'd all die?" I ask.

"It was their eyes," she says, setting the rock on the ground.

"What about their eyes?" I ask, watching her as she ties her long, wet hair into a buttery blonde knot on top of her head.

"The way they blinked. It was at the exact same time. I always had this thought that the eyes are the windows to the soul. I don't know where that came from, but I just I think it all the time. And anyway, it occurred to me that … well … I knew they were all sharing just one soul," she states finally and that it would have to be controlled by the leader.

"Wow, that's … insightful." I shake my head, amazed that she could think so clearly while being terrified. "Really smart," I marvel. "And how about that color? Of their eyes." That golden glow.

"That too. I knew they couldn't each have a soul with all of their eyes being completely black," she says, in a matter of fact way.

She didn't see what I saw, I realize. She didn't see the same bright fire-gold color that I saw.

Unsure what that means and unsettled by what it might, I decide not to mention it. I look down and see her bare feet on the rocks.

"Here, take my boots," I tell her, untying them from my feet.

"Are you sure?" she asks, sounding surprised and grateful.

"*I am*," I say, holding onto her as she steps into them, feeling my heart expand at the simple act of caring for her needs.

FOURTEEN

—— ❈ ——

We quickly find our way out of the caves once we walk behind the makeshift altar. There is nothing but a long corridor, the whole thing illuminated softly in pale silver light, a glowing ball of brightness at the end inviting us out.

Now, we're walking through what appears to be a meadow, an unending field of tall soft grass as far as we can see in all directions.

We're looking for the others. Figuring that, by the distance from the lagoon to the cave to here, they should be close by. Though, we can't seem to find the lagoon or the shore where we left them. We can't find the mountains either, the enormous ranges walling us in on both sides, which should be of some concern, but somehow is not. We just keep walking, deeper and deeper into the tranquil meadow.

"I have this feeling like we don't need to worry about anything," I tell her, my whole body in a state of total calmness. "I know we'll find them," I continue, trying to explain why the suggestion that we turn around, go back into the caves, and try to swim back to the shore where we left them, is not coming out of my mouth as it reasonably should.

"Yeah," she says dreamily. "Me too," she agrees, looking over at me, her face glowing in the mysterious sparkling light, her big blue eyes lit from inside her soul in a way I've never seen them before. There's a whole new way about her, like she's standing differently in herself.

"The light here is just ... spectacular," I marvel at the magical source of it, a huge shining silver disk hanging in the dark sky directly before us, almost close enough to touch.

I know it's the moon, this glowing, round, shimmering orb. Casting its soft silver light out in a luminous blanket covering this wondrous place and everything in it, including us, with her luxurious beams. We *both* know it's the moon. In Primitus we're told all about the incredible things, like the moon, that no longer exist. Everything Eve supposedly destroyed is carefully catalogued in our minds. She turned the moon red then sent it into the sky at midday, where it was seared by the sun and never seen again. And yet, here it is, looking just as it's said to have looked: mysterious, alluring, soothing, radiant. Alive and well and right where it belongs, illuminating the night sky, adorned by billions of glistening stars.

We both know it's the moon, but neither of us mention it specifically. Maybe if we talk about it, it'll evaporate somehow. We just … accept it. We just take it all in. We take in the mysterious meadow, the stars, the moon, and each other. All of it. Just being here. It feels like a balancing force—like some kind of medicine. I can almost feel it all healing us as we walk beside one another. My bare chest and skin absorbs the night air, bare feet in the soft grass, all of it energizing me. I feel a force like life itself surge up out of the ground, through my feet, shooting up my spine, and out the crown of my head, pulling every part of me towards the center. Arranging me, syncing me with nature, bringing my body and soul into harmony.

I glance over at Ruby, but I don't just look at her. I *see* her. All that she is, her striking beauty, her mental strength, her calm nature, her strong presence, her soft heart. To look at her is to know I haven't even scratched the surface of who she truly is. She's yet to know herself, and already she is a miracle, a wonder, a goddess.

She is overwhelming.

So overwhelming, that it stops me. My chest expands

with breath, with life. My heart pounds. I place my hand gently on her forearm. She stops, and turns, her eyes flick up to meet mine. I pull her towards me, then take hold of the other arm too. I look down into her eyes, like deep powerful oceans, terrifying and alluring. Staring into her, feeling the energy she radiates, the feminine force, *the energy*, so powerful, so beguiling I lose myself in. I lose myself in her eyes, and then in the glow of her skin and the long tendrils of blonde hair falling down around her neck.

Just like she did in the cave, Ruby leans in before I do, and she presses her lips to mine, more deliberately this time. When she kissed me in the cave it was like a wake-up call, an alarm clock that had been going off for some time but that I'd only just heard. This time, her kiss is harder, more forceful, and it's like a drug. A mind-altering, psychedelic trip to another reality that makes the entire world melt and the universe dissolve. All of existence pulls into us like it's nothing more than electric current in a closed circuit.

I'm not sure how long we stand there, kissing in the silver moonlight, our hands running through each other's hair. Holding onto each other's faces. Feeling each other's bodies. And I'm not sure how long ago it was that we started walking again. How long ago it was that she stopped kissing me, looking up into my eyes with a satisfied smile, her mouth pink from the scruff on my face. I think we've walked a good distance since then. We must have. The moon is much smaller and sitting directly overhead now, but I can't be sure.

I also can't tell how far we've gone. Time itself feels *off*. Distinctly so. It feels stretchy, elongated, filled with more space, infinite space. Like however much space or time we may want or need we can just create by stretching it out further. Perhaps we could even contract it, condense time, or make it run backwards.

I hadn't noticed it at first, but the longer we kissed, the more I began to get the feeling that time can be dissolved altogether. That it's only a matter of figuring out how.

As we walk, I look over at Ruby and she smiles at me, her skin aglow, eyes shining bright. She glances down at my boots on her feet, laces swinging loose as they plod along. She stops to readjust them. Even laced as tightly as we can get them, they're still so big on her. But she insists on keeping them on.

"I like walking in your shoes." she smiles up at me with a dreamy look on her face. "It makes me my feet feel ... happy," she genuinely tries to describe. We both laugh at how it sounds once the words are out.

"Well, good. I like being barefoot. And I like having you wear my shoes. It makes me feel happy," I say.

"Well, good." She's flirting, I realize all at once.

"It is good," I say, flirting back, feeling like the world is an elastic rubber band and her and I are bouncing on it freely.

"Hey, what is *Earth*?" she asks from down in the grass, still working to retie the laces. "Why did the creature keep saying *Earth dwellers*? Do you know what that means?"

"I think I do know what he meant," I say.

"What?" she asks with a look of utter fascination.

"Another world existed," I tell her, "before this one, or well before what we know as Passus."

"Are we even on Passus anymore?" she asks.

"I don't know."

"Another world, huh?" Her eyes are wide.

"Yeah. We lived in it. You, me, everyone," I explain. "We had other lives. I mean these lives, but they were different. They were nothing like our regular lives now. There was no Antiquus and Primitus, no Animus, no incarnation numbers. The Destruction Story and The Cause, none of that existed in this other world."

"No?" she asks, standing up.

"Nope. That's all just been ... made up, like a story."

"Made up," her eyes wide. "Why? When? By who?"

"By who ... I'm not sure, not yet. And when? Not that long ago," I say. "It was done to control us and keep us from the truth."

"What truth?" she asks.

"The truth about what actually happened ... the truth about who we really are, where we come from, why we're here..." I tell her.

"Like the energy," she says to herself. "So, you don't believe what we're being told? Any of it?"

"No, I don't."

"But what caused *this* world, what caused Passus then? And what about The Events and The Unthinkable? Isn't that how it all happened? Because of Eve?"

"Something happened to start all this, to create Passus and everything in it. I'm not sure what, but it wasn't The Destruction, not as we're told, anyway. Something different happened, something else entirely. I know it in my gut," I tell her, locating for the first time the source of this knowing that's driven me for so long.

I watch a flash of understanding come over her.

"We're *all* being lied to," she says, nodding as she explains her thought, "just like *women* have been lied to since the beginning, like the creature said about what we really are, all the power that's inside us."

"Yes, that's exactly it. And you know how that felt when you found out. When that truth about yourself was revealed?"

"Like I was learning something I already knew but had

forgotten. It was like a piece of myself restored—the most important piece of all— one I somehow didn't even know I was missing," she tries to explain.

But I already know.

"I can see it in you, in how you seem. Different. Restored. It's beautiful—remarkable, in fact. Knowing the truth, it changed you instantly into more of who you really are, into a deeper and truer you," I describe as I look at her. "I feel like I'm meant to find the truth like that, but ... for all humanity," I tell her, and she nods, spurring me on. "The truth behind this whole world ... it's being kept from us," I say, searching for something just out of reach.

"We're *all* enslaved," she says and realizes all at once. "Men and women, enslaved by lies, lies about who we are, where we come from, why we're here…"

"Yes!" I exclaim, "Exactly. And I'm going to uncover the truth, to free us from this place," I pledge to her, taking her hand and kissing the back of it.

"I believe you're meant to," she says, studying me. "I believe in you, Roman. You'll do it. I know you will."

"*We* will. We'll do it together," I say, hearing myself getting over-excited, sounding like a fool but not caring. "We'll heal the whole world, you and I!"

She smiles a sweet little smile at me, then looks away, seeming unsure about what the future may hold.

"Yeah," she says finally, looking back up at me, but I can tell she's not sure. "So, the world before Passus, where we all lived … it was called Earth?" she asks.

"It was," I say.

After a long moment of quiet, "It's so strange," she remarks.

"Which part?" I joke, knowing it all sounds more than strange.

"Just, all of it. It's so strange how I feel when you tell it to me and when I hear the word *Earth*. That's the strangest part of all. Something about it, the word—*Earth*—it calls to me, if a word can call to a person. And when I hear it, the sound that it makes, it's like it's telling me who I am," she struggles to explain. "Like it's all right there in the word…" she trails off.

"I know. I feel it too," I tell her.

She stares off, then points at something in the distance.

"What's that?" she asks, I look towards where she's pointing.

"Looks like … a city," she says. "Think it's the armory?"

"Only one way to find out, right?" I say, and we start towards it.

"How do you know all of this anyway? All that stuff?" she asks walking beside me.

"I just know," I shrug, deciding not to tell Ruby the

other part, the part I told Iris about how I dream of a girl who tells me all this and many other things. I'm not sure why, but I don't want to tell her.

I don't want Ruby to know about Eve.

FIFTEEN

——— ✦ ———

As we draw nearer to what we thought was a city, we realize it's just a small town. A cozy little village nestled between twin buttes, two enormous flat-topped rock mountains sitting like guards on either side. In the distance is a sprawling prairie, where gentle breezes roll through miles of tall, golden grass like waves rolling through water.

When we arrive, it's twilight—real twilight, or so I'm suddenly remembering it's called—the time when the sun starts descending towards the horizon. Ruby and I stare at the brilliant burning sky as it begins to ignite into a glowing golden pink. Never mind that it was the dead of night just a short time ago and now appears to be approaching night again.

Since Ruby and I emerged from the cave, time seems meaningless.

As soon as we walk into the town, the air begins to feel crisp, and the temperature suddenly plummets, going from balmy to chilly to freezing all at once.

"It's cold," Ruby says, pulling my shirt tighter around her.

I wrap my arm across her shoulders. Just then, soft white powder begins falling from the sky. It swirls down slowly at first, then starts falling harder and faster until it's dropping like a wall of white all around us.

"*Snow*," she says, arms outstretched, letting it fall onto her hands.

"Snow," I repeat, nodding. "Remember snow?" I begin to wonder if this is all some kind of dream.

"I remember," she says, her voice awash in mystery. Her eyes shine like diamonds floating in crystal blue rivers, lit from some deep place inside her, aglow with the fire of her soul.

We walk down a road called Main Street, where people are coming and going, bundled in heavy clothes, walking in and out of shops. They look busy and happy, and I have no idea who they are.

"The two of you must be freezing," a voice says from behind us.

An older woman I can barely see through the blinding snow and from behind her knit cap and red scarf hands

Ruby a long coat. She places a pair of boots on the ground in from of me and hands me a heavy flannel shirt.

"Are you sure?" Ruby asks her, as the woman wraps the coat over Ruby's shoulders.

"Nonsense, I insist," the woman hushes her, and pulls out a scarf and hat as well, from where I don't know.

"Thank you," Ruby says gladly, as we both put the warm clothes on. By the time we're done, the woman is gone.

"Where did she go?" Ruby asks.

"I don't know," I say. "I can't see her anywhere."

That's when I spot something at the end of the busy street. A sign, lit in bright green and buzzing in and out. Though it's too far away to read, I know exactly what it says.

"The Green Owl," I whisper, and like moths to a flame, Ruby and I both start heading towards it.

When we get closer, the words become clear enough to read.

"How did you know that?" she asks me.

"I don't know," I tell her as we stand outside, looking in. The warm yellow glow through the windows, the smell of food, fresh and hot, all of it is hauntingly familiar.

"Let's go in." Her eyes light up.

But I hesitate.

"I don't know," I say, feeling uneasy, unsure as to why. But something is holding me back.

"What don't you know about?" she asks, exasperated. "It smells like *food* in there. Real food. Delicious food! And I'm starving!" She grabs her stomach.

"I know, me too, it's just…" I start, but I have nothing really to say.

"C'mon!" she grabs my arm and pushes open the door.

The sound of brass bells clanging against the glass door as we cross the threshold is a sound I have heard a million times before from this very door and from the very bells hanging above us, swinging and clanging as I look up at them. All the smells I have smelled, all the sights I have seen, all of it a million times before. But when? That is the only question in my mind. When was I here?

But the smells of meat cooking on open flames and soft buttery rolls rising in the warm brick oven nearly knocks me over.

I look around. The framed knick-knacks on the walls, the vinyl booths, the stool-lined counter, the license plates…

"Remember *license plates*?" I ask, pulling Ruby towards a wall of them. "Ruby, do you remember them?" I ask, pointing at all the tin rectangles scattered about on the walls. "Remember cars?" I whisper to myself, feeling almost dizzy.

"North Dakota," Ruby reads. "I remember *North*

Dakota," she says, emphatically, a puzzled look on her face.

"Me too," I admit, staring at the words.

"*Rugby*," Ruby whispers, just as the very same word rushes into my mind.

"Welcome to Rugby," the tranquil voice of a young woman announces from behind us. Ruby and I turn to see a girl around our age coming towards us. Dark hair is her most prominent feature—midnight black—all the way down past her waist, shiny and wavy, cascading over both shoulders. A few shorter locks tousled around her porcelain pale face fall near her eyes, obscuring them just enough from view to where I can't look directly into them.

"Rugby," Ruby repeats. "We lived in Rugby," Ruby declares, exactly what I'm thinking.

"Well of course you guys do," the girl laughs, her voice echoing in the most unnatural way. Her pink lips and pale skin appear to be almost shimmering. "Everyone knows who you are," she says casually. "Been a while since you were in here though. Almost seems like another lifetime ago…." she studies us with a warm smile, then takes Ruby's arm, "But it wasn't, I assure you. C'mon." She leads her towards the wall of booths, and I follow.

I can't hear what the girl is saying to Ruby, but soon they're chatting back and forth like old friends. Ruby throws her head back in laughter as the other girl talks away, a mile a minute, both smiling ear to ear. I get the most mysterious feeling as I watch them—as if, somehow, they're one person. I even see them merge into a single girl right in front of me. When I rub my eyes and shake my head, the two of them reappear again.

"Hello?" Ruby calls to me. Her voice sounds far away.

"Huh?" I say, noticing that the girl has already sat Ruby in a booth and I'm just standing in front of the table doing nothing. "Oh, thanks," I say as I sit, "kind of spaced out there for a minute."

"Well, I'm sure, you must be absolutely starving!" the girl exclaims, and all at once I become aware of how utterly and completely empty my stomach is. How empty it's been for too long.

"This is Lily," Ruby beams. "She tells me she and I are really old friends," she says, eyes squinting trying to imagine it, captivated by her mysterious new/old friend.

"The oldest," Lily remarks.

"It's nice to meet you, Lily," I say, trying to get a look at her eyes. But just as I do, she glances away and turns towards the kitchen.

"I'm just going to start bringing food out," she calls back to us over her shoulder as she walks away.

"My God, don't you just *love* her," Ruby remarks sounding absolutely enamored. "I mean don't you just feel this ... like *deep connection* to her? This electricity?" she asks, trying to describe what's going on inside her and looking charged with a million watts of power. I stare at her, but I don't answer. It's as if I don't have an answer to give her. "Roman?"

"I mean, I don't know … all of this is so eerie," I say, looking around. "It's all so familiar, her too, in a weird way, and yet, I don't know. It's also different and unfamiliar," I struggle, rubbing my forehead.

I start to seriously worry that I may be losing my mind.

Then Lily comes striding through the kitchen door like a goddess descending from the sky, bearing abundance, arms filled with an incredible amount of food and an enormous pitcher of ice cold water. I'm struggling to understand how she's carrying it all. It seems physically impossible, and yet, it appears effortless for her. Even the way she walks, or rather floats, across the floor, gliding towards us. It's all from another world.

"Isn't she so beautiful?" Ruby wonders aloud, marveling at her.

"Yeah," I agree, trying to look at Lily's face as she approaches.

Again, she averts her eyes, and this time I know it's intentional.

"This should be enough to get you started. I brought you our signature Bison burgers—"

"Bison burgers," I say, at the exact same time. Like I work here.

"Of course, right? They're the best! Everyone loves them. And here's a bunch of other stuff to go with them. All my favorites. Ruby and I have the same taste," she remarks as she sets down plate after plate. "And nice cold water," she says. "I'm sure you guys are thirsty."

On her words, I become aware that she's right. I'm so dehydrated, my lips feel dry, my head light.

With that, Lily turns and heads back towards the kitchen.

"Oh, I almost forgot," she whirls back around holding a piece of red cake I hadn't seen in her hands before. "Happy Valentine's Day," she says, setting it on the table between us. "Now, you let me know if you need anything else, okay?" she asks as she retreats again back through the swinging kitchen door.

"Something about that door," I say, staring at it. Watching it swing gently back and forth. "It's almost as if..." I nearly tell her what I'm feeling so strongly, that I work here, or used to, but stop myself. It's too insane to vocalize. Saying it out loud will make me feel even crazier. "What do you think she meant by *Valentine's Day*," I ask instead. Then I wonder to myself, "I mean ... am I losing it?"

"Roman, eat!" Ruby says, her mouth already full, and pushing a plate towards me. "You're just hungry." She smiles with her eyes since her mouth is full. "Eat!"

"You're right," I say, shaking my head again. Then I dig in.

"You guys did well," Lily remarks of all the empty plates. "Can I get you anything else?" she asks us.

"I'm good," Ruby says.

"Roman? How about you?" Lily asks as she starts clearing the table. I don't remember telling her my name or Ruby mentioning it.

"Thanks, I couldn't eat another bite," I say.

"Good!" she beams. "Do you guys have a place to stay?" she asks, stacking the plates on her arms, making them disappear from the table as rapidly as she set them.

Neither of us answers, seeing as neither of us knows what we're even doing here.

"You haven't been around town much lately, so I wasn't sure," she says. "But if you need a warm place to lay your heads, I know of one," she tells us, then she heads towards the kitchen.

"That would be great," Ruby calls to her.

"Ok, just give me a second." Lily waves as she disappears into the kitchen again.

"What makes you so sure we can trust this girl?" I whisper to Ruby, feeling suddenly leery of her hospitality, the fact that she knows my name, and everything else in this strange place.

"I just know. I mean, have you even just known something? Like, words or knowledge just placed in your head?" Ruby asks. "I've been feeling this … connection to her since we got here. I know we can trust her. I even know … that we are supposed to," she tells me with a serious look on her face.

I follow behind Ruby and Lily. Their arms are locked and they're talking away, looking just like the oldest kind of friends as Lily walks us towards an enormous house, or more like a castle fortress.

I wonder whose place it is as we walk up the long winding path to reach it.

"This is my friend's house," Lily answers, as if I had asked the question in my mind out loud. "She's out of town, but she's more than happy to have the two of you stay," she tells me over her shoulder.

"All right, *this* is by far the best room in the whole house," she says, pushing open a towering wood door leading us into a sprawling bedroom that's larger than a hundred huts in Primitus.

"The linens are fresh, and the towels. You should have everything you both need," she says, fluffing the pillows on the enormous bed.

I notice an elaborate painting on the ceiling high above. It covers the entire area over where the giant four-poster bed sits.

"What is that painting?" I ask her, pointing at the artwork as I walk near her to stand underneath it.

"That, Roman, is the battle of the fallen angels," Lily remarks, gathering more blankets from a giant cabinet and fussing with the bed. "Also known as the fall of the rebel angels. It's a depiction of the book of Revelations chapter twelve, verses two through nine," she says.

I hear the words *two through nine* echoing, but can't figure out if it's in the room or my brain. *Two and nine*, I hear again in Lily's voice as if she said it twice though I know she only said it once, out loud anyway.

"From the bible..." I stammer out, instead of mentioning the strange echoes I keep hearing when she speaks, remembering suddenly that there once was such a thing as the bible and trying to recall what was in it and what it was all about.

"Yes," she says. "The book of Revelations, *from the bible.*"

"What does it mean?" I ask Lily.

"And who is that?" Ruby asks her, pointing to the woman figure floating over the battle, high above the violent fray.

"Well the book of Revelations is said to be about the end of the world. It's said to be a *destruction story*," she emphasizes, then goes on, "but that's not what it is at all. Likewise, most people have taken this painting to mean inaccurate things as well; a war in heaven between good and evil, for example. Between God and the devil. But, what it's showing is merely the ending of one world and the beginning of another. Something that will happen. And when it does, some will cling to the old world even as it crumbles, they'll cling to the lower dimension and what was created there, even as it falls apart. They will cling to the time of man, alone, man without knowledge of the God inside him, even though the truth will have already been revealed. But they won't accept the truth, the truth about who they are, that the God they are waiting for, the powerful force they think is outside themselves, separate, is already here, walking the Earth, from inside them. Humanity's enlightenment to their truth, that God is here within them, that *is* the second coming, when the time of waiting will be over and the time to create the new world will be at hand. Those who don't awaken to this will continue to suffer," she says pointing to the warring men, desperate and raging, climbing over and clawing at one another.

"A destruction story that's not really a destruction story, because while it's the crumbling of one world, it's also the beginning of another," I surmise.

"Yes," she says seeming surprised, then pauses, "you understand completely." She sounds amazed. I can tell by her voice that she's looking right at me, but I don't take my eyes off the painting.

"So more of a *shift story*, or even … a creation story," I say as I study it, so many questions racing through my mind I don't know where to start. Namely, is she talking about Passus and Earth?

"Exactly," she says. "It is the creation story." She smiles, seeming to relish the answer.

"What causes the shift?" I ask.

"Awakening. The rising awareness within people. Expanded consciousness, and along with it a new understanding about themselves and about the world around them. The shift has already begun, we're almost at the height of it in fact," she answers.

"And what about the woman?" Ruby asks. "How did *she* get all the way up there? Above all the others? She looks so … *powerful* up there," she says, admiring her.

I look up at the figure draped in billowing fabric, trying

to grasp where I've seen her before—the image of this pregnant woman on a cloud in the sky—why it feels burned into my soul.

"She is *very* powerful, Ruby," Lily confirms. "You're right, but that's not why she's up there. She's really up there because her awareness expanded before the others. That's all, and she's showing them the way."

"Is she giving birth?" Ruby asks.

"Yes, she is. Just as Revelations twelve says: *'A great sign appeared in heaven. A woman clothed with the sun, with the moon under her feet and a crown of twelve stars on her head. She was pregnant and cried out in pain as she was about to give birth.'* She is giving birth to a child, and to a new world as well," she says, staring up at the woman intently.

"The sun and the moon and twelve stars? What's all that about?" Ruby asks.

"If you look at the sky, which the bible long urged us to do, Venus represents the woman, the moon beneath her feet, well this happens often in the sky, the moon is directly below Venus once a year around a holiday that once existed, called *Labor* Day, not coincidentally. But the moon represents her fertility, her sexuality. The moon represents a woman's power over a man," she says, looking towards me. "Do you know what I mean?" she asks, as though the question is an immensely important one.

"I think I do," I sort of stumble out, feeling caught off-guard.

Lily glances towards Ruby, and because she does, I do too.

"Could you ... *stop her* ... if she wanted to have sex with you?" Lily asks me, plainly. "Right now, could you really stop yourself if she wanted to *have* you?"

"I wouldn't really *want* to stop her," I admit to Lily, feeling strange, almost defiant as I do, and as if Ruby's not even in the room. As if Lily and I are talking about all of this in a private vacuum where we can't be heard.

"But what if you *did* want to stop her?" Lily asks.

I shake my head, "It would be challenging. Very challenging," I admit freely, which seems to take Lily by surprise.

"Good thing you wouldn't want to ... stop her, I mean," she fumbles out, looking towards the ground a moment.

"Right." I laugh nervously.

"Right, so Venus," Lily goes on, "having the moon at her feet is about *woman* ..." Lily gestures towards Ruby again, who does a little curtsey, making Lily and I both smile, breaking the tension that had been steadily building up. "It's about her being *on top* of her sexuality, in command of her own power, the power she has over you, and her power of creation," Lily says, and the room falls into a reverent silence.

"It's actually, really beautiful..." Ruby starts, then stops abruptly, her eyes misting and the whites going red as a swell of emotions rise up in her. "Man," Ruby gestures towards me, "being so powerful, so much stronger, submitting to a woman's power over him, it's almost ..." Ruby grasps, trying to explain what she's feeling, utterly unable to.

"Divine," Lily tells her.

"Yes, exactly," Ruby marvels.

"There's nothing more beautiful in any corner of the universe than a man and a woman aligned perfectly in this delicate dance of opposites, yin and yang, hard and soft, dark and light. It is both human and divine; the embodiment of our very nature. Where truth and love merge. Love and truth create the universe."

"Wow," Ruby breathes out, sounding overwhelmed. "So ... is that why she is giving birth in *heaven*? Because of this human and divine, because of man and woman being in perfect balance, is that how the child was created?"

"She is giving birth *to* heaven," Lily says. "And ... *yes*."

"Did she have to *die* to get there?" Ruby asks her.

"Yes, *many times*. But not in the way you're used to. She has died to the false world, as well to those who only believe in the false world. She's dead to them. But they're wrong. She has only died in the illusion, the illusion of life that they, who are suffering, are still living in. Much of humanity is unknowing of the truth, a truth so powerful she became invisible to those who didn't know it. She died to them when she became the truth. Those who believed the lies could no longer see her, not until their eyes were opened," she says, "and so she's giving birth to this knowledge, bringing it forth, bearing this wisdom, pouring it out for all the world like water from a jar, water that's unending. Just like life."

"That's so beautiful," Ruby remarks, her voice breathless. "If only life were really everlasting."

"Life is everlasting," Lily tells her.

"How's that? What about time?" Ruby argues. "Time runs out."

"Time doesn't even exist," she says. It's a very odd statement, one I'd find even odder if I hadn't just experienced the way time felt in the meadow as Ruby and I walked beneath the moon—stretchy and elastic. Not real. Nonexistent.

"You said it was the ending of one world and the beginning of another. Of a living heaven. Does this living heaven already exist?" I ask, feeling like Ruby and I may have even gotten a glimpse of it.

"Aquarius," she says.

"Aquarius," I repeat. "Where have I heard that before?"

"It's hard to say," Lily comments, then out of nowhere, she heads for the door. "Perhaps someone's been whispering it to you in your dreams," she says, turning back before she exits. "Rest well, Roman," she says looking right in my eyes for the first time. The blazing emerald color, like green fire, matches my own. "Sweet dreams." Then, "For your Valentine," I hear her whisper, but her mouth didn't move. Then her eyes shift to a table next to me where there's a single red rose on a long green stem. A flower that wasn't there before.

"Good night Ruby," Lily says as the door closes.

And then she's gone.

Ruby, finally done looking at the painting on the ceiling, turns towards me and walks a few slow steps. I walk towards her, and when we reach each other we're already tangled in an embrace. Her open lips move passionately over mine, her tongue moving into my mouth, mine into hers.

We stop to look at each other, both breathing heavy. I study her face, feeling her soft skin, and she studies mine. Then she kisses me on the neck and my entire body surges.

She takes a step back and undresses, kicking off my boots, peeling off the coat, until she's standing there in nothing but my shirt. Starting at the top, she unbuttons each button until the shirt falls off her shoulders and lands at her feet. I stare at her, trying to comprehend this woman in front of me, all that she is.

"You are so beautiful," I try to explain, but am at a loss, knowing no words can make her understand what I see as she walks towards me. How she's blooming before my eyes, like the rose beside the bed. How beguiling it is and how entrancing to watch, the force of nature inside her being revealed, her coming into command of her own power.

She pushes gently against my chest, and I sit down on the bed, my desire for her nearly uncontainable. My whole body so wanting of hers.

"Lie down," she whispers.

The thought of leaning back, away from her … it's the last thing I want to do. I grab onto her and kiss her again, more heated and more passionately than ever before, overcome with my yearning to have her.

She moves her lips a millimeter off mine.

"Lie down," she whispers again, her voice breathy and insistent.

Finally, I do, I lay down, my back sinking into the soft bed.

She climbs on top of me, her gaze locked on mine.

A few hours later, loud footsteps in the hall outside our room startle us awake. I start to sit up first, and then Ruby does. Peeling her face from my chest, she looks sleepily towards a window across the room.

"What time is it? What's going on?" she whispers.

"I'm not sure," I whisper back. I kiss her on the forehead, get up, and start getting dressed. She jumps up too.

"I'm not leaving your side," she says, pulling my button-down shirt over her head, and staying close as we walk to the door.

When I open it, there's Payge. Hands on her hips, eyes narrow, shooting daggers in my direction.

"Nice," she remarks, raising her eyebrows at me. "Are you guys coming, or what?" she questions impatiently, then turns on her heels and heads swiftly down the hall.

I had a strange feeling last night while I was in bed with Ruby. The longer we made love and the deeper and more intense our connection became, it felt as if time and even reality were dissolving. Now, as we stare bewildered out into a hallway that does not remotely resemble the one we walked through with Lily last night, I'm beginning to think that it may have been more than just a feeling.

"What is going on?" I mumble as I look out the door. "Did we ... do this ... somehow?" I scratch my head.

"I don't know," I hear Ruby say from inside the room, "but we'd better get dressed and go find out."

I look over to see her standing at the end of a bunk, putting on military style clothes, pants, and shirt, both black, and a holster vest—tactical gear. She shrugs and points to what must be my clothes, which look to be the same as hers, folded at the end of the other bunk. I don't stop to wonder what happened to the big luxurious bed we just climbed out of only moments earlier. I just walk over and get dressed.

Ruby and I leave the room and head down what is now a long white hallway, following where Payge had gone. At the end of the hall is a long flight of metal stairs lit with buzzing flood lights. We shrug to each other again and jog down what last night was a grand mahogany unending spiral with crystal chandeliers overhead.

By the industrial, sterile look of everything around us, and by the way we're dressed, it's clear this is some kind of barracks on a military base. Obviously, we're at the armory. I start to wonder whether the castle-like house we entered and slept in last night was either not the place we thought it was, or it changed into someplace else somehow—a question I have a feeling there is no answer to.

It's dawn, and the dull morning light adds to the eeriness as we walk past a few guards, a row of watchtowers, and steel fortresses. What now lines Main Street.

"I've never seen any of this before in my life," I say to Ruby, feeling uneasy, as we search for the others.

"The Green Owl," Ruby points down the road, and I search for the glowing sign, eager to see something I recognize, anything, "Look, it's gone," she notes of the concrete building now in its place. I shake my head in wonder. Then I peer down a side street where something catches my attention.

"I've seen that before," I say about a concrete and metal windowless building I spot at the end of a street called Boulder Avenue.

"The Animus symbol is on the outside," Ruby says, like she remembers the building too. Like she finds it as hauntingly familiar as I do. A place we've been before, but the memory of it just out of reach.

Ruby stares unblinking at the abandoned-looking building, seeming determined to remember what happened there when something occurs to her. Her mouth drops open, and she inhales sharply.

"Eve," she whispers to herself, then turns and looks at me, brow furrowed, like I'm some kind of a ghost.

EVE

SIXTEEN

———— ❈ ————

The first time I met Iris was a blur.

The Events had just happened, the tsunami and the first blood moon. It was during the morning assembly just after, on what would be my second and last day of school—ever.

I was seated awkwardly between Roman and Jude. Between my soul mate and my fate. I was uncomfortable, shifting about on the hard, wooden bleachers in the school auditorium packed with the entire student body and half the town. That's when I first noticed Iris seated just a few rows away.

She was so little. I noticed that first. That and how alert she seemed, how awake, like a little hummingbird hovering amongst vacant-eyed oafish teenagers. But mostly, she stood out, not because everyone around her was so much bigger or because they all looked more fearful than she did, but because she smiled at me. Over the course of my illustrious school career, seeing a smile directed towards me was a very rare thing. At that point, I considered Jude and Roman my only friends, even Phoenix was still just lurking around me ominously. Not to be outdone by Ruby, who I was about to encounter with her band of cohorts in the girls' bathroom where they'd beat me to within an inch of my life. So, Iris's big, bright-eyed smile more than caught my attention. It captured my heart in an instant.

When the assembly was finally over and the masses of students, teachers, and others melded together, I looked down at my side to see Iris walking right next to me. My little sidekick. The only other person in here, aside from Jude, of course, who didn't seem to believe the end was near. Or if she did, she didn't seem to be bothered by it.

"Hi, I'm Iris," she bubbled up at me, her voice brimming with confidence. She's so cheery, I remember thinking, on a day when most of the world was convinced our very existence was in peril.

"Hi," I said back. "I'm Eve."

She beamed, as if she's just met her favorite movie star. Then the crowd shifted, and she was gone.

Later, I asked Phoenix who she was, this young girl who looked so out of place.

"Oh, Iris Adler, she's some kid genius, some kind of

computer wizard. Supposed to be in fourth grade or something, but she's in ninth. They say she might even graduate next year, head off to college."

"Wow," I marveled, thinking to myself about how her life and mine must have been similar. "I bet she doesn't have a lot of friends," I said.

"She probably doesn't care about stuff like that," Phoenix shrugged.

Everyone cares about stuff like that, I remember thinking. Then I realized for the first time that no one is meant to be an island. Not really. That's not what we're doing here. We're here to swim.

After that chance moment, I never saw her again.

Not until she was placed with Roman in Primitus. By that point she looked much different. The confidence I'd seen and the light in her eyes were both gone. She was still in there, but buried beneath the trauma of living through the destruction of all she'd ever known, the deaths of parents and siblings. Then the mind-altering techniques everyone was subjected to in order to make them forget the world they'd once known. The constant mental torture of fearing for her life.

Now I watch her, sitting in a cell as if she's some kind of dangerous animal, locked in Shamus's prison. Under heavy guard, this tiny girl, like she poses some grave threat to everyone. Iris reminds me of myself in almost every way.

She's sitting on the dusty floor devouring the books I keep secretly placing under her rickety metal cot. She doesn't know where they're coming from, but she doesn't much care. She tears through them one after the next. Right now, she's nearly finished with *A Tale of Two Cities*, enwrapped in this story of revolution and resurrection.

"Crush humanity out of shape once more," she whispers to herself, thinking deeply about the words she's reading, "under similar hammers, and it will twist itself into the same tortured forms. Sow the same seeds of oppression over again, and it will surely yield the same fruit according to its kind," she murmurs, then looks up, thinking of all the things in her world that crush her like hammers: Primitus, The Cause, Servus. Remembering all the things Roman told her before he left, and trying desperately to piece it all together.

Then, she hears the familiar sound of Shamus's loafers on the stone floor walking towards her cell. The gritty tap of his toe striking first on the sand-covered surface, followed by the delicate click of his heel. He comes around a few times every day, mostly to belittle and mock her, or rant about his problems, and sometimes to do things that are far worse.

She stashes the weighty book beneath her cot, pushing

it deep towards the wall, afraid to even think of what would happen if she were discovered with it. According to the government, The Word and textbooks about The Destruction are the only books in existence. So, she assumes possessing a copy of *A Tale of Two Cities* would likely get her beheaded.

"Knock-knock," Shamus says in his devilish tone. He's standing right outside her cell, and he's not knocking. "May I come in?" he asks as he unlocks the metal gate, opens it, and walks inside uninvited. "What are we up to this fine morning?" he asks, lurking over her.

"What does it look like?" she asks, venom in her tone.

He glares down at her for a moment. As if he's trying to decide whether to take issue with her disrespectful tone, like perhaps he's about to backhand her across the face. But Iris knows he's not. She began to notice a few days ago that no matter what she said to him, he never did anything about it. So, she glares right back, clearly unafraid.

"It looks like you're bored out of your mind," he surmises finally, "just like I am. You look like you're in need of some … entertainment."

She always knows what's coming next when he says that. The very same thing that made me start locking my door when I was not much older than her.

For the next few moments, he just saunters around her

tiny cell making himself feel big and important. Iris sits in a tight ball on the floor in front of her cot, squeezing her knees to her chest. She's careful never to be in the bed when she hears him coming. She worries that one of these days he may take his deviant behavior to another level if she's in her bed when he comes to visit.

Finally, Shamus finds a spot he likes in the far corner. He stands there a moment staring at her, then he unbuckles his pants and begins to masturbate, watching her as he does, a sick kind of vulnerable look on his face.

She used to look away while he did it. She'd never seen a man's private parts before, nor did she want to. And she didn't understand the first thing about what he was doing. She only knew that it was wrong, and that it wasn't something she wanted to see. But he screamed at her to look at him, to watch him while he did it, his roaring voice thunderous and menacing and masking a desperate panic underneath.

So now, she stares him dead in the eyes and doesn't look away once until he's finished. Lately, she doesn't even blink as she watches him. Her back teeth grinding together, a blazing volcanic rage growing inside her.

He finishes with a grunt, propping his hand on the wall beside him, leaning all his weight into it, eyes closed. After a few seconds, he refastens his pants and walks out, leaving behind a mess of himself in the corner.

Staring at where he stood, Iris burns with anger.

She takes a deep breath and lets it out, then reaches under the cot and grabs her book. She opens it to where she left off and continues reading.

Roman paces in the main building of the armory, an oversized complex of large warehouses filled with enough bombs, guns, and armored vehicles to wage endless war.

"For the last time, we are in *Aurora Proper*," Bael tells Roman in an overtly nonchalant way, as they stand surrounded by enough weapons to blow up the world several times over, "… location of the one world government and central command of both Primitus and Antiquus. That's where we are, Aurora Proper, where the armory is," his tone condescending, dismissive of Roman's obvious frustration.

Beal hadn't mentioned that the armory was in such a place, or that *Aurora Proper* even existed, that it was even a thing in this already messed up world of theirs, which Roman has grown to hate and resent even more lately.

"No one has *ever* mentioned Aurora Proper," Roman drones out for the third time. "*We've* never even heard of it," pointing at himself, Cicero, Payge, and Ruby, leaving out Kali and Bael. "So, it is reasonable to think that you are keeping other things from us," he explains in a voice of controlled calm.

Roman is convinced that Aurora Proper sits atop the very spot where he claims that a town called Rugby once was, before the supposed destruction, which he narrowly proclaimed an all-out hoax in his mounting anger and frustration. But neither Bael nor Kali will even acknowledge Roman's "wild claims," his "'delusions" as Bael calls them. All this fuels Roman's sense of disorientation, his deep mistrust, and his growing aggravation.

So, Roman does what anyone in his position would do, he completely loses it. In his case, this means blowing up at Bael.

"What the fuck?!!" he suddenly screams right into Bael's face. "How the *hell* am I supposed to lead some fucking mission if I don't even know where we're going? If I don't even know where I am when I get there? If you don't tell me anything?!" he unleashes, then begins pacing about as he rants.

"God! It's like I'm flying blind! People expect me to accomplish fucking miracles! Save the fucking world, Roman! Save fucking humanity! Well tell me where the fuck I am first!" he yells at the top of his lungs. "Tell me what the fuck is going on here in this fucked up place!" he screams right into Bael's face again, as Kali, Payge, Ruby and Cicero look on awkwardly, eyes wide, mouths gaping.

Bael stands motionless, just staring blankly ahead. He

clearly does not enjoy Roman unloading on him, and he's clearly not taking it well. Then Roman learns another brand-new thing he didn't know before; what happens when Bael doesn't take something well.

Bael walks casually over to a huge gun rack, picks up an automatic rifle and starts firing it at random. Spraying bullets around the giant warehouse in all directions.

Everyone hits the deck as the machine gun unloads for what feels like an eternity, covering their heads, all screaming for him to stop and hoping for the best. Everyone except for Kali who, through a hail of bullets, marches over to Bael and smacks the giant gun out of his hands, sending it to the concrete floor with a crash.

Bael and Kali stare at each other in silence. Kali, intimidating in her black tactical gear, stands less than a foot away, her chest forward, right in his face, her eyes burning through his. Finally, Bael storms off.

Kali walks over to Roman.

"Stand," she commands him calmly.

Roman gets back up from where he'd been lying on the floor with his arms and body covering Ruby.

"Did you know, Roman, that we arrived here days ago?" she asks him. "Bael, Payge, Cicero and I?"

"No, I didn't know that," Roman says, surprised.

"We've been stuck here, in Aurora Proper, which is

where we are, like it or not, where there is virtually nothing and hardly a soul to be found. Waiting for days and days for you and Ruby to finally show up so that *you* can lead us on this mission. And now, we're all ready to go. Everyone except *you*. You don't seem ready to do anything but bitch about all your little problems." She levels him. "I'm going to give you thirty seconds, in which I want you to get your fucking life together. Then we are leaving. You are going to lead us out of here and on what will be a highly successful mission accomplished, where we will rescue Val, bring her home to Primitus, and restore the hope of humanity."

Moments later, they head off, a team beyond fractured. Divided, literally, into two combat vehicles, and figuratively. Roman is at the wheel of the lead vehicle, Cicero next to him in front, Payge and Ruby sitting silently in the back. Roman keeps looking at Ruby in the rearview mirror, her arms crossed as she stares out the window. Payge sits as far away from Ruby as possible, arms crossed, looking out the other window.

"Are they mad at *you*? Or are they mad at each other?" Cicero whispers to Roman.

"I don't know." He shakes his head. "Both, I think," he guesses. He's not sure what Ruby suddenly remembered when she saw the Animus building. He can't recall much about it, only that he knows he was there and that he was there with Ruby. Why had she said Eve's name? And why was Payge so angry with him, and with Ruby as well? None of it making any sense to him.

"Maybe that one's got the hots for you too," Cicero motions with his head to Payge, who just rolls her eyes and shakes her head in disgust.

"I don't think so," Roman says just as he starts to notice something outside and leans forward, looking up at the sky through the windshield. "It's changing," he observes.

The blue sky appears to be rolling back, and a turbulent, almost violent-looking black and gray sky starts to replace it, swirling and rolling in overhead, as if the sky itself is alive.

"What the hell?" he hears Cicero say, pointing ahead of them.

The road is splitting apart, asphalt ripping in two and rising ten feet high as it does. Roman lays on the brakes. Bael slams into the back of them. They all fly forward violently.

When Roman looks up, he sees the road has stopped splitting.

"It stopped," he says still studying it. "Is everyone ok?" he asks.

Just then, something rises out of the enormous crevice

in front of them, a swarm of giant winged man beasts.

"Are those … *gargoyles*," Cicero whispers, the long-lost word coming to him at the sight of the demonic screeching monsters. Just then, the vehicle lurches as they feel Bael and Kali back off their bumper. Without a word, Cicero and Roman burst from their doors and meet at the back where they open the badly damaged tail gate and start strapping on several machine guns each. Kali and Bael are already behind their vehicle doing the same thing.

"Stay here," he commands Ruby and Payge through the open back, both of them nod, terror-stricken.

Roman, Cicero, Kali, and Bael, an arsenal between them, walk past Roman's car and down the road towards the gaping hole the giant monsters came out of before they disappeared into the strange whirling sky overhead. Suddenly they hear a crash and turn to see a seven-foot-tall, muscled, man-like beast atop the armored vehicle and hear Ruby and Payge screaming inside. It moves in a bizarre and unnatural way—rapidly, and like it can flicker in and out of this dimension.

Roman takes aim, and with a single shot to the center of the skull, the winged gargantuan is flung off and crashes to the ground with a mighty thud. It's sprawled out in the dirt, right outside Ruby's window. Breathless, she looks at it, then up at Roman through the windshield just as the sound of screeching announces another one swooping in, again heading right towards Ruby and Payge.

"It's them they want," Roman says, thinking of the creatures from the cave.

"It appears so," Cicero remarks, just as more descend out of the volatile, rolling sky, landing with a boom all around Ruby and Payge, as they sit helplessly inside the vehicle.

Now there are three on the ground and two on the roof. They screech and howl and beat their enormous wings as they begin prying at the doors. The two on top rock the armored vehicle under their giant feet, like a toy, sending Ruby and Payge hurling about inside, screaming for their lives.

Bael, Cicero, and Kali fire at them, but it's like trying to shoot into a strobe light. Their rapid movements make them impossible to hit. When a bullet hits the front windshield, spider webbing it, Ruby and Payge look at them, helpless and horrified. But they keep unloading, trying harder not to hit the vehicle.

Roman takes aim again, and with a single round, he picks off the one outside Ruby's window with a kill shot to the back of its head. Then he fires at the one outside Payge's door, hitting it square in the chest. It drops to the ground. Bael, Kali, and Cicero stop firing and look at Roman.

"We'll just save our ammo," Cicero remarks.

Roman, laser focused, walks towards the monsters terrorizing Ruby and Payge, and fires, hitting one of the two on the roof. The last one left on the ground changes at him, tackling him before Roman even has time to react.

Roman rolls on top of the beast and starts whaling on him, his fists moving in the same rapid way until the beast goes limp beneath him. At the sound of gun fire, Roman looks back up at the vehicle to see the last one reaching inside from atop the roof and pulling Ruby out by her neck as Cicero, Bael, and Kali fire on him.

"Stop, stop!" Roman screams at them, afraid they'll shoot Ruby.

He grabs his gun and stands up just as the beast springs off the vehicle and launches into the sky, Ruby dangling from his hand, screaming as they rapidly ascend.

Roman fires a single shot, hitting the beast in the wing and sending it sailing towards the ground, still clutching Ruby by the throat. Fearing the beast will fall on her, he fires on it again. He hits it, right in the back of the shoulder, and splits them apart just before Ruby crashes to the ground. Roman's already in a full sprint towards her, a lifeless heap lying fifty yards away just next to the dead monster.

SEVENTEEN

—— ✠ ——

She was already gone before he reached her. He was gasping, him heart racing, mind numb, body flooded with adrenaline.

She died instantly when she hit the ground, that was clear to everyone, there was nothing he could do to save her now. But could he have done something differently before she was captured? Could he have killed the beast that snatched her, instead of killing another one first? One way or another, he let this happen, it was his fault. How had he failed to protect her?

That question was cutting through him like a sword as he sat there weeping over her limp lifeless body, holding her in his arms, crying out in anguish, the sky growing darker and more ominous overhead.

He knew he would have to leave her there in that strange

place, that there was no way he could bring her body with them. But he insisted on burying her. He couldn't accept the thought of her being exposed to the elements the way he'd seen all those corpses disintegrate in Primitus.

He sat for a long time, caressing the soft, silky skin on her face and arms, memorizing every detail of her, gently smoothing her long blonde hair away from her blue eyes before he shut them. Then he dug a hole in the dirt as deep as he could with his bare hands. Both Cicero and Kali offered to help, but he just grunted a word that sounded like no and pushed them away from her. He was focused, eyes all cried out of tears, determined to dig the best hole he could for her, all on his own.

Watching him leave her there was gut-wrenching for everyone, even Bael, who never once said a word. Never hurried him. Even as Roman stood at the foot of the mound of black dirt, paralyzed, unable to walk away for more than an hour.

Now, Kali and Bael follow behind him as he drives towards Antiquus in silence. Cicero stares absently out the passenger window. Payge sniffles intermittently, alone in the back.

"Why were you angry with me?" Roman asks Payge suddenly, his voice thin and hollow.

Payge looks at his reflection in the rearview mirror.

"I don't know," she says after a long silence.

Roman nods, the car falls quiet, heavy with grief.

"I loved her you know?" he says, the words just barely escaping.

"I know," she whispers after a moment, overcome with emotion, "and it made me so angry with you," she cries.

"Why?" he asks her desperately. "Why did you even care? *Why?*"

"I don't know," she cries out, sounding as helpless as she feels. "I just felt … betrayed. Like you were betraying me, or someone," she struggles "it makes no sense, but oh, I wanted to claw your eyes out when I saw you with her," she spits through clenched teeth, hands balled in fists of rage. "When I knew that you had been together. I wanted to kill you."

Roman looks at her in the rearview mirror for a long beat, taking her in, her rage so genuine, so apparent. He just observes it. Not trying to understand it, not yet. Then he turns his eyes back to the road, and they drive in silence the rest of the way to Antiquus—a route he remembers now, one he remembers driving before. No one says another word until they pull out of the forest tunnel into the clearing, and the castle behemoth emerges off in the distance before them.

Roman goes white at the sight of it.

"Oh my god," he says as he finally remembers. "Eve."

There's a tapping on the window beside him. Roman startles, and turns to see Kali standing outside his door.

He rolls the window down.

"It's been a really long day," she says, then pauses.

"It has," he agrees, coming back to himself, his role, what he's here to accomplish … so that he can get back to Iris.

Iris, he thinks.

"Let's back out of here, go into the woods, and find a place to camp for the night," he says.

"Regroup," Kali nods, "good idea." She heads back to the other car.

After the day he's had, Roman figures it'll be next to impossible for him to sleep, but he beds down anyway, climbing into one of the sleeping bags from the armory and nestling under a giant strange tree.

"You sure you want to sleep under *that* tree?" Bael asks him for the second time, seeming highly skeptically of the tree Roman is so drawn to sleep under—one Bael seems repelled away from. A sight to behold, it's as wide as it is tall, and covered with very large soft green leaves, strange yellow fruit hanging from its branches, like giant oblong lemons, but much bigger than normal lemons, and with bumpier skin.

"That's a citron tree," Kali commented walking towards it just as Bael finally retreated.

"Whatever it is, I'm sleeping under it," Roman declared as he settled in, Kali studying him.

"I'll keep night watch," she declares.

"All right," Roman says closing his eyes.

"You just get some sleep," she tells him, watching as he drifts off almost instantly.

"Roman," I whisper into his ear, raking my fingers through his thick, wavy hair. "Roman," I say again as his eyes begin to flutter and his body starts to stir.

He looks up at me, but he doesn't move. He just studies my face.

"Eve," he whispers, and I smile at him, knowing he knows who I am now. It's written all over his face.

"Come on," I tell him. "Get up, and follow me. I want to show you something." I stand up and walk away, leaving him still lying under the tree. "Come on," I beckon again when he doesn't move.

"Is this a dream?" he asks wearily. "Like when I usually see you?"

"Does it feel like a dream?" I ask him, knowing that everything is changing for him now, finally. That it's all beginning to merge.

"No," he says with a worried look. "It doesn't. It feels real, so real that I think it is," he confides, clearly unnerved.

"Roman," I say out loud. *Just go with it,* I whisper into his mind without using words.

After another moment, he gets up and follows me.

"I have so many questions," he starts, trying to put them all in order.

"I know." I turn to him. "That's why I'm here. I'm here to tell you everything," I say, just as I feel we're standing in the right place.

"This is one of many, *many* points where the lines of energy converge," I explain as I open a portal, slicing the air open before us, splitting it apart right in front of his eyes.

"Is this real?" he asks again, shaking his head and rubbing his eyes as the portal begins to widen.

"It's real," I tell him, grabbing his arm and pulling him through.

He flails at first, as we're swallowed into the Noosphere, but the airless silence is soothing and soundless. When white, pin-sized stars become visible, they're suddenly all around us and begin to stretch into trailing white beams of light. The space around us fades quickly from navy to royal blue as we warp faster and faster, until the Hall of Collective Records begins to materialize before us.

This is the Hall of Collective Records, the etheric warehouse of the Akashic. I place the words into his mind as we approach the colossal, white-columned castle.

How did it get here? he asks, hearing himself speak without using his voice or words.

It was constructed out of billions of years of pure consciousness and built into the very fabric of the universe.

We float through the mammoth entrance.

It's all that is, all that ever was, and all that ever will be. And all of it connected. Everything in the universe inseparably correlated with everything else in the universe. All events, people, conversations, thoughts, dreams, hopes, wars, tangled together on a quantum level, and all of it stored right here, I explain, and watch Roman glance down each corridor we float past baffled by how it goes on and on, like he's looking into a mirror of a mirror.

It's not an optical illusion? he asks, as the corridors begin shuffling past us, flying by like cards in a deck.

No. It's not an optical illusion, I tell him.

Is it … time? He struggles to comprehend.

Time isn't real. What we think of as time is merely existence.

Time is existence, he repeats, nodding as he does.

Yes, and the only thing that makes this existence what it is, is how we experience it. I know it's a lot to understand," I say, watching as he turns all this over in his mind.

Relativity, he says, and I can't help but grin.

Now there's the brilliant mind I met when I first arrived in Rugby, I say, watching it reemerging in him, the cloud that was placed over his consciousness lifting.

So... he starts, looking at the approaching white door in a knowing way, ... *is this when existence began?* he asks, just as we arrive at the luminous white door we're heading towards. A door that's at the very heart of the hall, not all the way at the far end as one might expect, if time were real and linear, the way we imagine it. But a door, the very one in front of us now, at the center of it all. *Is this why? Is it why we experience existence the way we do?* he asks, staring at the glowing white door, then looking at me. *I mean it's all relative to something, right...* he says, looking as if he almost knows what I'm about to show him. *Is it all relative to what's behind this door? All the other corridors and all the other doors... it all started here,"* he notes about how the luminous door before us and this corridor are inextricably linked with every other one.

Yes, I nod.

He stares at the gleaming gold handle in both wonder and fear.

Open it, I tell him.

EIGHTEEN

— ✦ —

We walk through the door and into a world of waist-high green grass, bush-shaped trees on long skinny trunks, where a pronounced and eerie stillness permeates the atmosphere.

"Is this place… *pre-historic?*" Roman asks in wonder, all the words and things he knew before the ascent beginning to flood back to him.

"It's the beginning," is all I say as we walk towards the center of Adam's calendar, the place where existence began.

"The birthplace of the sun," I say.

Just then, Shamus runs by. Roman flinches at the sight of him, then seems to realize just as I say it.

"He can't see us," I tell him, and I instantly watch Roman's mind go to work.

"We don't exist yet." He looks at me, figuring this is why Shamus can't see us. Just then, another *me* runs by us.

She's naked, she and Shamus both are. Neither of them seem to notice or care.

"Even before all the new lies, before The Word and all the things it's created, all the suffering and confusion, people were told other stories, ones they specifically weren't meant to understand. Like the creation story," I say, motioning to the scene before us now. "Everyone knew it, in every religion across the globe. For millennia, they were told of Adam and Eve and the garden of Eden—the very place we now stand," I say, watching Roman to gauge his understanding. "There's a vague mention of *another girl* in this the most well-known story of all time, but it's so cryptic, so obscured that most people don't even notice. Nevertheless, she is in the creation story, Adam's first wife. *Lilith*," I say, pointing to my naked, pre-historic self who is locked in an embrace with Shamus, *Adam*, in the center of the circle.

Roman and I watch as he lies her down in the soft grass.

"Shamus is Adam…" Roman says in wonder.

"He's *part* of Adam," I say. "Just watch."

The wind begins to blow as they roll around playfully in the tall soft grass. Lilith keeps positioning herself on top of Adam, and he keeps rolling her underneath him.

She rolls back on top once more, then she stops him.

"Like this," she says, Adam's hands clenched tightly

around her waist. He looks like he's getting ready to roll back over on top of her. But Lilith begins to move her hips.

"Relax," she says to him with a soft smile.

Adam closes his eyes trying to relax and enjoy. Lilith's head falls back as she moves herself rhythmically on top of him, then she begins to moan in pleasure. The more she moves on him, the more the grass and trees seem to blow, as if the force of the wind keeps increasing along with her pleasure—and his as well.

Suddenly, just before Lilith reaches the height, her face towards the sky, her hips moving rapidly, her breathing rapid, Adam rolls her over all at once, placing himself on top, her underneath him.

"No," she says, trying to roll over again, but he restrains her. He tries to continue with her on the bottom. She stares at him curiously as he does, studying him.

Then she rolls out from beneath him unexpectedly, stands up and walks off.

Adam chases after her.

Stopping just behind her, he wraps his arms around her and begins kissing her neck. She lets him, lets her head drop back then turns and starts kissing him as they begin to lower back down to the grass. Lilith tries to move forward on top of him, but he tries to do the same and easily pushes *her* back down onto the ground. She tries rolling to the top once more, but he's pinning her shoulder to the earth, a determined look on his face, but also an innocence, an unknowing of why he's doing what he's doing, not fully aware of what it all means. Still, he holds her there. Though she's resisting him, he begins again, doing as he wants with her, the way *he* wants it.

She burns him with a stare of mistrust, one of worry, deep concern for her own existence, which she clearly feels he's threatening.

"The energy," Roman whispers as he watches, thinking of Ruby.

Adam holds Lilith down, squeezing her arms harder, pushing her back deeper into the earth, thrusting into her forcefully. A look of fear flashes across her face, of knowing that because of his superior strength he can do whatever he wants. A look of dominance grows on his face, a look of ultimate power; having his own power as well as *hers*.

His hands squeeze tighter around her arms, not wanting to lose his grip on this newfound power, becoming lost in it, intoxicated by it.

She wiggles her hips away. He stops and looks at her. Then he begins again. Her head turns to one side, and she looks off with a disengaged stare, tears falling from her eyes.

I look at Roman, tears falling down his face as he watches her, shaking his head in dismay.

"How could he do that to her?" He seethes, balling his fists in anger at Adam. "Get up," Roman implores her knowing he can't be heard.

Just then, something comes over Lilith, and she turns her head back to look at Adam, moves her hands onto his hips and pushing him away. Then Adam, almost looking as if it's become a game to him, continues trying to have her how he wants her, even moving her hands to the ground. But she keeps moving her hips away underneath him, making it impossible, his frustration and his anger building.

He sits up and grabs onto her hips, trying to hold her in place exactly where he wants her, eyeing her threateningly as he pushes her lower back hard into the ground. Just then, a look of determination and self-preservation comes over her face, and she drives her knee up, square between his legs, sending him into a dizzying tailspin of mind-numbing pain.

He bends over sideways, clutching his low abdomen, and she rolls out from beneath him, gets up and walks off.

Roman looks at me, relieved. *As if it's over.*

"Watch," I tell him, and he looks back at the scene to see that there's still a woman there lying on the ground, it's Ruby. As I, Lilith, walk away. Then, out of Adam, who appears as Shamus, Roman emerges, walking out of Adam like a ghost. He stares down at Ruby, pain and sadness in his eyes, then he follows after Lilith.

"Did I just see what I think I saw?" Roman asks me, mystified.

"Yes, you saw why Shamus has spent lifetimes hating me, why he hates me still, though he doesn't even know I still exist. Why he hates himself. Why his struggles are all about power."

Roman points at Shamus, who's still doubled over.

"And he and I..." Roman starts, then breaks off. He can't even bring himself to finish the thought.

"You and Shamus began as one soul, Adam," I reveal. "Shamus is shadow, and you are light, and this," I point to the scene before us, "split the first male soul on earth into two," I say. "Adam." I point to Shamus still writhing on the ground in pain, "and Samuel." I point to the Roman that's now walking away with Lilith. "I was Adam's first wife, *Lilith*, the first female soul that this moment also split into two. Lilith and Eve, now me and Ruby," I say, pointing to Ruby lying flat on her back in the dirt, trying desperately to comfort Shamus, stroking his arm. He brushes her hand off him with a scowl. Then he turns his face back to her, a look of wounded pride, of anger, and of dominance—a ravenous, power-hungry look.

He takes ahold of her, placing her hips in front of him, and begins thrusting into her forcefully, holding her down, pushing her deeper and deeper into the dirt, grunting.

Ruby's face falls to one side, her tears raining down into the Earth as he rapes her.

Roman and I both turn away, it's too much to witness, too horribly sad, too tragic.

Off in the distance, we see Lilith and Samuel, our prehistoric selves, walking hand in hand towards the sea. The sun glistens on the water. An eagle and a condor flying above them overhead.

"The eagle represents the enlightened male, the sacred masculine," I say of the majestic, large-winged bird soaring high above Samuel. "The condor represents the enlightened female, the divine feminine," I tell him of the beautiful, large bird flying side by side next to the eagle and high above Lilith as she walks with Samuel—Roman and I, together, at the beginning of existence.

Adam and Eve, *Shamus and Ruby*, are no longer lying in the dirt when Roman and I look back to the spot where they had been in the middle of Adam's Calendar. It's empty, and the grass is changing along with the landscape and the sky, like a time-lapse camera.

Then, Ruby and Shamus walk by, *Adam and Eve*, their hair long and gray. She walks behind him, her head downcast. Behind her walks a young man.

"Is that Ansel?" Roman cocks his head to the side, squinting.

"Yes," I say, "the son of Adam and Eve is Ansel, *Abel*."

Then, we see ourselves, Lilith and Samuel, aged but looking well and happy, walking together hand in hand, a young man behind us too.

"Cian…" Roman says, breathless and stunned at the sight of a twenty-year-old version of the man who raised me.

"*Cain*," I clarify. "But yes, *our son*," I look at Roman, "the son of Lilith and Samuel. Cian and Ansel were once Cain and Abel," I say. Roman studies the way they look, their body language. Abel dark hair, dark flat eyes with black circles around them, skulking along, the same way Shamus moves through the world. Then he looks at Cain, his bright, sparkling emerald eyes the same as ours, the same as Cian's were, as is his sun-lightened hair and warm bronze skin. Cain, our son, walks tall and proud, happy and confident.

"But … Cain was *bad*. He was the evil one. I remember that from the bible." Roman looks at me, confused. "How can Cian be Cain?"

"Has anything turned out to be what you thought? What you were told it meant?" I smile at him. "Hasn't almost everything been the opposite?" I ask. He nods as he thinks.

"But I thought they were brothers?" he asks, looking on

as the two of them, both parting from their parents, meet in the center of the circle.

"They are brother," I say, reminding him that the souls of Adam and Lilith split, making the children of Adam and Eve and Lilith and Samuel technically brothers. "One shadow and one light," I say, as Abel pushes Cain, trying to goad him. Cain turns and walks away. Abel comes up behind him and shoves him again, in the back this time. Cain turns and shoves Abel off with a warning glare.

"What's in his hand?" Roman asks me, seeing the glint of something shiny hidden in Abel's closed fist. The one he keeps putting behind his back.

"A flint of iron that will later become the blade of the ax I found in Antiquus, the ax that saved my life. The very same one you used to kill Jakob," I tell him.

At the thought of the ax, the iron beast, Roman's face is washed in all his remaining lost memories, everything about his current lifetime flooding back to him at once, from his birth on December 21, 1999 in New Zealand, all the way to this very second and everything in between.

"I told you it was all connected to this moment behind the white door," I say, watching him, and he furrows his brow in wonder.

Then he turns his attention back to the two young men as the tension between them rises. Cain is walking away again. And again Abel, flint in hand behind his back, comes up and shoves him, this time it's so hard Cain is thrown to the ground.

"But I thought in the story, Cain killed Abel?"

"Just like the destruction story and the creation story and the word apocalypse and every other thing used to control people, the truth is weaponized and used against humanity to keep them locked in unknowing, as confused as possible. The fabled story of Cain and Abel is also not what you've been told. Abel killed Cain on that fateful day," I say, and as I do, Abel jumps on Cain before he has time to get to his feet, pinning him, much in the same way Adam pinned Eve, and begins bludgeoning him over the head with the iron flint.

Again, Roman and I both look away. Hearing the sound of Cain struggling, the iron crushing his skull as Abel takes his life, it's more than we can bear. Roman grabs my hand and squeezes it.

"Seeing Cian die once is more than enough," I say.

Watching Cian, the soul of our son, killed by Shamus in Eremis is more than enough for both of us.

"So, it was Abel who survived?" Roman says as he skulks away, leaving Cain lying limp in a puddle of blood.

"Yes. But if we knew that and we knew the truth, we'd understand why the world became the way that it did. Abel is all shadow, inhumanly so, just like Ansel," I tell him. "He is the product of two half-souls, both shadow sides, created with stolen power, a product of unwanted submission, spiritual pain, disharmony, and dysfunction between male and female. That is what his soul is made of, and thus it is pure darkness. Cain is pure light—our creation," I say, our matching green eyes meeting, "a creation of the divine feminine and the sacred masculine, of those two opposing energies when they are perfectly aligned, both in their power in love and truth."

Then Lilith walks wearily towards where her son is lying dead, her face frozen in shock. She falls to the earth and cries out in anguish, a high screeching sound that sends the birds streaking across the sky, the condor and eagle fleeing. Samuel comes running and collapses onto his son, holding his lifeless body in his arms, just the way Roman held Ruby.

Roman's eyes well with tears, and his jaw tightens, anguish turning to rage.

"So ... evil won in the beginning ... and now evil is winning again." He looks at me, panic coming over him. "Evil *already won.* Shamus killed Cian, Ansel's still out lurking in the world, Ruby's dead," he says, tightening his jaw again. I look at him, knowing he's not ready to grieve her, not with me. Not yet. So, I focus on helping him understand the very thing he failed to hear when he was busy killing Jakob and I was ascending into Aquarius.

"Roman, there is no good and evil," I say.

His brow furrows, and he shakes his head.

"No, you're wrong," he says. "There is. There very much is. Look, I don't know where *you've* been, but the world is shit—"

"I've been right there with you," I say.

"No." He shakes his head. "No, you haven't!" He yells, and the whole hall begins to shake. I glance at the door we entered through, watching it rattle like tremors before an earthquake. "There is nothing but suffering now Eve. *Lilith*," he corrects himself, spite in his voice, pain, and darkness.

"That is because it's the last epoch, Roman," I try to explain.

His face goes ashen.

"You left me, your soul mate, in the fucking *last epoch*?" he scowls, his eyes burning. "Oh, but I'm sure *Jude* is there with you though, right? In this paradise, this living utopia? In fucking Aquarius! Of course, he is. He's probably the damn king of it! And I bet you guys are having a really *good time* there without me," he insinuates venomously. "Do you ever think, Eve, that maybe you two were always a much better match?" he asks, going from angry to wounded and bitter all at once. "Because I did," he spits, "I thought it *all* the time. Seriously, how could I not?"

"I didn't know you thought that," I try.

"Um, let's see, I thought it when I watched you kiss him in the auditorium, right next to me. I thought it when you had an all-out panic attack that he was missing. You were so worried, so focused on him, even though I was right there with you. Even though I never left your side! And certainly not when you needed me most," he accuses. "And where was *he*?" he asks.

Then he begins to laugh to himself as he realizes something.

"God, it didn't even matter … everything I always did for you … it didn't even matter. I am such a fool." He shakes his head.

"Roman, you're not a fool. It mattered, it all mattered. I can't even describe to you how much it mattered."

"Don't lie, Eve. I may be a damn fool, but I'm not an idiot. I mean, *Christ,* Eve, from the very first second you saw Jude you couldn't take your eyes off him!" He assails me with the truth. "Whenever he was there, it was like I wasn't even in the room," he says. "And now you're both gone from the terrible, evil world I'm still stuck in … pretty *convenient,*" he surmises, then thinks better of it. "Pretty *evil,* actually. So, don't *you* tell me there's no evil in the world. Evil is all there is in the world! What else but evil would require a little girl like Iris," he says, his voice breaking at the sound of her name, "to endure the things she does? Huh? The things that lay ahead of her are all sorrow, all suffering. Iris and I, and all of us, we have to really work to see that there is good in the world, and we cling to it for our very lives, but we *know* that there is evil. And where are you!? Off in some secret paradise! Some impossible place the rest of us will never get to! Coming down from on high to preach about how there's no good and evil" he screams. Again, the hall quakes, but more violently this time. Even the ground beneath our feel trembles. Pieces of the hall start breaking apart as the shaking increases, the trees and grass of Adam's Calendar begin crumbling into large chucks of falling concrete.

"Don't you tell me that there's no such thing as good and evil. It sounds like nothing but an empty lie coming from you, Eve. *Lilith!*" he accuses, screaming my name at the top of his voice. So loudly, the older gray-haired me looks up from her grieving to try and find the source of the noise. When she does she sees a snake slither by. Captivated by it through the tears of her grief, she picks it up and holds it, studying it.

Roman, watching her in horror, turns and looks at me like he's looking at the devil itself. He starts shaking his head.

"I don't even know you," he says, sounding afraid.

Then the earth beneath our feet begins quaking so violently, I nearly lose my balance. Out of instinct, I reach out to grab onto Roman. But he pulls his arm away from me, as if for his life.

"Don't touch me," he warns. "You bring me nothing but pain and misery." His eyes filled to the limit with water, tears he refuses to cry. His heart overflows with grief and suffering. He's holding all the pain now instead of holding me. Pain he refuses to let go of.

Our matching green eyes meet, but for the first time ever, he looks right through me.

"Don't do this," I beg him, shaking my head, knowing deep down inside what's coming next.

"There is good and evil, Eve. And I know I'm good," he starts.

"Stop," I beg him. "Stop, *please*—"

"So, I guess that really does make you evil, just like everyone always said ... 6666," he reminds me, and himself, "I should have known all along," he says backing away from me, his eyes growing more and more fearful until he looks completely terrified. "I should have known what you were." he moves even further back. As he does, the entire Hall of Collective Records begins breaking apart, the gleaming white, Roman-columned beast slowly shattering like glass into a billion tiny pieces that go scattering off into space.

The sound is mighty, like the simultaneous fall of a thousand civilizations, the breaking of a hundred-billion hearts, the crashing of every wave that ever was in every ocean all at once, the total destruction of everything—all there ever was, all there is, and all that will ever be. And we both just let it fall away around us. Him, not seeming to care in the slightest, continuing to back away from me even though that seems to be what's causing it. And me, just standing there as the space grows between us, helpless to make him see the truth, certain that now he never will, and wondering what it all means. Cian's words about the numbers two and nine begin to echo in my mind.

"Nine represents completion, the end of a cycle, fulfillment, the beginning and the end, the alpha and the omega, nine is the universe itself."

I stand there, looking at Roman, the sacred, ancient warehouse of the Akashic records imploding all around us, bursting apart, and the *two* of us like an atom bomb, ticking since the beginning, always destined to cause the end, standing in what's left of Adam's Calendar, the place where it all began.

999, I think to myself, the day Cian first brought me here. The numbers floating out into the ether between us.

Roman stares at them, then we both watch as the nines turn upsides down into sixes. The number 666 floats in the vacuum of empty space between us.

"We may have just destroyed it all," I say, voice shaking.

"Even Aquarius?" he asks, eyes so flat and dead it's impossible for me to read him at all.

I nod. It's all I can do, standing there fearing the worst.

"Good," he spits, a dark cloud of hate falling over his eyes.

ROMAN

NINETEEN

———— ✠ ————

I wake up to the sound of Phoenix's voice—the voice of a person I now remember with perfect clarity. A voice from my life as Roman, before the last epoch began, before Eve left me here.

But even still, it's a voice I'm beyond confused to be hearing.

"Where in the world did you come from?" I ask, wiping the sleep from my eyes, straining to see.

"Look at you. What a piece of shit," she says, bending down, hovering over me, the sun, a yellow glowing fireball right behind her.

I squint, then I rub my eyes again and start to think that maybe I'm still in my dream from last night—the worst dream I ever had about Eve. The one causing a knot, right now, in the pit of my stomach.

"Such a skilled fighter," she proclaims, but I know her well enough to know she's actually mocking me. "In hand-to-hand combat there's no one better, they say. A deadly archer to boot. A sharp shooter, a *sniper,* in fact. The best there is, they say. The best there's ever been. Apparently, you must be. I mean, you must be *so* good that even though you should probably be preparing to save the world, prepping somehow for the mission of restoring the hope of humanity, but instead you're napping, in the shade under a fucking ... really weird tree." She stands up, hands on her hips, looking at the truly bizarre tree I'm lying under, the one I now feel compelled to flee from.

"That must mean you're an even better warrior than I am," she challenges, drawing her sword and squaring off.

"Could you give me a second to wake up?" I ask.

"By all means." She bows and starts walking away, then she turns and whips a knife into the tree a millimeter above my head.

"Jesus!" I shout, looking at her in shock.

"One," she laughs, as she points to herself, "to zero," she points to me, then turns and heads towards where I see some of the others are gathered near the vehicles, sitting around eating.

"Where in the hell did you come from anyway?" I shout as she's walking away.

"There's no time for any of that bullshit. Come on, Prince Charming, you've got a princess to save," she calls back as she goes.

She's right, but my head is pounding.

"Hey," I call to her, "wait a minute, you're a *new* soul. Why aren't you in Primitus?" I yell, truly wondering where she's really been all this time, how she got out of being in Primitus.

But she just sticks her two middle fingers up in the air to answer me as she continues walking over towards the others.

Sparring with Phoenix is not going well. Not for me, at least. She's having a grand old time.

"Yeah, you are *not* living up to the hype," she concludes, besting me for what feels like the hundredth time in a row, pinning my back against a tree, the tip of her sword touching my throat.

"What is going on with you, Roman?" Kali asks from the roof of one of the big military vehicles nearby, which she sits atop.

"You know what, I've had about enough! From both of you!" I shout, pushing Phoenix's sword away.

"Careful Roman," Kali warns, "Or she'll do to you what she did to Bael a couple hours ago."

I realize I haven't seen him around yet today.

I look at Phoenix, and she shrugs, a smug look on her face. Then she slices her throat with her finger.

"He put up more of a fight than this, I'll tell you that much." She raises her eyebrows.

I drop my sword to my side, exasperated.

"Just saying," Phoenix quips as I walk away

"As if this mission wasn't going to be hard enough. As if we aren't already laughably outnumbered," I shout.

"Don't worry. I'm prepared to take his place," she shouts back at me as I walk towards where Kali and Payge and Cicero are to get a drink of water out of the open back of the vehicle Kali is perched atop.

"Are you *trying* to have them see you?" I ask Kali, who looks like a mighty condor in a giant nest sitting up there like that.

I motion towards Antiquus. It's far enough in the distance but still certainly visible.

"They already know we're here," she says dismissively, then she flaps her arms, mocking me.

"All right, between letting Phoenix decapitate Bael, *unimpeded*, I might add, and the damn 'theater of war' which also makes no sense at all to me—just pick *one*, and please explain it," I demand, then pour as much water as I can into my mouth at once.

"Some people are not built to understand the theater of war, or even war itself. You, Roman, are one of those people," she tells me.

"Well, seeing as I'm about to go fight one, I'm not sure that's a good thing," I say to her between gulps as if I'm joking, but I look her square in the eyes to show I'm clearly worried by what she just said.

"Oh no, it's a compliment, a *very* high one," she corrects my thinking. "You see, Roman, war is extremely *low consciousness*. Warrior consciousness is one of the lowest states of human awareness. War, fighting one another *physically*, killing one another for things and ideas, pride and honor and ego and having to be right or better somehow by some new definition," she rolls her eyes, "it's one of the very lowest forms of human experience. We get virtually nothing out of it from an evolutionary perspective. As a collective, humanity transcended war at the end of the Middle Ages. That's what the Renaissance was all about," she says, as if this is just common knowledge. "So, what I'm saying is that people like you really *don't* understand it, because you've evolved so far beyond it," she says.

"So then why has there still been war?" I ask, the next and only logical question.

"Because of the more evolved souls, souls far beyond warrior consciousness, like you, but the ones with *darker tendencies*. They use war to manipulate the less evolved souls into giving up their power. It's just easier than anything else, using their fears and their base instincts against them, to trick them into handing over their lives to those who like to hoard things, like money and people, the liberty of others. War, profit, control, repeat, war, profit, control, repeat," she recites about ten times, then continues rambling on about it. After another minute, I conclude that I either don't have the attention span for this right now or, like she said, the ability to comprehend it. Though my blank stare doesn't seem to be stopping her long-winded lesson.

"All right, all right." I wave my hand. "What about Bael?" I ask. "I mean, Jesus, she cut his freaking head off." I motion to the sheet-covered heap on the ground twenty yards away.

"He was a terrible person, Roman," she tells me, "very, very dark." And that's all she says.

After a moment of quiet, "Yeah … I got that sense," I tell her.

"Good," she says, "You know, I was beginning to worry about your instincts." She gives me a concerned look.

"So, is that it?" I ask, awestruck. "He was very dark, chop off his head, the end?"

Kali rolls her eyes, like it suddenly pains her to speak.

"He was planning on killing you," she rattles out casually.

"Really?" I ask, not totally shocked.

"I mean, he didn't say as much, but I knew he was going to try," Kali says.

"Okaaay…" I say skeptically, then wait for more of an explanation. When there's not one, "Geez, talk about trial without a jury. Remind me to sleep with one eye open."

"Look, it's more complicated than that. It's just, it's a lot to explain," she says, growing impatient.

"You just sat here and explained the fucking *theater of war* and the history of the world from the beginning of civilization through the fucking Middle Ages all the way to right now!" I shout, officially and completely out of patience.

"That's different," she informs me.

"You know what? No," I say. "Kali, give me a break. I'm done being kept in the dark. I don't care what it is. I just want the truth," I demand, crossing my arms for good measure.

Kali starts smiling at me.

"You want the truth, huh?" she asks, a strange look on her face.

"Yes! Damnit," I demand, growing a smidge leery at the odd look on her face. "I thought I made that very clear in the armory! How can I possibly succeed if there are all these important things I don't know? If there are all these lies and secrets!"

She smiles down at me, what I instantly realize is a smile of knowing but also one of compassion.

"You're not supposed to," she says, then stares at me and waits.

"Not supposed to what?" I ask after a moment, flustered.

"Succeed," she plainly states, dropping the word down on me with ease, like a grenade into a foxhole.

"What?" I ask.

"The universe is trying to tell you something, but you haven't been paying attention. You're unable to see the bigger picture, or too busy looking at something else," she scolds, sounding deeply and almost personally annoyed. Then, her eyes turn more compassionate, her voice softer. She goes on. "You are being set up to fail from every angle, at every possible turn. Can you not see that?" she cocks her head to one side, studying me with a look of absolute wonder.

What a bizarre thing to say, I think to myself. What is she talking about? How could she know something like that?

What kind of higher knowledge does she possess?

"Oh my God, you're in the Aion Dorea." I say to her as

it hits me, as my mind keeps peeling open and the memories I'd lost keep jumping out at me. "*Kali...*" I say, remembering being told the name, "*and Bael,*" I motion to the man lying dead in a heap.

Kali nods, affirming it.

"And Druscilla and Claudius," she says. I recall that it was Jakob who told Eve and I their names, along with Kazaar, who tried unsuccessfully to kill Jude. Eve saved him. And there was one more named Thea. The six of them are the *other* half of the clandestine shadowy group we met miles below Antiquus. They are the ones that, at the time, were already residing in Primitus ... and would be, as Jakob had said, for the *foreseeable future.*

"How long did you know all of this was coming?" I ask. "I mean, all of this," I say, trying to encompass *everything*, thinking of when Animus first showed up, then when the world crumbled and Aurora was formed, and when Primitus and Antiquus first began, then when Eve left and everything changed again, always getting worse and worse. The box of life squeezing me tighter each time and filling up with more unimaginable things to endure.

"My entire life," she says. "I knew all of this was coming, all of it." She looks at me. "And I was not afraid. I was born at this time for this purpose, to fulfill *this* destiny, just the same as you," she tells me pointedly. "Roman you cannot be afraid to fail or to die or to suffer. Only failure and death and suffering can give birth to truth and peace and life, *real life*." She stares at me as if to say that none of this is real. "And yes, Phoenix did just save your life, but she only delayed the inevitable. She offered you a stay of execution because she loves you," she says without inflection.

I glance towards Phoenix, unable to hide my shock.

"Ah," I stammer, then looking down, rubbing the back of my neck.

"Don't get crazy Romeo. Not everyone's *in* love with you. You're in my soul family, dipshit," Phoenix says, seeming nonchalant about what she's saying save for her caramel eyes, which are locked dead on mine. She waits a moment for her words to sink in. Then she takes a deep inhale and goes on, her voice vulnerable and raw.

"You have helped me every time we have ever incarnated together, every time *I* have ever lived. You're usually my brother," she tells me. "And you have saved my life, saved the lives of the people I loved, aided and assisted me selflessly, sacrificing yourself every time, *for me*," she starts to crack, "one life after the next." Her eyes mist. "Roman, you are the most loyal and true soul I have ever had the good fortune of knowing. There is no way I was going to let you come this far just to have that dark force," she motions towards Bael, "put out that powerful light of yours, right at the last minute no less, all so you didn't have a chance to illuminate any others." She struggles to get the words out. "You know, loving *her* wasn't the only thing you ever did in this world."

"How did I not know? I knew all my lives, other people's…" I struggle to accept what she's telling me. "I've always had all that knowledge … through all my lifetimes."

"Not in this one," she tells me. "This time, you only thought you were seeing everything." She laughs, shaking her head, "but all you could really see was her, as if you were almost blinded to everything else, *the bigger picture*—the one time when it probably matters most." She laughs in spite of herself. "You've been completely obsessed with *her*," she tells me, not in jealousy, but almost in wonder, "and with yourself…" She sounds disappointed in me. "As if the fate of the entire universe depended on it. On the love between the two of you and nothing else," she says, then walks off, overwhelmed.

As I watch her walk away, seeing her so differently than I ever have, and knowing how right she is, about everything…

"I'm sorry," I call to her, but she just keeps walking. "I mean it, Phoenix. I'm sorry," I say again. She raises her hand in the air in acknowledgement, as if to say she's got it.

As we load up, preparing to head to Antiquus, I begin to wonder if Phoenix has already seen what happens. If she already knows, if she knows when my light goes out, and that it will, as Kali said—

I wonder if all Phoenix truly did was just delay the inevitable.

PART THREE

SWAN SONG

TWENTY

———— ❈ ————

There is an ancient belief that swans sing a beautiful song just before they are about to die, after having been silent for most of their life.

These are the kinds of things my strained and splintered mind is recalling at this point. Random bits of once lost information, arbitrary nonsense I knew before the last epoch began, expressions, like the swan song. A likely irrelevant ancient belief that, if it's actually true, I find frankly sad and more than a little disconcerting.

Regardless, this is what lodges itself in my brain while we drive up to Antiquus, the imposing grand kingdom of old souls where I now know I once lived. It was the last place I was with Eve, before she left this dimension behind for a better one.

And I'm still thinking about it, *swan song*, as Kali,

Phoenix, Cicero, Payge and I storm through the towering bronze gates. And as we infiltrate the mammoth courtyard and enter the sprawling limestone fortress, taking command of the common area and then the great hall after that. Instead of thinking much about what I'm doing, I'm wondering if this will somehow turn out to be my swan song. Or if it's not, wondering if I'll have one and when it will be—if any of this nonsense is even real. That's what's on my mind as we kill or maim more than fifty Sage and Dragon Souls, one right after the next, fighting with incredible stealth and near superhuman precision. The five of us in complete synchronicity, and me at the center, directing it all.

Once we've secured ourselves safely inside the grand hall, breathless, I tell Kali what I've been thinking about.

"What an utter waste of bandwidth." She rolls her eyes at me and laughs.

"What?" I ask.

"Imagine what you could do if you were actually in the room. *Good God Roman*, get your head in the game!" Kali yells, jarring me.

"Right," I say, refocusing on the task at hand. Find Val and get her out of here safe and alive, get her back to Primitus, give her to Shamus, Claudius, and Druscilla, and get Iris, and then ... *well*, I'm not sure what after that. I'm not sure what will happen or how I'll live within the confines of my current life in Primitus after everything I've been through and learned since I left. I doubt that the option will even be offered given what Bael was planning.

So, maybe this is my swan song? Maybe it's all our swan songs. I look around at Cicero and Payge and remember what Druscilla said after she so casually sliced the throat of Iris's teacher for seeing a fraction of what we've now seen; *she knows too much.*

They can't let me live. I'm a threat. I know too much, I realize.

"Focus, Roman. Get out of your head and lead," Kali instructs.

"Right," I repeat, looking around the great hall.

We were thinking we might find Val holed up in here, though it appears the sprawling circular space is all but empty. There's just one person in the entire familiar grand theater—Phoenix's younger sister, Sequoya.

"I thought you'd never get here." She smiles from where she's seated, in the white throne-like chair beneath the Zodiac flag hanging high above, right next to the Aurora flag. It reminds me of the day I sat in here with Eve trying to explain all of this to *her.*

"Nice throne," Phoenix comments.

"You like it? It's new," Sequoya clarifies. "Made special for me after Eve pulverized the last one."

"What are you doing here?" I ask her.

"I'm the oldest soul—the *next* oldest that is, after Eve, of course." She studies me intently, the way everyone seems to be lately.

"I'm sorry. You said she *pulverized* her throne?" I ask. "Eve?"

"With an ax," Sequoya points out. "Probably the single greatest thing that's ever happened here."

My mind turns to the ax Eve talked about last night in my dream. The very ax I used to kill Jakob after what he did to her. The ax that, along with me, kept Eve alive through her darkest time. I wonder if, as she chopped wood endlessly in the hollow, and when she pulverized the throne she would never sit upon, she was being fueled unknowingly by her pain. Vengeance, like a lifeline across the universe—dark and purposeful. I try to imagine the staggering odds, the near impossibility of the very flint that Abel used to kill Cain, *Cian*, the son of Lilith and Samuel, the son of Eve and I … at the beginning of existence …

"Roman." Kali nudges me.

"Oh, um," I look at Sequoya, who, like everyone else, is looking at me, "why aren't you…" I start, not sure how to phrase what I want to ask her next. "Why are you here? Why aren't you in *Aquarius*?"

"The hell's Aquarius?" Cicero whispers to me.

"I chose to stay back, to help others," Sequoya says, and I nod.

Then it occurs to me.

"You get to *choose* when it comes to something like that?" I ask, thinking again of Eve, in this place that reminds me so much of her. If she really did have a choice, then maybe there's a reason she left me here without her. One I haven't thought of.

Maybe it wasn't about Jude.

"We have *every* possible choice in Aquarius," she says. "And both Phoenix and I chose to stay here." She smiles at her sister. "The rest of our family is there waiting for us," she says, beaming.

"What is she talking about?" Cicero whispers, but I ignore him.

"Wait a minute, but I'm an *older* soul than you," I say to Phoenix. She shakes her head and rolls her eyes.

"There's no such thing as incarnation numbers, you idiot," Phoenix says. Then Sequoya motions for all of us to follow her, and everyone starts walking.

"He is literally killing me," Phoenix jokes to Sequoya, putting her arm around her sister.

Sequoya leads us out the back of the great hall, where Eve and I once followed Jakob.

First, we head down to the Subterranean, the vast dwelling of Mountain Souls, a place I've never been.

When we finally reach it after navigating a strange labyrinth of tunnels and steel vault doors. it reminds me of being inside a giant, hollowed-out mountain. I gaze up at what looks like a million caves covering the mammoth walls like a honeycomb.

The whole place is eerily silent.

"Not a single Mountain Soul was left after the ascent. Every one of them already in Aquarius before Eve and Jude broadcast the truth, a great deal of both Dragons and Sages as well."

"At some point, someone is going to tell me what the fuck she is talking about," Cicero announces.

"The Destruction Story is just that. It is a *story*. It is not what really happened when things changed. Shamus caused The Events as well as The Unthinkable. The same Shamus who's now been installed as your King of Kings. All this has been erased from his mind. He was raised by a man named Cian," Sequoya says, pulling Cian's will out of the cave she stands at the mouth of, handing it to me. "Shamus knew about the higher dimension, which is where he caused the bigger challenges humans now face here in the third dimension; no births, no food, the environment gone haywire. Though someone else was pulling his string so to speak, coaching him along," she explains.

Cicero, already an avid conspiracy theorist, tries to keep up. He nods but looks more shocked and more surprised with each new thing she reveals.

"Would you like me to go on?" she asks Cicero off his baffled look as she hands me a tablet that she had stashed in the same cave. "No one knows I have it," she says to me, booting it up. "No one else has seen it. It's completely offline, obviously. But, well, it's for you. From Eve."

She looks at me in a gentle way.

"I'll look at it later," I say as I take it, no idea what may be on it.

"No, go on. By all means," Cicero tells Sequoya.

"It's not too much?" she asks. "You just look..." she says, evaluating his pasty, pale, bewildered face.

"Oh no. I always look like this when people take everything I thought I knew about the world and blow it to smithereens," he jokes.

"All right, good, because we need as many people as possible to know the truth now," Sequoya emphasizes. "Come on, I'll take you to where Val's hiding out and tell you everything else on the way."

As she leads us all down into the tunnel system deep below Antiquus, Sequoya explains everything to Cicero and

Payge. As we walk through the winding interconnected passageways towards the remote location where I met the Aion Dorea—one half of its members anyway—when I came here with Eve on the night she got her grandfather's ashes and his will, now in my hand. And all of this on the same night we first made love. I let my mind wander back to her, letting my heart and my body remember how she feels ... but only for a second.

Then, I start to wonder if the reason she insisted that Jakob allow me to come with her to this remote place was because she somehow knew I would one day be coming back here without her, and she was trying to prepare me. I wonder when she knew she would give me the key realizing suddenly that it was always destined for me.

Then, I push her out of my mind completely. I will her out. I return to myself, my battle-ready state, despite that Sequoya has told us we're completely safe down here.

"Remember, you are *supposed to* leave here with *Val*," Sequoya comments. "I mean, you do realize that I've been instructed to help you find her, right?"

"Right," I say, remembering the theater of war and realizing Kali was most definitely correct. I'll never get used to it. "But won't Karl Alastair want to put up a fight? Make it look ... *real*."

"No," she laughs, "not if he can get away with doing

nothing instead. Karl Alastair is harmless at this point. He's the least of your worries. A meaningless figurehead, he's literally passed out drunk right now in one of the abandoned Sage towers, and pretty much always is. Even Ansel can barely get in touch with him most of the time. And technically, I'm in charge too, though just another figurehead, really."

"That's right," I remember. "You can do anything you want," I say, as Eve had said when she was the Zodiac.

"Yeah, not that there is anything to do, really," she says as we begin to walk past the aquifers.

"Is the water still being dosed with scopolamine?" I ask her.

"Ok, well I guess there are *some* things to do around here," she admits. "I did take those roots out of the water supply, and now it's running pure." She smiles proudly.

"Nice." Phoenix says.

"You would not believe the difference that it made around here. We don't have a big population, nothing like Primitus, but everyone started acting differently almost overnight. Just waking up. Coming together, forgetting about being Dragon Souls or Sage Souls and just being humans. Now Karl can hardly get any of them to want to fight, which is his only real job. We're down to just the dark Dragon Souls and a few handfuls of Sages, and mostly they want to stick to computer stuff—spying, and hacking, and launching bombs from behind a screen and keyboard," she says as we approach the familiar wooden door. "That's why everything looks so chaotic and disjointed, why there's almost no cohesion to the attacks and bombings and wars, just random violence," she explains, Cicero Payge and I all nodding, realizing she's right. "Anyway," she says, "Val's in there, but I need to get back," she says before hugging her sister and heading out the way we came.

We find Val in the mysterious enchanting library where I met the Aion Dorea. She's sitting at one of the six desks in the large round polygon room, giant crystal chandelier illuminating her as she reads, looking as pregnant as ever.

From what Sequoya told us, Val's been hidden here, deep underground, because she's the most important weapon in Ansel's arsenal. Biding her time, waiting to be "captured" again, she's been learning from Pythagoras and from the millions of books that line the walls. She's learned a great deal in the past six months she's been here.

"The first three months after the ascent, I was still in Primitus," she says. Payge, Cicero, and I all nod, remembering when she sat next to Shamus on the balcony. "I was a prisoner who was made to look like a Queen," she tells us. "I was scared all the time. Shamus was horrible to me. He treated me like a piece of garbage, a thing he owned. He was so angry when Ansel said that I had to come to Antiquus for a while, and when he knew I was going to be captured soon, Shamus broke every plate and glass he could find, screaming and ranting for days before the 'terrorist attack,' which was already planned.

"It was all planned," I marvel, stunned by the sheer magnitude of lies I'd accepted so blindly.

"Yes, and there was nothing Shamus could do about it. The decision had been made. I was there when Shamus was given a clear choice: live with it or be 'assassinated.' Either way, it had to be done, according to Ansel. I had to be stolen away to reignite the fighting, which had begun to wane," she says, Pythagoras standing behind her protectively.

"It worked," I say, "the... *theater*," remembering how I felt when I heard the news of the attack and that Val had been taken to Antiquus. "I was so angry and so terrified. I'd been starting to wake up, to question things, then that happened and *boom*, I snapped right back to how I'd been. Fearful. Re-believing all over again that unordered soul assimilation was the problem, thinking, with every bomb that went off after that day, it was because you were here as a new soul in Antiquus."

We all go quiet, thinking of mind control, propaganda, and war.

"It's a delicate dance," Pythagoras says into the silence, "as keeping humans unknowingly enslaved has always been. He can't starve them *too* much, and he can't kill too *many* of them, but he's got to keep them from waking up. To keep their consciousness as *low* as possible. So, he uses suffering, war, and desperation. He systematically instills feelings of helplessness and smallness, using things like class, identity, and ego. He breeds anger and division using lack, and scarcity, by pitting neighbor against neighbor, erasing the concept of family. Making you believe you are King Souls or new souls and distancing you as far as possible from your truth. Then, he gives you a mortal enemy, one who's like a ghost. A faceless threat who's out of sight, unpredictable, and who could strike at any time. This breeds powerlessness, dependence on authority and above all *fear*. What's important to realize is that this is about frequency, vibration. Things like fear, jealousy, dependency, these feelings vibrate at the lowest possible frequency, keeping human consciousness low. Things like sovereignty, independence, love, truth and justice vibrate at the highest of all frequencies. Thus, if you want to keep humans from enlightenment, from knowing the truth of their own power, the lower the frequency of a feeling, thing, or circumstance, the more of it you have in your society. These things have been used throughout history, one or two of them here and there to control people, but now, in the last epoch, Ansel's pulling out all the stops, using every tactic at once. To the point where no one even expects justice now, justice is nonexistence. The truth is not only impossible to find, but society at large will attack you for speaking it, and you are made helpless in every regard, property of the state, accepting all these lies in hopes of starving off supposed human extinction."

"But why? To what end?" I ask.

"To block the final human evolution, to try and prevent it altogether, or to put it off for as long as possible."

Again, the room falls silent. These are sobering thoughts, humbling, for how they force me to self-evaluate. To see all of the tricks I fell for and understand why I fell for them.

"Enlightenment is a personal journey," Pythagoras says to me, as if he knows where my mind is at and telling me I'm in the right place.

"Why does Ansel want to stay here?" Payge asks. "Can't he go to Aquarius?"

"No, he can't."

"Why not?" Payge asks.

"He's not a full-blooded human. Only humans can transcend past the third dimension of Earth, because of our unique DNA. Ansel doesn't have the same human DNA.

He doesn't have the same potential. That's why he's working to keep as much of humanity here as he can, so *he* can stay. Earth, even Earth's lower dimensions, is much better than the place where he comes from."

"Earth?" I ask. "But I thought a new world had been created?"

"A new world has been created, *is being* created as we speak. After six mass ascensions of humanity it's almost complete. But that new world is not Passus, it's *Aquarius*."

"The truth, manipulated. Again," I note, Pythagoras nods.

"Exactly, Ansel's favorite way to deceive is to weaponize the truth, flip it on its head. It's the best way to increase confusion. The truth is that Aquarius is just life on Earth lived in a higher dimension, which is reached by achieving a higher state of conscious awareness. When enough humans are enlightened, when they know that the source of power is not outside themselves, but within, when they realize they are nothing and everything, life and death, creation and destruction, darkness and light, and that they are creating reality, then Aquarius will simply become the experience for all humanity."

"What about Passus?" Cicero asks.

"Passus is nothing but a new name for the lower dimensions of Earth. *Rebranding* what's left of the third dimension as it's dying, as more and more human consciousness rises beyond it. Soon, the third dimension will be completely gone, closed, sealed off. Very soon there will be a space separating Aquarius from all that's left below. It's what the bible calls The Abyss in the book of Revelations."

"That's a terrifying thought," Payge says, wide-eyed.

"If you're stuck here in this world of illusion, enslaved to it, I'm sure it is, but if you're a free being and you know that … *you are*, if you know and feel that energy of *I AM*, then you can't wait for this dimension to finally finish crumbling away already," Pythagoras says, his brown eyes twinkling behind his glasses at the thought.

"So, it's safe to say that Passus doesn't mean peace as we've been told it does?" Payge assumes, to which Pythagoras laughs.

"No, but you can tell people anything you want when you control all their information, when they have no books or evidence, no way to find out otherwise. No one to teach them the truth, that Passus is Latin for suffering. And that every time you say it and every time you hold it in your mind it's like a tuning fork, keeping you attuned to the lower frequency and vibration of dimensions three and below. Bringing you down, quite literally. Sound is the most powerful thing of all that can be used to enslave humans, *or to liberate*. The vibration, frequency, and energy of everything you hear matters a great deal because it infiltrates the consciousness. Humans are much more dynamic beings than they've ever been allowed to understand here in the third dimension. So that they will stay here as unknowing prisoners, sleeping slaves," Pythagoras ventures so far as to say, knowing we all know he's talking about us.

After digesting as much as I can, I want to ask more questions. Then, I wonder suddenly if *this* is really my leadership role, if maybe I'm supposed to lead a mission of the thinking kind more than the warring kind, especially given what Kali said.

"So, what is Ansel if not a full-blooded human?" I ask.

"He's a different kind of being from another place, a star called Draconia. It's in another galaxy. He's a Draconian, him, Sourial, Rasuil, Druscilla, and Bael all are, or *were*," he notes of Bael being dead. "On their world, they are reptilian creatures, but when they incarnate here through a child created at a very low frequency, they appear as human. They don't have a human soul, the soul is what manifests the DNA, so they can't get to anything higher than the third dimension of Earth. All human souls, no matter how dark they may seem or how asleep, can transcend this dimension. Their DNA can be activated and they can awaken in the blink of an eye. Preferably, it happens in mass."

"How?" I ask.

"When the truth is unleashed, and when it spreads like wildfire," he says. "When it's such powerful truth that nothing can stop it."

"But what truth? Which truth?" I ask.

"The most important truth. The truth of who you are," he says. "That's when you wake up to your own power, to the reality that the things, people, or ideas that seek to have power over you are all built of lies, and the only thing that gives them their strength and their authority is you, by believing in *their* power instead of your own."

The room goes silent, yet again, but for a much longer time. Then finally, Val interjects a question of her own, one directed at us.

"Do you guys know how the Berlin wall came down?" she asks.

"I don't even know what that is," Payge says, sounding baffled.

"It was a wall that stood after the last World War, dividing the city of Berlin, Germany in half. On the east side of the wall was an authoritarian communist regime where all aspects of life were under government control, on the west side there was a free democratic society. People were not permitted, and many died, trying to go from one side to the other. Then, one summer night in 1987, David Bowie, on his Glass Spider tour, played a concert in West Berlin in an outdoor venue at a park just a stone's throw from the wall," she says, excitedly.

"Were you there?" Payge asks, enwrapped.

"No, I read about it," she tells her, pointing to all the books around us, drawing Payge's eyes up the enormous shelved walls and igniting her fascination. Then, Val goes on.

"The people on the east side discovered they could hear the music if they were close enough to the wall, so they tried to, congregating as close as they could get, trying to listen to David Bowie, but the regime's forces pushed them back. The government wouldn't let them get close enough to hear music that they wanted to listen to. The concert, and in particular, a song called "Hero," planted the seeds that grew into the spirit of revolution, of awakening to the knowledge that they were really being kept there against their will. Sleeping slaves, unknowing prisoners. By 1989, anti-wall sentiment and protest demonstrations had grown and grown reaching their height on November 4th, when half-a-million people gathered at the public square in East Berlin to demand political change. The people rose up, insisting the government open all six border crossings along the wall. Then, on November 9, 1989, a political spokesman was giving a press conference, and he had the task of announcing the new regulation, but he hadn't been part of the discussion about them. He was handed a piece of paper to read but not given any further instruction. At the end of the press conference he read aloud the note, and one of the reporters asked when the regulations would take effect. The man hesitated, figuring it must be effective immediately. So that's what he said. Then, in a news broadcast seen across the east and west, the anchor proclaimed, 'This November ninth is a historic day. Starting immediately, boarders are open to everyone. The gates of the wall stand wide open.' It wasn't true. The guy had messed up, but masses of people began gathering at the wall, at the six checkpoints between the two sides, absolutely demanding the guards open the gates."

"What happened?" Payge asks, eyes wide.

"Neither the guards nor their superiors wanted to take responsibility for using force to try and control what was an unmanageable swell of people insistent that they were allowed to be let through, so ... they just opened the gates," she says. "The people flooded from one side to the other, moving as freely as they wished, celebrating, popping champagne, climbing atop the wall, tearing it down with their bare hands. The moment they thought they were free to do what they wanted, they *were* free to do what they wanted. Unknowingly, they created the reality they wanted, they manifested it. They changed the very shape of their world, quite literally, with the thoughts in their minds," Val finishes, and we all just stare at her.

"That's incredible," Cicero finally says.

"Do you want to know the wildest part of all this? What had already been decided was that the regulations would go into effect the *following* day," she says. "But nobody in the public knew that."

"The people held the power all along," I say. "They could have declared the wall *and* the government illegitimate any moment they wanted to. They just didn't know it."

"As long as they were united," Cicero adds. Payge and I both nod, and I wonder if we're all thinking the same thing ... that humans are not meant to control one another.

"Control is an illusion," Payge says.

EVE

TWENTY-ONE

—— ❊ ——

When Iris hears Shamus lumbering down the long stone hallway towards her cell, she launches into her usual drill. First, stashing the latest book I've secretly given her deep beneath her cot; she's torn nearly all the way through *Lord of the Flies* in just a few hours. Then, she backs herself tightly against the rickety metal bed frame, her arms hugging her shins, knees tucked under her chin.

This is the second time today he's coming to 'visit.' The last time he spent twenty minutes pacing around her cell like a rat in a cage, complaining aloud about the scheming and insubordinate High Council, and the 'idiotic troll,' a man named Ansel. Iris, as usual, stayed quiet during his rant. Then he committed his ritual heinous act standing uncomfortably close to Iris, a few feet in front of her, closer than ever, before finally leaving.

Roman's been gone almost two weeks now, and Iris has begun to consider the possibility that he may not be coming back.

The light gravel grinding sound of loafers shuffling over sandy stone stops right outside the bars of her cell. Iris stares ahead at the wall in front of her, just listening. Listening to the jangling of the metal key as he puts it into the lock, the loud flip of the bolt as he turns it over, the slow creaking of the cell door swinging open, bringing herself fully into the moment at hand. The usual fear and apprehension she feels when he's walking into her cell, the feeling of wanting to jump out of her own skin burst through the ceiling and rocket off into the sky, that feeling never shows up. Instead, rooted down into her body, feeling the sandy floor beneath her, and the musty air moving through her lungs, she finds herself skipping straight to the anger and rage. The same blood-boiling ire that always rises up inside her when he's finished and gone.

He ambles across the tiny room. Iris sees clearly, how he's lost in the dizzying maze of his own head, his white-gray hair disheveled, his gaunt frame and narrow shoulders hunched.

"Druscilla is threatened by my power," he mumbles to himself like he's hatching some plot in his mind. "Ansel hates me, never listens to my ideas. He just loves to control me, his whole life is about controlling me," he reasons, sounding as unhinged as usual. "All of them, they're all against me. They're all my enemies—"

"Just shut up already!" Iris yells, enraged as she is exasperated. "It's not personal, you idiot. What makes someone your ally or your enemy all depends on what you want to do. If they're aligned with that, they're your ally. If not, and if they want something completely different, then why are you trusting them in the first place?" she asks him plainly. "What do they want to accomplish? What do *you* want to accomplish?" she asks rhetorically.

He just stands there slack-jawed, stunned into silence. Iris studies him, her eyes burrowing through him.

"Do you even know what you want to accomplish?" she grills him. Off his silence she goes on, "No, you don't," she evaluates, "that's your problem, you don't know your purpose," she charges. "And haven't you ever noticed that all you ever talk about is every little thing everyone else is doing to you, all the people who aren't as smart as you, and the zillion and one ways you're somehow not at fault for the miserable state of your own life?" she challenges him, unabashedly.

Like a deer caught in the headlights of an oncoming truck, he appears frozen in place.

"And the way you treat me, the things you come in here

and do, it's nothing but a sad reflection of who *you* are, a sick, broken and pitiful excuse for a man. I thought about screaming my head off or kicking you at just the right moment," she taunts him, "but I know I'll be the one who gets punished in the end for your vile act. I want you to stop. Don't come in here and do that ever again. It's not okay," she draws a line in the sand, her voice big and confident.

He doesn't respond, just starts to retreat towards the door.

"That's right, run away. Run and hide from who you are, as if you can ever get away from yourself. I don't care what you do, but go funnel your purposeless wandering self-loathing through someone else from now on," she shoos him, "Go on, keep your little insignificant life small and unimportant, keep being angry and ineffective and weak, continue being powerless parading around as powerful. Go on," she shoos him again getting to her feet now.

Shamus strides to the cell door, and walks through, almost running from her. He closes it with a gentle click, eyeing Iris curiously, cautiously as she stands facing him in the middle of the cell, arms crossed, eyes narrow, in classic Iris style.

The next day, earlier than normal, Iris hears Shamus' shuffling steps heading her way. She goes to hide the new book she's started, Tolstoy's *Anna Karenina*. Then, she thinks better of it and leaves the large leather-bound volume wide open on her lap.

He reaches her cell and she hears the familiar sounds of the door unlocking, but she doesn't look up from her book. She reads on. Though she feels a little nervous of what he might do, her instinct tells her he's not going to do anything. And that being herself might somehow save her life. So, she reads on, as if he's not even there.

"What is that?" he asks voice neutral, plain.

"Tolstoy," she remarks absently, with a turn of the page.

He stands just inside the cell practically touching the door, looking down at her across the small space. Appearing ready to make his escape if things turn too challenging.

"Anna Karenina," Iris elaborates, noting his demeanor, his curious lingering.

"What is it about?" he asks, biting his already chewed fingernails, furrowing his brow, but staying put safely near the door.

Iris lifts the heavy book sarcastically.

"It's about a lot."

"Well, what is it mostly about?" he asks, then goes back to nervously chewing on his nubby nails.

"I guess I'd have to say it's kind of about men and women, and their… difficulties, in their relationships together," she tries to explain one of the most complex novels in a sentence. "It all happens in a place called Russia, it just feels so real," she ventures, hoping he won't take the book from her, or worse.

"Russia," Shamus nods thoughtfully. Then he turns around and walks out, closing the door but not locking it before he goes.

Iris, staring at the unlocked bolt, is startled when Shamus reappears on the other side of the cell.

"What do you think of Druscilla?" he rushes out, seeming to regret asking her the second he does, "Never mind," he shakes his head and turns to walk off.

"She can't be trusted," Iris says, recalling how she saw her slice Ms. Medea's throat so casually, as if human life was utterly meaningless.

Shamus stands there a moment, thinking on her words. Then he looks behind himself and all around before taking the key from around his neck.

"You can have this back," he says.

Iris walks over to the unlocked door, and opens it.

Shamus hands her the key.

"Better hide that good," he warns her. She nods. "Wherever you're hiding those books," he suggests then departs, leaving Iris standing in the wide-open cell door.

TWENTY-TWO

— ✠ —

We can never escape our darkness. We must confront it. We must go towards what we are afraid of. We are afraid of our darkness and our power. And we must go towards them both to become whole.

This is the thought swirling through my mind like a brewing storm as I stand over Ruby's grave, the solitary mound of black dirt that Roman clawed out of the earth with his bare hands. It sits all alone out in the middle of nowhere, the lonely little center point of a thousand-mile radius of barren windswept nothingness.

I drop down to my knees at the end of it, where I know her feet are. I place my hands atop the cold, wet, packed dirt, thinking of her in there, still and dead, and I weep tears of bitter sorrow for her. My body lurches forward, and I collapse down, my ear directly on the mound, lying my head at her feet, sobbing for this beautiful girl, who was just … *becoming*. Who had just gotten her first glimpse of herself, all that she is or *was*, and all she might become. She had just seen with her own eyes and felt with her own body and heart what love really was for the first time—true love, this force that travels unbroken across dimensions, the force that creates worlds. She'd only just begun to understand this life. To understand love and truth; the only two things worth fighting for. The only two things that are real throughout the whole of the universe.

"Love is a *force*, and truth is not good or bad. It is merely *powerful*," I hear from behind me. I sit up with a sharp inhale.

"Ruby," I whisper. I stare at her face, angelic and lit like the sun.

"Eve," she smiles, "my other half, my twin flame," she says, and I watch as the glowing light around her heart intensifies, burning a brighter, hotter yellow and extending out far beyond her. Though I'm several feet away, the light reaches me—the love energy of her heart; pure, unconditional, source love. It blankets me with tranquility, with calmness, and with complete serenity.

I stand up, bathed in the golden light of her love—universal love.

"You're an angel, Ruby," I tell her.

"Yes," she smiles, her brilliant eyes shining.

"I've been able to see angels since I ascended." I tell her of how I see angels and archangels, light beings that reside in the highest realms of Aquarius, those who passed on from the third dimensional world and have not reincarnated again.

"There are so many of us here now because the end has come," she says, and I nod. She's telling me something I already know. That the third dimension is set to become void, that it's already happening, and that soon it will collapse, anything still here being pushed downward when the third dimension becomes a vacuum—an empty, impenetrable space between everything above and everything below. That's why I witness angels who look like Ruby working tirelessly here in the third dimension, why I see them everywhere now, surrounding almost every person, an army of angels, guiding them along their journey, whispering in their ears. But I never see anyone around Roman.

"Am I all he has?" I ask her, and she nods that I am.

"You're working hard to help him," she says.

"I am," I say. "I think I'm just not enough," I admit for the first time, this dark idea that's been whirling around me. But she doesn't say anything about it. She just looks at me, her blue eyes locked on mine, a path of energy like an infrared laser running between us.

"He loved you," I say finally, and begin to cry again. "His heart, his beautiful heart," I weep harder. "It's shattered ... because he *really* loved you, Ruby, so much. He saw you, and it was with pure love, all of you, all that you might have ever grown to be, you already were to him," I tell her. "I saw all of it in how he looked at you," I tell her as the tears of some bottomless sorrow wash down my checks like two rivers, like Weeping God.

"He is extraordinary," she says, "how he can love so powerfully, and he's not even whole yet. But he will be. We're all getting made whole this time, finally."

"Are you here to help him, to protect him? To be his guide?" I ask, hopeful. Knowing I'm doing all I can. "Me alone, Ruby, I'm not enough. I can feel it," I whisper, and I watch my fear rise out into the yellow light of her heart. An orange ring, bright and alarming, like a warning.

But she just smiles at me, the glow of her heart increasing outward again, this time even further, encapsulating me even more.

My fear collapses away, and my tears vanish. My heart feels light, almost airy, like she's making room, opening a window in the center of my being. Then she walks towards me and stops just an inch away, her ocean blue eyes channeling source love directly into mine.

A loud high-pitch ringing begins in my ears, five-hundred-twenty-eight hertz. And it's not just in my ears or in my head, I realize. It's everywhere all around me.

Then, a low humming starts. A deep, audible vibrating hum. It's the most soothing noise there is, a sound that's like a feeling, like the sound of home. Like the chant of Tibetan monks echoing off the walls of the cave of my soul, the ceaseless, earth-vibrating *om*. The hum travels through me, *preparing me*, I realize.

Our souls have merged through Roman, and now they are becoming one again finally, she tells me.

The humming grows louder, coming up out of the earth beneath my feet, tuning my whole body as it envelops me. Then, it becomes so loud, blasting into me through my ears, that I feel it splitting open the seed of my mind. Then the spacious, airy feeling, and the pure light from my heart expands like a gentle breeze billowing up through the crown of my head, infusing into my third eye.

She's opening my soul. *Our* soul. Then she steps forward. All at once, her sheer illuminated body disappears into mine.

Our soul, that was once split in two, has merged back into one.

ROMAN

TWENTY-THREE

— ✠ —

"Us coming together caused the universe," Eve's voice rises out of the tablet, her face aglow in soft light. She is radiant. "We are the big bang, Roman. The two of us, and well, really the four of us—original man and woman, and the light and shadow sides of each."

I click it off and stow it away, burying it deep between the sleeping bags from the armory—standing at the open tailgate at a complete loss. I push her words from my mind. I shove them from my head. Because I don't understand them. I don't understand the first thing about what she's saying to me. And I know there's no way for me to figure it out.

So, instead of trying, I just get on with loading Val's heavy travel bag, which is mostly filled with books. I told her books were going to be a problem. They were books that she would never be able to keep. But she insisted.

"You can't actually say no to me, you know that," she'd said, handing the bag right back to me without unloading any of the books.

"Why's that?" I asked her gently, holding the heavy bag again.

"Because look how pregnant I am," she said, leaning back, her giant round belly protruding between us. "Do you know how long I've been pregnant?" she asked me.

"A long time." I said.

To which she simply nodded, then waddled towards the back door, where Cicero helped her carefully climb up into the vehicle. After closing her door, he walked back to the tailgate and joined me in staring absently at Val's bag, brimming with contraband.

"Tell me Cicero, do you think I'm a good leader?"

He paused, both of us just staring down at the big bag of illegal books.

"I mean, you act like you're terrified of her, so I guess she's going to just do whatever she wants." He shrugged.

I looked over at him.

"You're right," I told him. "I am terrified of her." I slammed the door shut.

Stopping along the deserted roadside in the middle of the dead zone feels like a bad idea the first time Val tells me I need to let her get out so she can pee. But by the fourth time in just the first couple hours, with the first three stops uneventful, I'm starting to feel more comfortable with it. Hell, I may even be letting my guard down.

Standing at the back of the big truck to keep an eye on her, I open the tailgate, fish the tablet out from where I'd shoved it, turn it on, and hit play.

"Phoenix was right, on the last night I'd spend in Rugby, when she said to me emphatically, that we—you, me, Jude and her—were *not* the four beings, no matter what people might ever think or say. I asked her how it was possible that we could look so much like something that we weren't. Truth be told, I didn't believe her. But she was insistent, in that way she always was when she just *knew* something. 'We're just not,' she assured me. And her eyes were like steel. And, of course, she was right.

Even though the four of us came into this existence together, entering through the four corners of the earth on the very same day and at the very same moment, we weren't the four beings foretold in the story of the end of the world. And there's a simple explanation for that, as it turns out. Because Absolute Time was wrong. Newton got it wrong, Einstein knew—"

I click it off again. Then I open one of the large black gun cases in front of me, throw the tablet in, slam the top down, and spin the lock, watching as it whirls around, losing all hope I'll ever understand what I need to understand to leave the third dimension before it collapses into nothing … or whatever's going to happen. And if I'm never going to be able to understand, how am I ever going to help Iris? And I will *not* leave her behind.

Val comes waddling up from behind the little bush where she squatted, I pour her some water, knowing that it'll only make her need to pee again in another twenty minutes. But I do it anyway because it's what she told me to do.

I hand it to her with a smile, comfortable with this arrangement. Her telling me exactly what she needs or wants, me providing it and protecting her.

"You've really come around, Roman," she says, breathy from her twenty feet of walking, sipping her water in gulps intermittent with her labored panting. Her eyes convey a certain mysterious kind of wisdom unlike anything I've seen before—confident, grounded, and deeply rooted in herself, what she is, and what she knows.

"Tell me," I say to her, "what do you know about Absolute Time?"

"Newton?" she says, perking up like I gave her espresso instead of water. I nod. "Well, he got it *wrong*, I mean, for starters. A big thing to get wrong," she emphasizes, and then starts talking more rapidly, "because time, well, I mean time is ... time is everything *and* it is *nothing* all at once, like the universe, like the number *nine*. It is the means and the end and the beginning. The arrow of time is, well it's why we're here! Einstein, Einstein knew that," she proclaims, her eyes lit with the fire of her soul.

Nine ... two and nine ...

"Can you tell me more about this?" I ask.

After I help her back into the car, I climb into the driver's seat, buckle my seat belt, and look over at Cicero and back at Payge.

"I'm the leader of this mission, and I'm telling you both right now, pay attention. Val's about to explain the mysteries of the universe," I say. "And as we now know ... this is not a drill."

Payge and Cicero, eyes wide, look to Val.

"It's really not difficult to understand. Roman, you're making it sound a lot harder than it really is. It's literally two things. Ok, look, in all the knowledge that humanity has, we've really only figured out *two* things for sure, but these *two* things are all we need," she says.

Two and nine. Two and nine, the numbers Eve repeated into my mind somehow. Two and nine, like Revelations two through nine...

My mind snaps back as Val goes on.

"Now, supposedly, no one has ever been able to bridge the gap between these *two* things, but that's where the answer lies, in connecting these two things. So, think of these two things we know for sure as pillars, okay?"

We all nod. Then, she opens her right hand.

"Here we have quantum theory, which tells us, very basically, about matter on a quantum level—so think *small*, like atoms and subatomic particles. Quantum theory proves that when these tiny subatomic particles are observed by a person, they behave differently under the exact same conditions than when they are *not* being observed. So, we know, for certain, that the presence of an observer, of human consciousness, alters the behavior of matter on a subatomic level."

"What??" Cicero asks, sounding stunned.

"I know, right? Is that not the craziest thing you ever heard?" she shouts, almost giddy, then quickly goes on. "Ok so, over *here*," she holds out her *left* hand, "the only other thing we really know about the observable universe is Einstein's theory of general relativity, which tells us that, very basically, what we perceive as gravity is really just a consequence."

"So, time is how we experience it. Time is existence." I recount what Eve told me in my last dream of her. "And gravity is a consequence. That's connected, somehow, right?"

"Exactly, Roman," Val confirms. "Space-time."

"Wait, wait, wait, wait, forget time, or space-time, or whatever, how is *gravity* a *consequence*? What does that even mean, Val?" Payge grills her, growing frustrated.

"No, Roman is right. This makes it easier to understand. All right, look, imagine space-time is a box, and in this box you can only fit four things—three spots for space and one spot for time. So, inside this box you've got space, space, space, that's three dimensions of space—the third dimension—and you've got time, which is really just existence. In other words, time is just how we experience it. So, space-time is how we experience the third dimension. Let me repeat that. Space-time is *how we experience the third dimension*. That's all it is. Simple, right?" she asks.

We all nod.

"Ok. Einstein's theory explains that gravity is a geometric property of space-time, so what this means and why he also says that gravity is not a force, but a consequence is that what we perceive as the force of gravity is really just how things unfold based on how *we experience* the third dimension. Ergo, Einstein proved, mathematically by the way, that what we call gravity is in fact only a consequence of how we experience the third dimension. That whatever gravity is we're creating it."

"So, the bridge is *us*," I say suddenly, as I realize. "We are what connects the two. The link between quantum physics, us affecting matter by our present awareness, the link between *that* and what Einstein proved, is us. We are shaping the world with our minds, with our awareness, with what we focus on. We are creating gravity. We are consequences. That's who we are," I say, and everyone falls silent.

After a moment, Val goes on.

"Ergo, how can there be good and evil? Really?" she asks, and no one can answer. "There is no good and evil," Val states, the very thing Eve tried to tell me in my dream, the thing I wasn't ready to hear. "There is no good and evil, there are only consequences, which are us. We are the consequences of what we've created. Because of Einstein's proven theory, we *know* that this is true. That's how advanced ancient civilizations like the Mayans, the ancient Egyptians, the Lumerians, the Atlanteans, translated the same theories which they knew well before Einstein came along. They looked at the mathematics, and what they saw was that there is no good and evil. There can't be. The third dimensional world of limits and control, I call it the control matrix, wants us to perceive that there is, like some fixed force, *evil*, like gravity, which is not a fixed force at all, but relative. The universe is truly relative to how we experience it, and how we experience the universe shapes and creates what it is. We are the holy grail, the thing we've been searching for, the bridge between worlds, it's us."

"How do you know all this?" Payge asks in absolute wonder.

"Pythagoras taught me. The Aion Dorea are the keepers of this *forbidden* knowledge. The gift of eternal time, that's what Aion Dorea means, they've been guarding the gateway at the third dimension, holding the knowledge of the higher realm."

"So, we are not King Souls, or Guardian souls, old souls or new. None of that is remotely real," Payge realized.

"Not remotely," Val confirms.

"It's all an illusion, just like control," Payge says. "Completely fake. False identities created to hide the truth, to hold us here. We are none of these things. We control gravity. We can dissolve time. We are consequences," she states boldly.

"That is the truth of who we are," Val tells us.

We all fall silent again, just steeping in all we've just learned, what we've come to understand, *who we are.*

"All right, Val," Payge speaks first into the silence, eager to learn more, "now that we know who we are, where did we come from? And why are we here?"

"I am going to need to pee again before I tell you that." she holds her round belly.

I pull onto the side of the road, noticing that it's dark out now, wondering when the sun went down. It's as if time sped up while Val was teaching us. And it gives me an eerie, uneasy feeling.

I unbuckle my seatbelt and grab the large caliber AR stashed under my seat.

"I'm coming with you this time," I tell her, "that's that."

"I'm coming too," Cicero says, grabbing the largest gun near him, an AK 47. He clicks the safety off and racks it.

"I'm not staying here alone," Payge says, grabbing the twenty-gauge shot gun that's become her weapon of choice.

"You guys," Val says. "I'm just going pee." Val opens her door and waits for me to grab her hand.

"And we're all coming with you," I tell her as I help her climb out.

She grabs her forehead suddenly.

"Ow!" she exclaims, her voice so loud and abrupt I startle.

"What is it?" I ask, but she doesn't answer. It appears she can't.

"My god," she says finally, about a minute later, taking her hand off her head.

"What is it?"

"Headache," she says, breathless, "so painful."

"Is it better now?" I steady her as she takes a few tentative steps, holding her elbow. "How do you feel?"

"It just came out of nowhere, sharp and sudden. It's subsided now, mostly," she says. I hold her arm as she walks. Payge and Cicero follow close behind us. Both of them acting just as nervous and alert as I feel.

EVE

TWENTY-FOUR

He drives through the night, the still world outside a blank canvas that will stretch on and on as far as he needs it to. Inside, complete silence, only the low vibrating hum of the engine reverberating in his chest under the slow, deep rhythm of his breath. The steady beat of his heart like a metronome, syncing the infinite with his consciousness, plugging him in to the universe as he melds together all the things Val taught them before she fell asleep.

His hands rest gently on the wheel. I sit unnoticed behind him, watching his thoughts dance around his head, numbers in a language, a story. Ancient sacred knowledge flowing out from within him like a gentle winding river. The symphony of life.

Sitting between Val, who's nestled against the door on the left, and Payge, who stares out her window on the right, I just watch his mind flow. I listen to the music of existence:

Time doesn't exist
Time is existence
Existence is how we experience it; existence is us
Where did existence come from
Us coming together caused the universe
We are the big bang
Two opposing forces, male and female; Adam and Lilith
Two opposing forces drawn together, magnets
Our bodies & minds are magnets, opposites that attract
Magnetism creates electricity
Our hearts are electricity
Our two hearts beating as one is love
Love powers the universe
Humanity creates electromagnetism
Electromagnetism is stronger than gravity
Gravity binds the universe together
Gravity is not a force, it is a consequence
It is a geometric property of space-time
How we unfold based on how we experience the third dimension
How we unfold shapes existence; we create gravity
We are consequences, the consequences of Adam and Lilith

There is <u>no good and evil</u>, only <u>darkness and light</u>.
How we <u>experience</u> this dimension shapes <u>reality</u>...

The only thing keeping us locked in the third dimension is how we experience the third dimension... Change how we experience the third dimension, change reality. With focused awareness time dissolves, and we exert the power of creation over our experience. Relativity and quantum mechanics, bridged by us, focused human consciousness in the middle.

We are here to transcend three dimensions. We are here to dissolve time, and to exert the power of creation over our experience...

How we interact with existence is the arrow of time. The arrow of time. Arrow...

Roman looks up into the night sky out the windshield, and directly in front of him is the constellation Orion, the archer.

Orion, Ophiuchus, the arrow of time... across the universe... love... across the universe... arrow...

Just then, Val moans, startling Roman out of the state of flow he'd slipped into. He glances back at her in the rearview mirror, checking to see that she's all right. Her hand is again on her head, her sleeping face contorted in pain. Roman keeps his eyes on her as much as the road until he sees her settle back to sleep.

But now his mind has come down from its higher state.

He looks back at Val again and begins to think of the conversation they had today as she packed her bag to leave with them.

With one hand propped on her low back, she walked around the room she'd lived in for six months, gathering her necessities, stepping unconsciously over piles and stacks of books spread out everywhere like landmines as she loaded up a large, ruffled, pink duffle bag.

"You know, Roman, I've seen you fight," Val said as she waddled back and forth across the room for this and that, making him very nervous that she'd fall. "I've seen *all* the footage, everything there is to see. Even today when you fought your way through the gates and into Antiquus. Pythagoras studies all of it," she said casually, shoving an alternating combination of long cotton night gowns and books down into the bag.

"Why would Pythagoras study the footage of me fighting?" Roman asked her.

"Pythagoras was always trying to figure out *what* you were fighting for. Always studying how you moved, the look in your eyes," she said continuing her packing. Then a few silent moments went by.

"What *are* you fighting for?" She looked up at him finally.

Her direct question caught him off-guard.

"I'm fighting for Iris," he stammered. After a moment, "I guess, mostly when I fight, it's for her in one way or another. It's either for her protection or for her survival or for her basic needs. I'm fighting for her life," he struggled to articulate.

"Are you fighting for your own?" she asked, looking as if perhaps this was what Pythagoras was trying to determine.

"I've never really ... thought about it that way, but I mean, yeah. I am. I'm fighting for Iris's life when I fight for my own life," he reasoned.

"You see, that's not what I asked you." She waved a book at him, then started packing again. "That's not the same thing," she said.

Just then, he thought of being in the cave with Ruby, about the binding link between their two lives they'd discovered.

"Actually, it is. Her life is linked to mine. If I die—"

"If you die, Iris goes to another male Keeper. If you die, in most instances, she likely would not," Val said.

"But, well, if I was dead and she was ... with any other Keeper other than me, some other *man*..." He struggled with even the thought. "For her, what she'd have to go through, how her life would be..."

Val was quiet.

"Why?" he asked her finally. "Why does he want to know?"

"He's trying to understand you, how it is that you fight the way that you do," she said casually, as she continued to pack.

"Why does it matter? Is it because no one else can fight the way I do?" he asked.

"No. Because they *all can*. You're just the only one who's figured it out for whatever reason," she said.

"Not more of this hope of humanity stuff," he began uncomfortably. "It's not me, *you've* already taken that role," he said, motioning to her round protruding belly.

"No, see that's where you're wrong. I am not the hope of humanity, and neither are you. *We* are not the hope of humanity," she said, looking him dead in the eyes. "Even this baby is not the hope of humanity," she remarked boldly of her pregnant stomach. "Human consciousness is the hope of humanity."

Roman clearly didn't understand what she meant.

"You see, Roman, I think I know why you can do what you do, how you're doing it. Pythagoras is right to think that *why* you are fighting causes you to be able to break the three-dimensional laws of physics."

"All right, why?"

"You are not fighting for Iris, not Iris *alone*," she tells him, like she's somehow inside his mind. "And you're not fighting just for yourself to stay alive to keep her alive. Existence is about more than just being ... alive," she told him. "What I told Pythagoras, what my intuition tells me, is that you are fighting for *love and truth*," she said pointedly. Then she asked, "What do you feel like when you're fighting?"

"I don't know how to answer that," he struggled.

"Why?" she asked, knowingly.

"Because there's no 'me' when I'm fighting. The 'me' that I know isn't there. I feel like *I'm* gone when I fight, but it's weird, I'm also bigger somehow too. Like I'm not myself and at the same time all of myself, *more* than myself, I'm everything," he struggled to describe.

"*You* are surrendered to love and truth, so you reach the highest form of human consciousness, your highest self. 'Roman' can't do those things. Roman *is* gone when you fight, you become nothing, nothing but a focus point of love and truth, which is what existence is, thus you become one with the universe, you become everything. That's why you're able to dissolve time and to exert the power of creation over existence, to create what is happening. It is my belief, Roman, that love and truth are living alchemy. *We* are the bridge between what is happening and what we want to happen. It is human consciousness that shapes and changes reality, and when you fight you are physically altering the space-time around you, because all of your awareness is focused on love and truth. The universe is love and truth so you become aligned. When we live in love and truth we are living alchemy."

"Living alchemy," he repeated as he tried to understand.

Roman snaps back to himself, his hands gripping the wheel, everyone else in the car fast asleep, a dense heavy fog outside. He switches on his high beams, and the moment he does, he sees Primitus in the distance.

Somehow, they're already all the way back to Primitus.

"The dead zone," he whispers to himself, wondering if the mysterious space between Antiquus and Primitus is somehow contracting as the dimensions bleed into one another.

Even here, on the outskirts of Primitus, things have clearly changed. The giant white castle still looms larger than life, but an eerie, dark, twilight now blankets the barren desert. The kind of disorienting dimness that comes just before the full darkness of night. Roman wonders where the blinding sun and bone white sky have gone, and he has a sinking feeling, a knowing, that it has everything to do with the pending collapse of the third dimension and he's not sure it means consciousness is rising. He worries it may be going the wrong way.

His heart starts to pound against his chest, his palms sweat and his thoughts immediately turn to Iris. To what she's had to endure, and if she's safe. He wonders what their fate will be, him and Iris, as well as Payge, Cicero, and Phoenix. They have to return to deliver Val, but now they knew far too much. He figures they'll be used for propaganda before Druscilla disposes of them, or tries to.

How will he get them all out of here, to Aquarius? How were the things Val taught him going to help, what did it all mean? How would relativity and quantum physics get hundreds of millions of people out of the third dimension before it collapses? How was he going to explain living alchemy when he barely understood it himself, how was he going to save everyone. His mind races frantically, looking for solutions until he remembers the key. This has to be why Eve gave it to him. The key has to lead to the answer to getting to Aquarius.

His anxiety building, he glances in the rearview mirror to check on the vehicle behind him, his reinforcements. Kali at the wheel, Phoenix asleep next to her. Phoenix, who insisted on coming despite Roman thinking it was a very bad idea. Being a new soul, unregistered and undocumented ... there's no telling what they may do to her. But she wanted to help, and she wouldn't take no for an answer. And Kali. Roman couldn't predict what Kali would do once they arrived any more than he could predict the moment of the coming collapse.

He sighs, heart burdened and heavy, and glances back at Val, noticing her skin, a grayish pale white, not pink like usual, the way she's slumped against the door more than nestled, her lips blue, her chest still—

Roman's heart stops; he knows she's dead.

PART FOUR

LIVING ALCHEMY

EVE

TWENTY-FIVE

— ✦ —

Roman gives Cicero a shove, startling him awake.

"What?" Cicero jumps, eyes wide. His hand on his gun the moment he sees the look on Roman's face.

"What?" Cicero asks him again, but Roman just shakes his head rapidly, unable to speak.

"What is it!?" Cicero demands, his unease turning to alarm.

"Val," Roman whispers finally, then pulls over at the edge of the foothills of the western mountain range, Primitus not far in the distance. He puts it in park and stares ahead, his breathing rapid and shallow.

Cicero whips around, and upon seeing Val, he immediately bursts from his door and races around to her side. Roman, both hands on the wheel, tries catching his breath, but he can't.

Aneurysm, he thinks, recalling the headache and the sudden surge of nausea she complained of before she drifted off, the moan she let out in her sleep, gripping her head in pain.

"Aneurysm," Roman whispers inaudibly, to no one, between gulps of air, and trying to somehow digest that she's gone, and what her death may mean for the whole of humanity. He's suddenly ransacked all over again by the loss of Ruby, a rush of bottomless grief devours him.

He failed her. She died because he failed to protect her. And who hasn't he failed? What girl who he's been charged with protecting hasn't been either taken prisoner, or dropped from the sky by a flying monster, or died in her sleep just feet from him? All on his watch. So much failure, just as Kali had said before they stormed Antiquus: "The universe is trying to tell you something but you haven't been paying attention. You are being set up to fail from every angle, at every possible turn."

It's clear to him now that Kali was right, he's not supposed to succeed. He's being set up to fail at every turn. But why?

"Roman!" Cicero screams, sounding like he's at the other end of a mile-long tunnel instead of two feet behind him. Then Roman hears Payge scream and begin to sob, but it's just a faint wobbly murmur somewhere in the distance. All the chaos exploding around him sounds like some kind of underwater play he's hearing from above the surface.

His breathing choppy and erratic, his arms tingling and numb, hands still on the wheel, Roman stares ahead at a large boulder his high beams are lighting up. He sees something crouched behind it, something moving. Something small.

"Iris," he says, his chest rising and falling furiously. He looks to his left where both Kali and Phoenix are yelling at him, telling him things, important-sounding things, but he can't hear any of it. He stands up out of the driver's seat. Leaving the door open he walks past Kali and Phoenix, past Cicero performing CPR on Val's lifeless body, like it's all a scene happening someplace else, to some other Roman in some other dimension. He walks slowly, like he's being pulled by a tractor beam towards the gray boulder that's illuminated, breathing in swallows and gasps, until he reaches it.

She's curled in a ball, covering her head with her hands, crouched down with her entire torso between her knees. She's shaking like a leaf.

He stands over her in shock. To Roman, the world seems silent and still, even as a helicopter goes flying by overhead, kicking up sand and sending a tornado of wind whirling around them. Roman's not sure if he's imagining it but he and Iris are in the calm center of a swirling vortex.

Head huddled between her knees, Iris still doesn't know he's there.

Roman crouches down.

"Hey," he whispers, "Iris."

She jerks her head up. Shock, then wonder, then relief, then tears filling her eyes. She throws her arms around him. He holds onto her, overcome with emotion, as the tornado of wind and sand spins around them.

After a moment, she pulls back and holds out her hand.

"I got your key," she says.

"How?" he starts, baffled, as she places it over his head, "How did you get it?"

"Shamus gave it to me. He never found what it unlocked anyway."

"He gave it to you?" Roman asks, shocked.

"Yeah," she says.

"Why did he do that?" Roman asks.

"I don't know really. He is kind of afraid of me," she says.

"He's afraid of you?" Roman can't conceive of what she's telling him. "I don't understand."

"He was awful at first. He did awful things in front of me," she says, Roman's heart sinking at the thought. "But then, one day I just told him off, I just—"

"You lectured him," Roman says knowingly. Having been on the receiving end of so many of Iris's lectures, Roman knows better than anyone the fire she has inside, how smart she is, how strong willed.

"You can be scary," he admits, "in the best way possible."

"I let him have it, Roman," she says with a little smile.

"I can't even imagine."

"I wish you could have seen it," she says, overwhelmed suddenly by all she's been through in his absence, and so grateful that he's back.

"You're incredible, Iris, you know that?" he tells her, "I mean that, I'm so proud of you," he brushes the hair out of her face tenderly.

"I could just see right through him," she explains, "right into his dark heavy heart, so filled with anger, and hate. Almost like the exact opposite of you," something inside her recognizes for a moment how Roman and Shamus seem to be two halves of one whole.

"I'm so sorry I couldn't protect you, that I had to leave you here," Roman admits painfully. "

"It's ok. For some reason, I don't think you were supposed to," her instinct tells her, a thought that eases Roman's mind ever so slightly.

"So, what on Earth are you doing out here?" he asks.

"I don't know, something inside just told me to come out here. Shamus always says that he's pretty sure I know everything, that my instincts are never wrong, so I snuck out, and I ran here as fast as I could. Then a second later, you just pulled up."

"Your intuition led you straight to me," he marvels at what is nothing short of a superpower.

"Roman," a voice calls.

Iris and Roman turn to see who it is.

"Jude?" Roman stands. He can't believe his eyes. "Where did you come from?"

"Come on, I'll explain. We need to get out of here, and I want to show you this beautiful place I know of," Jude says, motioning them towards the helicopter parked behind him.

Just then Roman notices a swarm of Primitus guards and police drones barreling down on them. He grabs Iris and turns to run, but then drops to his knees at the sight of Phoenix putting herself in between the guards and drones, as they take their firing positions, and the awaiting helicopter.

"Go!" she screams at him, and he fights to his feet, Iris in his arms. Shielding her head, he sprints to the helicopter in a hail of gunfire, Iris screaming.

As the black metal blades begin to whirl a loud chuff-

chuff rises into the desert air joining the screaming and the gunfire in a chorus of chaos. Sand blows wildly as Jude hovers the Apache a few feet off the ground. Roman leaps in, a single superhuman bound as bullets ping and ricochet off the fuselage as the chopper ascends rapidly, the matte black copter quickly disappears into the abyss of night.

Roman looks down at the desert below. In the stream of headlights from the very vehicle he'd been driving only moments before, he sees Phoenix lying dead in the sand.

"No," he exhales, a mix of disbelief and devastation.

"She sacrificed herself for you," Jude tells him, knowing what Roman is looking at and how he's feeling from the energy radiating through the cabin. "Like you've done for her so many times so that she could accomplish what she came to fulfill in those lives."

Roman stares down at her lifeless body as they fly farther and farther away.

After a long silence, "Is it what she was born to do?" Roman asks Jude, struggling to conceive of the idea that a person's life could be to die so that someone else could live.

"Yes, one of the many things she came to do, and accomplished," Jude says as he expertly pilots the craft through a strange kind of sky.

"Where are we going?" Iris asks looking out the window at the wavy atmosphere.

"We're going to Alaska," Jude says, "we're just taking a little short cut."

His soothing calm voice is the last thing Roman and Iris hear before they both drift off to sleep.

The northernmost tip of the continent, that's what they're flying over when Roman and Iris awaken. Jude's home, the closest thing someone like Jude has to a home anyway, being born the way he was; fifth dimensional, virtually unattached to life in the third.

"Am I still dreaming?" Iris asks in all seriousness of the sundrenched wonders below, rubbing her eyes in disbelief.

"The most incredible place in the third dimension," Jude remarks as they fly over glaciers and forests and tundras, "in my humble opinion at least. It's so full of life," he says as Iris and Roman take in the polar bears, whales, and seals below and the sky filled with birds all around them.

He sets the Apache down on the bank of a frozen jade lake, a forest on the other side, a snow-covered ridge high above, a massive caribou perched atop. The caribou stares into the cabin of the helicopter, looking dead into Roman's eyes.

"I feel like I know this place," Roman says, the caribou's eye-contact unwavering.

"Eve links you to this place. She's paved a path for you here, an energetic path to help you find what you're looking for. The two of you, the connection between you," Jude begins, but then trails off seeming lost for words. Finally, "It's a divine union, it's the highest form of love in all planes and all dimensions. It already exists in higher places. And when both of your souls are finally whole again, the love of your divine union will save all humanity."

"How will our souls become whole?"

"Hers already has, she's merged with her twin flame. Ruby. They are one soul."

"Eve and Lilith," Roman says, remembering how they split in two.

"Yes, and finally, in this lifetime after eons and eons her soul is whole again."

"How?"

"You," he says simply then begins climbing out of the Apache.

"Wait, I don't understand," Roman says.

"You will," Jude tells him as he hops down into the snow, "Come on."

A few moments later, Jude and Roman stand at the edge of the ice.

Iris is crouched behind them examining Cian's will,

which Jude had somehow grabbed from the back of the truck where Roman had left it. Iris declares it fascinating.

"It's a cipher," she says, trying instantly to decode it.

Cian's nightstand sits out in the very middle of the lake. Roman and Jude look at it from the shore, the key in Roman's hand.

Roman glances back at Iris, Cian's will open in the snow as she studies it.

"She's fine," Jude assures him. "I'm not going to let anything happen to her," he promises. "Go on. Go see what's in it."

Roman nods, placing his trust in Jude. Then he sets his sights on the little wooden relic and starts walking across the ice towards it. He glances up to see the caribou again, but now he's gone, and he notices the snow on the ridge is gone too, replaced by mud and a river, rushing toward the ice below. Fearing it'll be lost, washed away by the snowmelt, or worse, fall through the ice, Roman runs towards the nightstand.

He nears it, then sliding down onto his knees, and grabs the front near the lock.

Fumbling with the little key.

"Come on," he shouts trying to get it into the lock, wondering if this key will even work to open it, and why suddenly he's so convinced that it will. He glances back at the shore. Iris is still head down, working on trying to read some coded message in Cian's will, and Jude is watching him. He waves at Roman from the shore.

Roman begins to wonder if Jude tricked him, if this is all a trick, just as the key slides in. Roman looks at the nightstand in shock. Then he turns the key, takes a deep breath, and swings the little door open.

ROMAN

TWENTY-SIX

———— ✦ ————

I stare into the nightstand in disbelief.

There is nothing inside it. Absolutely nothing.

I sit back on the frigid ice staring into the emptiness, wondering how it's possible for something so small to look so gaping and cavernous, so hollow and grand.

There is nothing to hope for. There is nothing to help me, to help humanity. No more Val, nothing in Cian's nightstand, no secret weapon, no holy grail.

Staring into the gaping emptiness it somehow becomes me, and I become it. I am the emptiness. I cannot be defined, and in that I cannot be contained. I am nothingness. I am limitless.

There is nothing I need. I AM.

At that moment, the ice beneath me snaps, then there's a loud crack, like a baseball hitting a wooden bat. The next thing I know, the spot where I'm kneeling along with the empty nightstand are both underwater.

The sting of hypothermia, the weight of water filling my lungs, I descend rapidly towards the bottom, surrendered, I am death as I am life. The burning cold turning to warmth, the weightlessness, the world going dark, one sensation bleeds into the next. I close my eyes and let myself be swallowed away.

Then I feel her touch, the gentle way she rakes her fingers through my hair, it sends a rush of electricity charging through me. I smell grass and feel the warmth of a late afternoon sun on my face. I hear her laugh echoing around me, filling the universe. And another laughter, that of a child, a little girl.

I open my eyes to see Eve staring down at me, tiny grin on her lips, a breezy little smile as she looks at every part of my face.

"You were napping," she says, then lowers her lips towards mine, pressing them softly into a long deep kiss. I feel the warmth of her love travel through me. I feel her energy mixing with mine, swirling into an electric figure-eight between us, a closed circuit; our two hearts beating together as one.

I reach up and grab onto her cheeks, kissing her slow and hard, feeling every cell in my body aligned to hers.

I don't know how much time passes, because there is no time.

The next thing I know the kiss is done and she's looking into my eyes, her face still close to mine.

"Must have been some dream," she says then she sits back up.

With a little smile, she moves my head from her lap gently into the soft grass and stands, her flowing white dress billowing in the breeze.

"Come on," she says.

I watch her walk to the front of a perfect little stone cottage with and giant flower garden and a rope swing hanging from an enormous ancient oak tree in the front. I get up and follow her as she walks towards the house, passing a little blonde-haired girl around three years old as she swings. Her wintergreen eyes are the eyes of my child, the child Eve and I have had in nearly every one of my lifetimes with her. Payge's eyes. And I instantly understand how my love for Ruby made her feel betrayed. I think of telling her somehow that Ruby and Eve were one soul, *are* one soul, but then the thought dissolves and I realize she already knows. This is Aquarius, the fifth dimension, she already knows.

Standing in the doorway, Eve turns around to look at me, the glow of the sun lighting her from every direction.

She's pregnant, her belly round and full, looking like she's due any day. I walk towards her remembering what happened with Jakob, what he did to her, though I'm unable to grasp what's real and what's not, what things really happened and ... when.

When I approach, I feel the magnetic force between us.

I wrap my arms around her.

"I'm so happy you're here," she breaths out, her eyes looking up into mine. I place my palm gently on the top of her belly.

"Do you know?" I ask her.

She smiles and throws her head back with a laugh, then runs her hand over the back of my neck, pulling my eyes towards hers.

"Yes, I know," she says, then pressing her forehead into mine, "so do you. He's ours," she tells me, her emerald eyes two sparking jewels.

"How do you know?" I ask.

She places both my hands atop her belly.

"Close your eyes," she says, and when I do, I see and feel and know the child. I know the moment he was conceived, I know the very second it happened during the night Eve and I were first together, right after she got Cian's will. I know every hair on his head and what he'll look like and when he'll be born. I see him when he's grown, what he'll be like, what kind of father he'll be and why he's coming into the world. And I know who he was, before. There's nothing about him I don't know.

Opening my eyes is like returning from a trip to the furthest reaches of the stars.

"We have to go back," she starts, her voice tender, "to the third dimension, to Primitus. You know that, right?" she asks, and I know that too.

"Iris," I whisper.

EVE

TWENTY-SEVEN

When Roman entered Aquarius, Jude returned to Primitus with Iris. He assured her that Roman was going to be fine, that he would be back, and that Eve would be with him.

"He just … disappeared," Iris fretted of how she watched Roman pixilate into nothing. Though he felt like he fell through the ice, he entered Aquarius the same way I did by dissolving into it.

"The most important thing now is to not be afraid, everything will be revealed," Jude told her. "That's when the new Earth will just become where we are, when all is *revealed*, and the last of humanity awakens."

"Like the book of revelations," she said.

"Exactly. It's not scary, all that it is is the revealing of truth on such an enormous scale the entire world completely altered, onto a higher plane. This is all part of the record of what happens, of how this dimension ends," he explained as they flew towards the walled-off desert city. "But between now and then there's work to do," he told her.

"What do we need to do?" she asked, having just learned about the existence of Aquarius and the coming collapse of the third dimension, and ready, willing and able to do whatever it was going to take to save not only herself but as much of humanity as possible.

"The people must turn against the power structure they've been fooled into believing controls them. To understand the full truth, they must see the darkness behind the illusion and they must see the power within themselves, one another and the power of their unity."

"How in the world are we going to make that happen?" she asked.

"It'll be easier than you think. When people have been so betrayed, when their whole world has been a lie used to enslave them unknowingly, and when they learn the truth and start to see the world of lies falling down around them, they are filled instantly with the knowledge of all the power they always had. It's getting them the truth, that's the only challenge. Once they know enough … there is no stopping it, like a speeding bullet train. Planetary consciousness rising cannot be stopped once it gets beyond a certain point, that is the force that collapses the third dimension and expels the darkness; it is the minds of humanity and the light and love in their hearts. Love and truth. We only have to deliver the message."

Iris thought a moment.

"Oculum," she said, "we'll hijack it and beam the truth right into their faces. We'll take the tool being used to enslave them and we'll use it to liberate them instead."

It was a brilliant plan, Jude told her, and that he believed she was more than capable of hacking into the system. She beamed excitedly at the thought and the challenge. Remembering, quite suddenly, how she'd planned to study computer science, hopefully at MIT, before the unraveling of the world, before Animus and everything that followed. Then she began to wonder about the future, and what her life might be like when all this was over.

"Can people do jobs in Aquarius?" Iris asked, not understanding how a place that sounded so perfect functioned, what people did all day.

"Of course! Every person has a very special gift, that one thing they do where time just melts away. Like me, I'm a spiritual guide in Aquarius, it's how I serve humanity. We're all called to serve the world by doing the thing we love most, whatever is the song of our heart. That's why we're each so different, why we're talented at different things. When we use our gifts, we serve humanity; we create a human paradise."

She was enthralled at the thought of what a world like that must be like, how magical and wonderful, how happy and joyous.

Then he began preparing her for the task at hand, which turned out to be, of course, just her using her gifts to serve humanity.

"Consider it practice for Aquarius," he said, then went on to explain that he would need to stay out of sight until the very end.

"Spiritually, humanity must discover that they are their own savior, that the source of all life lives within them. That the light of the world is already here, inside them. That they have the power to create the reality they want. So, I won't help or interfere, but I'll be nearby," he told Iris as he brought the Apache down outside the city gates, "I'll be right there with you. You are protected."

And with that, she felt ready.

Iris walks into Primitus on her own and is immediately spotted by the drones. She's picked up shortly after that by guards who bring her back to Primitus Castle.

Once there she quickly discovers that the government is covering up Val's death—from the welcome banners to the signs of celebration and the enormous pictures of Val hung everywhere. All of them seeming to carry on as if Val is alive, and that the hope of humanity rests soundly in her.

But something incredible is happening, the people are questioning what they're being told. They hadn't seen her yet, not live on their Oculum feeds or on the balcony with Shamus the way they used to see her before. Though there appears to be an elaborate story of her return, and a manufactured mood of celebration, there is no proof. And proof is what they are demanding.

That's why masses of people are gathered outside the castle—they are demanding proof. As Iris is escorted through the gates, she notices that every different type of soul is there, together, united in their demands for answers. In the front, standing on makeshift platforms and leading the chants of rebellion she sees Payge and Cicero. All the souls in Primitus, appear to be clearly and loudly united in their suspicion and mistrust for the established powers of Primitus and Aurora. And in their unity, the millions gathered, hungry for the truth, demanding answers, are a powerful sight to behold. Now, all she has to do is deliver those answers.

Even more gaunt than before she left, deep dark circles under his eyes, sitting in his gilded throne, drunk, the moment Shamus sees Iris he's blanketed in relief.

"Is it bad out there?" he asks looking terrified, before taking a giant swig from a canteen of grain alcohol.

"Where are Druscilla and the others?" she asks him. The castle appears empty, the monitors where Ansel would appear, which were always on are now off.

"Who knows? Gone," he postulates, sounding careless and looking anything but. Iris was used to seeing Shamus drink, but she never saw him this drunk before, hardly able to hold his head up, eyes half-mast.

"They left?" she asked, skeptically. "How?" Given the mob of millions waiting outside she wondered if it would have been possible.

"Who knows," he repeats, "who cares? I just want to tear the whole place down," he tells her, taking another long drink. "Did you know that … none of this is real?" he whispers to her waving his arms about to mean … everything. "Val is dead, the people know it. It's all lies. Strange shadowy beings make all the decisions. I have no real power, nothing is as it seems," he rambles hopelessly on, then goes to take another swig, but Iris grabs the canteen before it reaches his mouth. "Hey," he protests, studying her for a long drunken moment, "where've you been anyway?" he asks, then remembers, "Hey, wait a minute, you escaped!" he accuses her, his finger waving in front of her face.

"Guard!" he yells and the guards at the far end of the long room start heading towards them.

She swipes his wagging finger out of her face, then gives him a threatening look that sobers him up enough to remind him who he's dealing with and how much he needs her right now.

He waves off the guards.

"Yes, I left, I had to go somewhere but now I'm back, and I'm going to help you. I have a plan," she says.

"I was hoping you would say that."

Sourial's broadcasts are simple for Iris to hack into. She isn't sure if Sourial or Ansel know she's doing it. She doesn't have time to care at this point. Right overtop the usual broadcasts of fear and lies, Iris has been revealing the truth. The truth about Val, when and how she died, including the proof Cicero and Payge have supplied her with, the truth of their history, the truths about their leaders and the shadow forces behind them, that their entire society has been built to enslave them by keeping them in suffering so that dark entities weren't forced off the planet by their rising consciousness. And the whole of humanity is awakening.

But the mass awakenings have one drawback—Ansel. The more he loses control, the more he steps up the stakes, dialing in on every method and tactic, bombings, mass shooting, staged terror attacks, even creating natural disasters, blaming it all on them, until much of the world is ablaze.

From what Jude had told her Iris knew that the rising waters would come next. The last part of the collapse of a dimension is always chaos and fire, followed by a great flood he told her.

Iris knows it's time to share the last revelation she has, what she decoded from Cian's will. The message that appeared on the parchment when she placed it on the wet snow to decode it.

The creed of Aquarius, the way of life:

"Humans are not designed to be controlled by other humans," she spoke into a camera, a live feed into their Oculum devices. "We are born as free, sovereign beings, each and every one of us.

We are of the earth *and* we are of the stars. We are human and divine. We are the very image of God, the source of all life. We are God-made into flesh.

But our truth as humans is that we are not *just* sovereign; *we are not islands.* We are connected to all things and to one another. *We are one.* But, we are not *just* one, we are not meant to be as a single organism. True oneness only exists when sovereignty is recognized, and honored first. When oneness is a choice made by sovereign beings the love that we are flows free, and creates the Earth anew."

After she delivers the last message she instructs everyone to head for higher ground.

"The waters are coming," she warns.

Through billowing smoke and blinding heat, Roman and I walk up the white marble stairs towards the door of Primitus Castle.

Ansel descends immediately out of the sky followed by Sourial, Rasuil, and Druscilla, and then a massive wave of others like them. Their human forms have disintegrated away revealing their reptilian bodies. The four dark Aion Dorea land with a mighty thunder, surrounding us.

In the distance the rumbling of water, thundering across the desert as the oceans cave under the pressure of the collapsing dimension. Ansel and Sourial each grab one of my arms and swoop me up, at the same time as Druscilla and Rasuil grab Roman and ascend into the sky.

A round platform buried beneath the desert sand begins rising swiftly into the air on what seems to be a never-ending giant metal pole. Ansel and Sourial and I land with a mighty clang on the platform as it continues rising higher and higher. Then Roman, flanked by Rasuil and Druscilla, lands beside us just as flood waters from both sides of the earth meet in a mighty roar beneath us. I look towards the mountains at the masses of humanity huddled on the highest ground, the raging waters only a few feet below them.

Pythagoras, Bronwyn, Kali, Claudius, and Thea materialize on the platform. Like Revelations 12 and the painting on the ceiling in Phoenix's house there are twelve in the sky, twelve stars, all gathered around me, Venus. Pythagoras, Bronwyn, Kali, Claudius, and Thea, Ansel, Sourial, Rasuil, Druscilla and Roman, and finally Clio and Jude.

Iris is seated next to Shamus on a makeshift throne atop the highest peak of Primitus Castle, the raging waters covering most of the castle below.

"Shamus, hand down the charges," Ansel orders him.

After a long silence, "I won't," he yells, defiantly.

"You," Ansel seethes, eyes fixed on Iris.

Suddenly, he's soaring towards them. Shamus stands, protectively, to defend Iris. Ansel reaches for Iris's arm, grabs ahold of her, and pulls her out of her chair. She screams. Shamus yanks her back, somehow overpowering Ansel.

The entire platform around me gasps at the unlikely turn of events, of a skinny beat-down man holding his own against a superhuman reptile alien.

Just then, I drop down to my knees on the hard metal platform and start breathing heavily, moaning in pain.

Ansel gets ahold of Iris again.

But I can feel the frequency rising, I can feel Shamus's soul merging with Roman's through love for Iris, as the waters churn and swell and thunder booms in the stark white sky.

Ansel yanks Iris up once more. Without a second thought, Shamus races up on the ledge of the balcony, grasps her leg and pulls her back by forcing his own weight forward. Iris goes tumbling back down onto the balcony as Shamus falls down into the tumultuous flood below and is instantly swept away.

I glance over at Roman and see him experiencing the very same thing I experienced when my soul merged with Ruby's, the glowing light around him expands, knocking Druscilla and Rasuil from the platform.

Roman rushes over to me, the light around both of us growing brighter as I begin to give birth, sitting back, panting, and screaming out, Roman kneeling in front of me. I cry out again and know this is it. The waters begin to rapidly recede. The white sky parts, falling away, revealing blue.

"No," Ansel says.

He turns back to look at Iris, with a menacing scowl,

and then he's sucked into the sky along with Sourial, Rasuil, and Druscilla, and all the rest of the dark ones, a wave of black launched into space.

Iris stands and rushes to the edge of the balcony and looks up into the sky. A tiny star, far in the distance, gleams.

I scream out one last time, the last push, and give birth to the first baby born in the fifth dimension.

A baby boy.

Roman hands him to me, and I weep at the sight of him again, as I look down into his sparkling green eyes.

"Hi," I whisper. "We did it, welcome to the new earth. Welcome to Aquarius."

THE END...
Or is this just the beginning?

ABOUT THE AUTHOR

Tiffany has said that the story of The Oldest Soul had been "making its presence known" for several years.

Eve first sprang into her mind—like a bucket of cold water in the face—while on a walk in 2011, she promptly went home and wrote the first 4 pages (which have remained unchanged since). But she filed Eve's one-of-a–kind journey away in her mind when work on other projects beckoned.

"I've been a writer of all forms of stories since I was around seventeen and the success of a couple of my TV pilots took me further from Eve's story, but what I didn't realize was that I was always amassing inspiration for what would one day become *The Oldest Soul.* Everything in my world somehow always circled back to Eve."

In the spring and summer of 2015, in a matter of months, she breathed life into ANIMUS, or rather, it breathed life into her … "The story is a force of nature—and seemed to move through me like an incredible breath of life from someplace else."

Tiffany has always said that stories "know what they want to be." And that as a writer she feels it's her job to "show up and get out of the way." Never has that felt so true than when Eve is telling her story.

"Elaborate worlds infused with real human emotions and strong characters with thought provoking stories are what fill my soul." Tiffany has spent the past few years creating such worlds in the form of original feature screenplays and TV pilots as a screenwriter. She lives outside of Atlanta with her husband, their two beautiful daughters and Chloe — the best dog in the world!

Made in the USA
Columbia, SC
15 December 2017